KAT TALES

KAT TALES

A Rae Robin Novel

iUniverse, Inc.
New York Lincoln Shanghai

Kat Tales

iUniverse, Inc.

For information address:
iUniverse, Inc.
2021 Pine Lake Road, Suite 100
Lincoln, NE 68512
www.iuniverse.com

ISBN: 0-595-30231-9

Prologue

It was a spot in the woods that seemed almost supernatural. A small bare spot surrounded by five trees in a perfect circle, as if someone had planned it.

It was Katherine's special place. Where she went to be alone. Think. Escape. Only she knew about it. Only she and whatever farm pet followed her there. Today it was "Flex." Flex was Katherine's favorite cat, for which she had particular respect. Flex had shiny black hair and mysterious green eyes, much like Katherine. Flex was the best hunter on the farm. She could out-run, out-jump, out-hunt, and out-fox every animal and human on the farm.

"You remind me of myself," Katherine said with a little smile as she rubbed the cat's jaw, "although it doesn't take much to show up those idiot stepbrothers of mine."

Deep down Katherine knew she was not considered a normal girl. She didn't care. Other girls didn't have the family she had; three lazy, stupid stepbrothers and one loud, obnoxious bully of a stepfather. It was their fault, she rationalized, that she had taught herself to behave more like a boy than a girl. Katherine smiled inwardly, what they hadn't counted on was that she would become better skilled with a gun, knife and whip than the all rest of them put together. The smile left her as she realized it had also caused them to resent her and leave most of the work up to her. "Kat do this, and Kat do that!" she mimicked under her breath. Flex looked at her as if trying to understand. "I don't care if they don't like me, Flex. You seem to like me. Probably because we're so much alike," she said as she stroked the cat's beautiful coat. "I shouldn't blame the boys. After all, it's not their fault they're stupid. They get it from Boris." Kat shook her head as if trying to release her latest conversation with him. She tried to pretend it didn't hurt when Boris told her no man would ever want her the way she carried on. Long ago Kat had learned to dismiss Boris's bullheaded ideas that he loved to shove down other's throats. Ignoring him usually worked, but not this time. He wasn't giving up, and this time, it was wearing on her.

"Flex, you'd know what to do!" Kat said. "You never hesitate. I know those Toms get you sometimes, but you still manage to take care of your kittens, hunt your prey, keep yourself out of danger, look magnificent, and keep a good attitude. Flex, tell me, what should I do?"

But Flex's attention had been diverted. On the other side of the clearing was a forest rodent who had become too bold. He had come out of his hole to get a look at Katherine and Flex. Flex sprang at the rodent and with one accurate strike, broke his neck, picked him up, and hauled him off.

"Well, you didn't waste any time with that one!" Kat said with a surprised smile. "I guess you're not going to help solve my problem today. I'd better get back."

Kat took her time as she walked back to the house. Her mind returned to her problem. She was nineteen, way past her prime, as Boris often told her. His words echoed in her head. "Girl, it's time you got married. That's what women are for. Tend to the house, help with the chores and keep the bed warm. You're to marry Harley Sneed and you ain't puttin' it off any longer."

"I won't do it! He's as old as you! He reminds me of a rat with his beady eyes, humped back, and pointy little teeth. He's a rat and you're a pig." Those had been Kat's words just hours ago.

Kat knew Boris was done waiting for her to decide on her own. She knew the only reason Boris wanted her to marry Harley was because Harley's land was adjacent to his. If Kat married Harley, she could work both farms. Lord knew she did more than her fair share already, and when Harley kicked off, Boris would get his land and more than double the size of his farm. Boris had always been envious of Harley's possessions. Harley always seemed to have the money to buy new horses, plows, and livestock.

It had come to this point, and now Kat didn't know what to do. She had no other family or any real friends to whom she could turn. She lived a very secluded life on the farm. A plan was what she needed, a plan to free her from this dilemma; but nothing was coming to her. She emerged from the woods deep in thought…

Boris watched Kat come out of the woods. "This is perfect!" Boris thought. He put the big saucer of milk on the table and hurried behind his bedroom curtain. Boris decided to go to bed. His part was done. He and Harley had concocted this plan, and the rest was up to Harley. Once Harley spoiled her, she would *have* to marry him, and then, one day, Harley's farm would be his. Boris congratulated himself on being so clever. He had no problem drifting off into a snore-filled sleep.

CHAPTER 1

When Kat entered the house she saw a big saucer of milk on the table. Shaking her head, she picked it up and muttered, "Everything on this farm would be dead if it weren't for me." Kat headed to the barn to give the saucer of milk to the kittens.

There was barely enough daylight left for Kat to find the spot where she always set the saucer for the kittens. Boris and the boys must have headed over to the Buckley boy's farm for a night of whiskey drinking, Kat thought. Boris and his sons loved to drink. In fact, for Henry and Clay in particular, it was what they seemed to live for. Kat thought it made them even more dumb and lazy.

Kat set down the saucer and the cats came running. She took a few minutes to stroke them as they drank and purred with appreciation. She stood up and walked toward the front of the barn in the darkness. Unfortunately, her head was down, as she was still deep in thought.

He was waiting for her, hiding behind the gate of an open stall, already rock hard just thinking about it. "Settle down, Settle down!" Harley told himself silently. "That got you into trouble before." He had a problem releasing too early. Years ago, his young wife used to make fun of him for it. The second time she made fun of him was her last. Harley, consumed with rage and humiliation, pushed her down the stairs. He considered himself lucky. He was able to pass it off as a clumsy accident on her part.

Harley waited a bit longer. Once Kat was a step past him he pulled the shovel back and whacked her on the head. He was unsure about how hard to hit her. He didn't want to kill her or even knock her out. Just stun her enough so he could pin her down and do his thing. Then she would have to marry him.

He was surprised Boris had come up with such a good plan. Harley didn't like Boris, but he did like this plan. Harley had watched Katherine grow up and had lusted after her from the first time he saw her. She was only three at the time. He had often fantasized about catching her alone in the forest, but the opportunity just never arose. She was as quick as a mouse and made sure never to get close to him.

The shovel worked like a charm. Kat stumbled to the ground in a daze but was not completely knocked out. Harley grabbed her and flipped her over. He was really worked up now. To Harley's dismay, she began to struggle. Damn, he should have used a bit more force. Harley was angry as the bleary-eyed Kat flipped on to her stomach and attempted to crawl toward the stack of hay just on the inside of the barn door. He was furious as he reached for her ankle and yanked her back toward him. With great force he grabbed her by the arms, flipped her back over, and slammed her head into the ground. Hard. This time she was out.

"Damn," Harley said quietly. He liked it when they struggled. "Oh well, maybe this is better." Kat was strong, and she could have made things difficult. Harley looked at the unconscious girl's face. His eyes slowly drifted down to her breasts. He just loved little titties. He couldn't resist and had to take a look.

Harley reached down and ripped her shirt open. There they were. But the second he put his hand on her breasts it happened. He released too early. "Damn. Damn," he whispered. Harley unzipped his pants and frantically worked to get himself hard again. He was staring at Kat's breasts to help with his chore. He was just beginning to make progress when something drew his eyes from Kat's breasts to her face.

Harley's first reaction was confusion. Kat's eyes were now open. She didn't look scared or even confused; instead she looked calm, aware, and strong.

Kat made her way up to the porch on shaking legs. She sat up against the front door, her head resting on her knees, her body quivering from head to toe. "What am I going to do? Someone, please tell me. What am I going to do?" Kat pleaded, although no one was listening. She gasped as she felt something brush up against her. Her relief was tremendous, and she even felt a little comfort as Flex pushed her head into her hand for a pet.

"Oh, Flex! I'd give anything if you could talk right now and tell me what to do." The human and the animal looked at each other for a moment. Kat almost felt as if Flex understood. Then, Flex suddenly turned, ran toward the west end of the porch and jumped up on the rail. Flex took a final glance back at Kat before fleeing into the darkness of the night.

Kat jumped again as she noticed the corpse of a rodent Flex had left on the porch by her side. Kat stared at it for a few moments as a plan quickly took shape in her mind. It was just before midnight—she had much to do. She stood up and made her way to Harley's place.

CHAPTER 2

It was the smell of fresh coffee brewing that finally woke Boris. As he sat up and scratched himself, it occurred to him a wedding was about to take place. Boris was in good spirits as he went out to the kitchen. His youngest son, Trevor, was the only one up, and he had made the coffee.

"You boys stay out late last night?" Boris asked.

"No," Trevor replied, "we got home about midnight. Seems I can take less and less of those Buckley boys."

"Ah, they're good boys."

"No, they're not," Trevor replied. Trevor peeked out the window. "Hey, what are Harley's horses doing in our yard?"

Boris and Trevor, coffee cups still in hand, headed out the front door to get a closer look at the strange sight. As they stepped out on the porch, both men's heads turned. Their eyes drifted to the west end of the porch, where Kat's favorite black cat, Flex, was sitting quietly on the rail. The animal looked up at the men who emerged from the door only for a moment before she returned to sweetly licking the blood off her jowls from her latest kill. Boris and Trevor looked at the animal. Both men were puzzled. Something didn't feel right. It was dead still out. Then suddenly, as if commanded by an unseen force, Trevor and Boris slowly turned their heads to the opposite end of the porch.

Trevor dropped his coffee cup as his eyes rested on Harley Sneed in the porch swing, a pitchfork protruding from his bloody neck.

Boris wet himself.

🍁   🍁   🍁

Kat had been riding all night. She was tired and had a raging headache, but stopping wasn't an option. She turned the horse she was riding and the pack-horse she was leading south and headed downstream until she found the perfect place to cross. It had begun to rain softly, which fit her plan perfectly. The horses were strong and healthy. She knew they'd be all right if she pushed them. Just the first day or so, then she'd give them a break. So push them she did. Kat rode all day and deep into the next night. The Missouri landscape was beautiful this time of year. Yellow and purple flowers dotted the banks of the river, and the land was a lush green, but Kat didn't notice. Because she was so tired, she made herself take deep breaths of the fresh spring air to keep awake and alert.

Finally, Kat stopped for a few hours before sun up to sleep and rest the horses, only because she felt she had put enough distance between her and the men who were likely tracking her down. She tied the horses a short distance away yet still in her line of sight. Cleverly, she covered herself in chunks of bark from a fallen tree. Someone could walk right up to where she lay and not realize she was there. Kat snuggled up to her gun and quickly fell asleep. She was confident she had several hours' head start on the men.

When she awoke after just a couple hours of sleep, Kat went to work on the second part of the plan. The early morning sun flooding tiny ribbons of light through the tall trees, giving her just the light she needed to survey her supplies. After all, she had packed in such a hurry and had to now make certain she had everything she needed. Kat's eyes looked to the ground in front of her, at the contents of the bag of goods she had stolen from Harley's place: two pairs of pants, two shirts, a hat, strips of cloth, tobacco, scissors, a small mirror, some jerky, raisins, bread, and jam, three knives, a saw and an ax, ammunition and money. Plenty of money. "How original," Kat thought, "to have hidden it in the mattress." Kat knew she would soon be approaching a town. She took a deep breath and let it out a bit shakier than she intended. The real test of her new plan would come in town.

It was just twenty-four hours later, and a beautiful morning, when Kat rode into town. She kept her head facing forward in an attempt to feign confidence while her worried eyes scanned the people and landscape in front of her. Her first human contact since the incident was the man at the livery. That went fine. She boarded her horses and headed for the hotel. Kat took her items to her room and then stared out the window for over an hour. She then carefully checked herself in the mirror, took a deep breath, and headed down to the saloon.

Kat sat at a corner table, ordered a whiskey, and just watched. She watched how they talked. How they walked. How they stood. Even the way they drank. How they handled their money. The way they smoked. Thankfully, they left her alone. She had been in the saloon for about an hour and was definitely feeling the three whiskeys she'd had.

Back at her room, she practiced rolling cigarettes and even smoked one as she stared out the window, watching. The town was teeming with activity. If it weren't so overpopulated, it probably wouldn't seem so dirty to her. She knew this was a jumping-off point for people heading west. Many were passing through; this wasn't their town, so they didn't care if they left their trash behind or if their dogs urinated all over the boardwalks. As she rode into town she had caught several different odors. Food cooking, urine, and dead animal just to name a few. Right now, Kat was fighting a feeling of wooziness as the whiskey and tobacco mixed in her system. "If they can do it, I have to," she told herself. It was mind over matter, and Kat talked herself into conquering her feeling of sickness.

As the light of day began to dim, Kat headed for the street. The town was quieting down. She walked to the post office and read the job openings.

Help Wanted

Wagon Train heading for Oregon needs a Scout and Hunter. We leave from the north edge of town, 9 am, Tuesday, May 16th. If interested, ask for John Appleton at the hotel.

School Teachers needed out West. Opportunity in the territories to teach Miners' and Ranchers' children.

7 Brides needed for 7 Brothers. Handsome men. Make a good living. See Postmaster for details.

That one made Kat laugh. She turned to walk away when something caught her eye. She froze in her tracks.

Wanted by the Law

Katherine Yelta
Suspect in the May 13^(th) murder of Harley Sneed.
Suspect is 19 years old. Tall. Slender. Female.
Handsome woman with green eyes and long black hair.
Very dangerous.

Contact the Sheriff if you have seen a woman fitting
this description and to inquire about the reward.

Katherine slowly backed away from the sign. Quickly, she turned and began walking down the boardwalk. Her pulse was racing. She broke into a sweat. Kat could not believe her name and description were up on the post-office wall. She was up there along with a man who was wanted for brutally slaying two drifters and seriously wounding another. What kind of sick, disgusting person had she become? "Get a hold of yourself," she said through gritted teeth. "Stay calm. Stay calm!"

Just then, Kat's attention broke from her thoughts. Up ahead she noticed a girl coming out of the dry-goods store. She was almost as tall as Kat but looked to be a few years younger. The girl was quite pretty with beautiful wavy brown hair. Kat thought she look a little sad or scared. Maybe both? The girl turned north and quickly headed down the boardwalk.

"What is that stupid girl doing out at this time of night!" Kat thought. Just then, two men stepped onto the boardwalk from an alley. Kat didn't like the looks of them. They sneered at each other and began to follow the girl. Kat followed them.

The sixteen-year-old girl quickly looked behind her. She knew she was being followed. Kat noticed she was approaching another alley. "Don't do it!" Kat thought as she quickened her pace. "Don't turn down that alley." But the girl did. She threw a worried glance back at the men and turned down the alley.

"Damn. Damn!" Kat concern grew when she saw the men looked at each other and smile. They broke into a trot toward the alley entrance.

Kat reached down and pulled out the long skinning knife she had in a scabbard against her right thigh. She broke into a run, hoping to confront the men before they turned down the alley. There was quite a distance between her and the men. She preferred to confront them on the boardwalk rather than in the alley. As it turned out, she didn't have to do either.

Out of nowhere, a man on a huge black horse appeared in front of the men on the boardwalk. The horse, unaccustomed to the sound of its hooves on a boardwalk, pranced nervously in front of the men. There was something about this man's presence that rendered Kat's muscles useless. She stood frozen in her tracks.

"You know, fellas," the man on the horse said, "that's the bad thing about this town. They allow all kinds of animals on the boardwalk. My advice to you is to turn around and find something else to do tonight. I don't know how much longer I can control Bullet. He loves to trample snakes." The horse then lunged at the men with a little urging from his rider. The men dove into the street then quickly got up and ran across the street to the saloon.

Kat stood with her mouth open. All kinds of thoughts were rushing through her head. The two "snakes" hadn't scared her but this man had her shaking in her boots. He must be eight feet tall! No, it must just be his horse. She knew she needed to calm down and looking at him wasn't helping. For some reason she couldn't take her eyes off him. Although it was dark she could feel the intensity of his stare.

The man's eyes seemed to penetrate completely through her as he spoke. "I could see you had the situation under control. Hope you didn't mind that I stepped in, since I happened to be right here. Bullet loves to scare snakes. Have a good evening, son." And he was off.

Kat watched him go, not wanting him to leave, yet feeling great relief. If a man like that could spot "snakes" so easily, she figured her disguise must be convincing enough. Kat looked down the alley. The girl was gone. She must be part of the wagon train camping just north of town.

"What kind of parents would allow her to come to town alone at dusk?" Kat wondered.

CHAPTER 3

Kat didn't realize how exhausted she was until she was back in her room. She removed Harley's hat and stared at her reflection in the mirror. She felt her cropped hair. It wasn't as hard as she had thought it would be to cut off her long black mane. Kat was especially proud of the fine black dots she had put on her chin and upper lip. It truly looked like black stubble. She took off her shirt and with relief unwound the cloth that confined her breasts. Kat looked forward to the bath she had ordered. The steaming water called to her from the other side of the room. Kat undressed and looked at her body. She realized her build had helped her pull this off. She was slender and muscular, with long legs, narrow hips, and a small rump. Thank goodness Harley had been skinny and bony—his clothes fit perfectly. Add a hat, and Kat had to admit, she made a fine-looking boy.

As she lay in the tub she cleansed more than just her body. She cleansed her past. Katherine's mind went back through the years, to the faint glimpses in her memory of her real father. According to her mother, she was the spitting image of him with her thick black hair and green eyes. From what her mother had told her, Kat's father had adored his little girl. He died one night when a man burst into their camp in an attempted to rob them. Her father drew his pistol and both men shot each other. Katherine was just three at the time, and the happy little family was naively heading west at the time to start a new life. She wept for the father she could hardly remember.

Kat's mind continued on its journey. She faintly remembered escaping the confusion, with her mother dragging her into the darkness of the woods. They made it to a nearby farm—Boris's farm. Kat knew her mother had never loved Boris. She was merely finding a way to survive. Boris had literally worked her

14 Kat Tales

mother to death. She wasn't built for hard physical labor and constant verbal abuse. By the time Kat was old enough to relieve her load, it was too late. Her mother was too weak. Kat wasn't sure what had really killed her. She simply took to her bed one day and never got back up. She died weeks later with Kat by her side. That was ten years ago. Kat wept for her mother, remembering her as though she had seen her yesterday.

Kat even thought about Trevor, Boris's youngest son. He was the same age as Kat and the most normal of the three boys. He would defend Kat when Henry and Clay's words would become too harsh. He worked twice as hard as the other boys but was gone a lot. He often left for long stretches during the year to work with his uncle, Jacob, Boris's first wife's brother. Kat could tell he thought more of his Uncle Jacob than his own father. Who could blame him? She was certain she'd never see Trevor again. She wept for Trevor and the relationship they had never had time to develop.

Kat's thoughts turned to the events of the previous week. It amazed her how her life had been so uneventful for so many years, only to become frenzied and complicated within the span of a week. She thought of the terror and the horrible feeling of helplessness when she knew she was about to be raped. She remembered the feeling of complete control and focus that overtook her body and mind as she decided not to let it happen. And she remembered thrusting the pitchfork through Harley's neck with precision. It was her intention to kill him. She squeezed her eyes tight and vowed to never let that scene run through her mind again.

It seemed unreal now. How afterward she went to Harley's house and calmly rifled through his belongings, taking whatever she thought she could use, including all his money. Going out to the corral and picking out the two best horses he had and letting the rest escape. Riding back to Boris's farm late in the night. Dragging Harley from the barn and propping him up in the porch swing. She wondered now why she had done that. She didn't weep for Harley or the life she left behind.

Finally, she thought of Flex and smiled with fond remembrance.

❧   ❧   ❧

Kat got up at sunrise. She had breakfast in the saloon: a big plate of eggs, ham, and potatoes, and a plate of flapjacks. She downed a cup of coffee and a glass of milk and then sat back to smoke a cigarette. She was getting good at it. She didn't really like it, but it completed her disguise perfectly.

She was startled when she heard a voice say, "It's always you little guys that can put back so much food. I remember when I was a young lad. Seemed like I could eat forever and never fill up." It was the eight-foot-tall man from last night who had confronted the snakes. Kat decided he was only a little over six-foot tall. It didn't help her calm down. Kat sat up straight. The man offered his hand. She extended hers and remembered to tighten her grip as hard as she could as he shook her hand. "Name's Jack Parker. What's yours?"

Kat froze…a name…a name? She hadn't thought of a name. She'd just been given a number tag at the livery and signed her name with an x at the hotel registry, pretending to be illiterate. She had paid cash up front—that was all they cared about. "Name's…uh, John…John Deer."

"Are you part Indian?" Jack asked. "Sounds like that has some Indian origins."

"No," Kat replied.

"What's a young lad like you doing in a town like this? Are you looking for work?"

"You sure ask a lot of questions," Kat replied. She was beginning to get a bit annoyed.

"Don't take offense. It's just my way of looking out for you, son. I have a brother about your age and I would want someone to do the same if he was out on his own."

"You have a brother about my age, huh?" Kat asked, because she truly was curious. "How old is your brother?"

"He's fifteen."

"That's interesting," Kat said. "Well, nice to meet you…Parker, was it? I've got to go. I have a job interview I can't be late for."

"And I'm leaving town this morning," he replied. "You take care of yourself, Deer. Steer clear of snakes." And he was off.

On the way to the livery, Kat chastised herself for forgetting to give herself a name. That was a big mistake. She tried to think of anything else she might have forgotten. She almost blew it with "Jack Parker." Well, at least now she knew how old she was.

CHAPTER 4

Kat squinted in order to make out the figures she saw ahead of her on the prairie. She had just passed the last building and was heading toward the wagon train camped about a mile north of town. She kicked her horse so she could move closer, giving her a better look.

It looked like two men on horses, but what was in front of them? It took a second to sink in, and when it did, Kat gasped. She couldn't believe her eyes. It was the girl from the alley again. She was walking all alone on the open prairie in the direction of the wagon train. It looked like she was carrying a couple of bags of supplies. Kat squinted again to make out the men on horseback. By God, it was the two snakes from the night before! Kat kicked her horse into a full run just as the men had urged their horses to pick up speed. They didn't realize anyone was behind them. They were too busy concentrating on what was in front of them.

Up to this point, the girl had been oblivious to the fact that anyone was behind her. Some instinct must have finally kicked in, as she looked back and saw the men closing in on her. In a panic, she dropped her bag of supplies and began running, but she was too far from camp.

Kat urged her horse to move faster. Her packhorse had come untied and was running free next to her. Oh well, she'd deal with that later. Kat passed the two men just before they reached the terrified girl. Kat squeezed her thighs against the horse's sides, reached down with one hand, and grabbed the back of the girl's dress. That wasn't enough, as the girl started to stumble and Kat began to lose her grip. Quickly, she reached over with her other hand and grabbed the girl under her armpit. The girl bounced up in perfect rhythm with the horse, and Kat was somehow able to hoist her up on the horse's neck. The girl almost went completely over the horse, but Kat balanced her in time. Kat then grabbed her thigh and was able to get her to straddle the horse while sharing the saddle with her. It wasn't pretty, but it had worked somehow. By this time, Kat and the girl were just a short distance from the wagon train. Kat glanced behind her and noticed that the men had peeled off to the east and disappeared into a grove of trees.

Kat and the girl didn't speak until they entered the camp. As the horse came to a stop, Kat dismounted. She asked the girl, "Can you get off by yourself?"

"Yes," the girl whispered. When she got off the horse, she began to cry. "Thank you."

"What's your name?" Kat asked, not acknowledging the quiet thank you.

"Laura," the girl muttered, her eyes on the ground in front of her and still full of tears.

"You need to be more careful," Kat scolded. "What were you thinking going out alone like that?"

"I know!" Laura screamed through her tears. "I don't have a choice! There's no one to help me! No one! And now I don't have any supplies." She was thoroughly sobbing now.

Kat felt badly. This Laura must be without any family and without any idea how to survive on her own. In that instant, Kat felt lucky she had been left to fend for herself and not raised like normal females, who were raised to be helpless, to depend on family and especially men. What happens when women like Laura are left all alone? Often bad things, Kat concluded.

"Sorry." A crowd of wagon-train people had started to gather. "Don't cry," Kat whispered. "I'll go back and get your supplies. You wait here." Kat turned around and ran smack dab into her packhorse. "Ow, those horses have hard heads," she thought as she rubbed her nose. At least she didn't have to go find him on the prairie. She turned him around and began to retie the packhorse to her mount. She looked up and saw a familiar face. He was silently chuckling, his arms loaded down with Laura's supplies.

"Kid, that was a sight to see! You should have seen how you looked trying to haul her up on your horse." He was laughing so hard by now, he could hardly get the next words out. "And then...running into your pack horse...it's like it's the first day you've spent in your body."

"Yeah. Thanks. And shut up," Kat replied.

"Kid, don't be mad at me," Jack Parker said with more composure this time. "It was also amazing. Well, not the part about running into your horse, but the rescue. You're to be commended." He was still trying not to laugh.

"Just give Laura her supplies." Kat looked at Laura, and noticed she was actually smiling through her tears now. Kat chuckled and said, "Laura. Jack Parker. Parker, this is Laura."

"How do you do?" Laura said to Jack. "And what's the name of my rescuer?"

Again, Kat froze.

"His name's John. John Deer," Jack interjected.

"Oh." Laura asked, "Are you part Indian?"

"No," Kat replied.

"What are you doing here?" Kat posed the question to Jack.

"I'm applying for a job."

"You can't apply for the hunter job. I am," Kat said.

"Well, yes I can," Jack replied, "but I'm not going to. I'm interested in the position of scout. It's more my area of expertise."

"Oh."

Kat stepped back as a man with a very round head and bright red cheeks approached. "Hello, fellas. Name's John Appleton. You need a job?"

"Yes." Jack took the lead. "I'm interested in becoming your scout. You'll find no one better for the job. This is my partner, John Deer. Don't look like much, but he sure can hunt."

"Well, as luck would have it, you're the only two that have applied for jobs, so I guess you're hired. Our last scout wasn't much good. He went out on the prairie and never came back. Maybe he got lost or something. And the hunter—he died of syphilis."

"Well, that is lucky," Kat replied. "When do we pull out?"

"Right about now."

Kat tied her packhorse to one of the wagons and rode beside Jack a good distance ahead of the wagon train. There were fifty-six people in the wagon train, eighteen units altogether. There were couples, young and old, a pair of brothers, and several families. Kat found it very interesting to be a part of this parade west. These people didn't know her and she didn't know them. It was a completely fresh start. Her plan was to get as far away from her past as possible. A past that had only restricted her. A past that wouldn't allow her to be who she wanted to be. She was certain she didn't want to be a man forever, but it had been an interesting experiment so far. She felt an incredible sense of freedom in the presence of people who did not see her as a woman. As a woman, she had always felt a little conspicuous. As a man, no one seemed to notice her. She liked that. She could never get the job as hunter for a wagon train as a woman! It certainly would not have been safe to travel alone, and she would not have been able to talk so freely with men like Jack Parker and John Appleton.

John Appleton pulled his mount alongside Kat and Jack. "Howdy. Thought I'd fill you two in on our day. We'll break for lunch about noon. Cook will heat up some beans and cornbread. We'll stop again for a half hour in the late afternoon to rest the horses and then travel again till dusk. Jack, we're relying on you to keep your eye out for trouble during the day and find us a nice, safe place to camp at night.

"Kid, we need you to find us some meat for our evening meals. These folks are thrilled to have you both with us. This is their first time West. For some, it's their first time traveling at all. Most of them are leaving because they've got nothing to keep them where they were. I don't think they understood the dangers until we had our first tragedy. We were crossing the river and one wagon was swept away. That's how Laura lost her parents. Laura rode with Cook on that crossing because we thought their wagon might be too heavy. It's sad, cuz now she has no one. It will take some time, but she'll be all right. She's young and pretty. Some young feller will marry her. Well, fellas, I'd better get back to the train. Gotta make sure no wheels fall off. I hate it when we have a delay because of equipment failure." With that, John Appleton was off.

"That's too bad about Laura's parents," Kat remarked. "That's got to be tough, a young woman like Laura trying to make it on her own. Especially in a new town."

"Maybe she'll find a 'young feller' to marry her," Jack said with a sly smile. "Maybe a 'young feller' like you."

Kat just looked straight ahead. "No, that's not going to happen."

"Come on, kid. I saw the way she looked at you. You're her rescuer," Jack teased.

"Shut up," Kat said.

"Settle down, kid. There are worse things than having a young lady after you. I'm going to ride ahead and see what I can see. Want to come along? Maybe you'll find some supper for the folks," Jack said.

"Sure." Kat and Jack kicked the horses into a canter and rode ahead of the wagon train.

It was a beautiful day. Not too hot for late spring. They rode until they reached a rocky plateau with a stream running through it. Jack and Kat dismounted and climbed to the top of the rocky ledge to get a look ahead. The horses munched on grass at the bottom of the hill. Jack was several paces ahead of Kat and had made it all the way to the top of the ledge. He lay on his stomach, perched on his elbows, and held his telescope up to his eye. As he scanned the landscape ahead of him, Kat made her way up the hill. When she reached Jack, she realized something was wrong.

Jack froze as a rattler lay coiled and rattling beneath a rock about three feet from his head.

"Don't move," Kat said in a low voice. She pulled at her pistol then thought better of it and returned it to her holster. She then reached for her knife, pinched the blade between her thumb and forefinger, and let it fly. It was a direct hit. The snake went limp, its head pinned to the ground with Kat's knife.

Jack approached the snake, cut its head off, and then pulled Kat's knife from its head. He picked up the snake's long body, looked it up and down, and then looked up at Kat. "Thanks, kid." He walked up to Kat and slapped her on the back, hard. "For a minute, you had me worried. I thought you were going to shoot it and ricochet a bullet off all those rocks into my head."

"I thought about it," Kat said with a smile, "but then I'd have to do the scouting, too, and that wouldn't leave me enough time to have fun."

"Well now, that was smart thinking, kid. I guess I did know what I was talking about when I told Appleton you were the best hunter in the area."

"I was wondering why you did that," Kat said.

"Here's part of tonight's supper," Jack said as he handed the snake's large, lifeless body to Kat.

Kat just stared at it.

"What's the matter, squeamish about snakes? This one sure isn't going to hurt you after what you did to it."

"I know. I just have never eaten snake before, but I've heard it's good. So, did you get a look before you realized you had become snake bait?" Kat teased.

"Yes. It would have been a great lookout point if it hadn't been for the rattler. I could see for miles. Nothing but prairie as far as the eye could see. Looks like we'll go for a while without many trees or water, so we'd better fill up the canteens and water barrels."

CHAPTER 5

Kat and Jack came across a covey of quail to help round out the evening meal. It was almost noon as they headed back to the wagon train, which would soon be stopping for the midday meal. While they were still in the shadows of the trees, Kat and Jack brought the horses to a stop. Some men on horseback had approached the wagon train. Jack pulled out his telescope and peered through it.

"What is it?" Kat asked. "Troublemakers?"

"Depends on who you consider to be troublemakers," Jack said, still peering through the looking scope. "Looks like a posse."

Terror filled Kat. She had to think quickly. "Let's wait here for a minute; they could be troublemakers. If they start acting up, we can ride in and surprise them. Let me take a look," Kat said as she reached for the telescope.

"Fine," Jack said and handed her the glass.

Kat looked through the scope. There was a man talking to Appleton. He handed him a piece of paper. She sure wished she could see what was on that paper. She then looked at the five men on horseback. Clay, her stepbrother. That asshole! He was hunting her down! He cared more about Harley's missing money and horses than about her. She was angry, really angry. One man rode up and down the train checking out the wagons and the horses. He had stopped behind the wagon where Kat's packhorse was tied. Oh, no! Kat couldn't believe it. It was Trevor! Trevor was hunting her down, too. Would he recognize Harley's horse? Trevor turned and rode back to the group of men. He didn't say anything. He must not have recognized the horse. The man talking with Appleton tipped his hat and mounted his horse. The posse rode off in the other direction.

"So, who do you think they're looking for?" Jack asked in a serious tone.

"Don't know and don't care," Kat replied.

"Don't care?" Jack asked. "Why not?"

"I just think there are a lot of innocent people condemned for things they didn't do, or maybe did do but had a right to. People sure are good at being the judge of others when maybe they should take a good look at themselves."

"I agree," was Jack's reply. "I'm going to fill these canteens. Why don't you drop off the meat to Cook, grab whatever canteens you can handle, and ride on back to the stream? This air's so dusty I'm sure those folks are thirsty."

Kat's heart was beating wildly as she approached the wagon train. John Appleton waved a greeting. "Howdy," Kat tried to say in as firm a voice as possible as she approached Appleton. "W-who were those men and what did they want?" Kat asked, mad at herself for stuttering.

"It was a posse," he said. "They were looking for this woman. Said she killed a wealthy farmer. Stole some of his livestock, belongings, and his money. Killed him with a pitchfork while he slept. Said he was a nice old man. Just goes to show, you never know who the crazies are."

Kat stared at the drawing of herself. It did look like her, or how she use to look. She studied Appleton's face as she handed the picture back to him. It was obvious he did not suspect her. Her gaze then shifted to the people on the wagon train. None of them looked her way, only Laura, who offered a friendly wave. Kat reluctantly waved back.

"Where's Jack?" Appleton asked.

"He's filling canteens. I've come to gather up more to take to him. It's going to be a long, dusty road from here on out. I'll be back shortly."

Jack watched as the kid approached him at the stream. "Is everything all right?" Jack asked in a serious tone.

"Yes," Kat replied.

"So, was it a posse?"

"Yes," she replied again.

It was like pulling teeth! "So, what did they want?" Jack asked, mildly frustrated.

"They were looking for a...um...murderer."

Jack was becoming impatient. "Did they have a picture?"

"Yes," Kat said.

"And...what did he look like?"

"The murderer was a woman."

"Oh. It must have been the one I saw on the post-office wall. If she looks anything like the drawing—wow! So, they actually formed a posse to find her? Maybe I'll find her first," he said.

"So you could collect the reward?" Kat sneered.

"No," Jack replied. "Well, we better get back. I'm sure those folks are thirsty, and you, you're probably starving!"

Back at camp, Kat helped herself to beans and cornbread. She sat on the back of a wagon to concentrate on her meal. She had just put the first bite in her mouth when Laura plunked down next to her. "Hi, John. Mind if I sit here?"

"Suit yourself," Kat replied suspiciously.

"Mr. Parker said you saved him from a rattler today. He said you threw your knife at it and pinned its head right to the ground. It that true?"

"Yes, I guess it is," Kat replied.

"How did you learn to do that? Did your father teach you? My father didn't teach me how to do anything like that. He was a doctor. I know how to sew. I know how to cook and I'm very good at school learning, but that's really all I know how to do. I was wondering," Laura said with her head down, "could you teach me to throw a knife and maybe…shoot a gun? I'll find a way to repay you."

"Why do you want to learn?" Kat asked suspiciously.

"Because knowing how to sew, cook, and learn from books doesn't keep you alive. Maybe if I knew how to handle a pistol and a knife I wouldn't be so scared all the time. I know everyone's expecting me to just up and marry someone so he can take care of me, but to tell you the truth, from what I've seen of men so far, I'd rather do without one. No offense, but I just don't trust men. They either scare me or they make me feel—I don't know—dumb or bad about myself."

"I'm a m-man." There was that stutter again. She was going to have to get over that.

"I know, but with you it's different. You're a different kind of man. Oh, I think that sounded bad, but believe me, in my eyes it's good."

"Yes, I'll teach you. Just because you're a woman doesn't mean you can't do it. It doesn't mean that at all. Here's what you need to know before we even start. You must want to do it. You must practice every spare moment if you want to be good at it—and I will never marry you. Do you agree to all those things?" Kat said.

"Oh, John," Laura replied, "you are so funny." She jumped off the wagon and went to help Cook with the dishes.

Kat sat there dumbfounded. "So, did she understand or not?"

Just then, as if out of nowhere, Jack appeared. "Kid, you look perplexed. Did Laura say something to 'confuse' you? Get use to it. Men will never understand women."

"I guess not," Kat whispered.

The wagon train pulled out a short time later. Kat rode alongside the train and Jack rode ahead to do some scouting. The mid-afternoon sun was heating things up, and Kat wished she could take off the cloth that bound her breasts. She also had to scout out a good place to go to the bathroom. She spotted it about fifteen minutes later, a grassy knoll. She would wait for the train to move ahead of her and then she could "squat." Some things you just couldn't disguise.

When Kat fell in line with the wagon train once again, she thought about Laura and how she would teach her to throw a knife and shoot a pistol. She hadn't ever taught anyone before, but she had taught herself. Laura did seem smart enough and she was definitely willing to learn. If she learned quickly enough, maybe Kat would teach her to crack a whip and ride a horse. Kat wouldn't be around forever to watch over Laura and she needed to learn these things if she intended to be alone in the world.

As Kat rode she became increasingly aware of how hot it was getting. She was accustomed to riding in the woods, not out on the open plains with the sun beating down on her every minute. The land here was flat and the horses' hooves kicked up dust with every step. The dust seemed to make her feel even hotter. Maybe it was because her skin couldn't breathe. She was absolutely dripping with sweat and could feel a little river of it running between her breasts. She longed to grab her shirt and rub but knew she couldn't.

The fact that she had already found food for dinner was a relief. The afternoon break did little to revive her, but finally the time came to pull over for the evening meal. They were lucky enough to come upon a stream. The tired, hot people washed their hands and faces, watered the livestock, and rested from the first long day across the prairie portion of their journey.

Jack Parker had returned from his day of scouting. Kat listened in as he spoke with John Appleton about what he had seen (or, to be more accurate, what he hadn't seen). Kat wasn't surprised to learn his biggest concern was the extreme heat. Jack recommended making more frequent stops if the heat continued, and maybe rerouting north sooner than they had anticipated. Kat figured rerouting would slow them down, but silently agreed it might be necessary to prevent people and animals from dropping due to the heat.

Kat took extra time to wipe down her horses. They were hot and tired, too. Kat noticed that the prairie grass was different than the grass back home. It seemed tougher and not as green. Hopefully it gave the horses the nourishment they needed.

After caring for her horses, Kat walked upstream to find a private place so she could do her thing.

"Hey, kid. Where are you headed?" Jack asked.

"I was looking for a little private spot to do a little private thing."

"How about that rock over there?" Jack pointed it out. "But watch out for rattlers. A bite down there is sure to be fatal. I'm heading over to that watering hole. Give me your canteen. I'll fill it up."

Kat handed him the canteen and went off to "the rock." Boy, a dip in the stream sounded great to her right now, but she knew she couldn't risk it. After doing her thing, she headed down to the watering hole to retrieve her canteen. She looked on the ground and saw the canteens. She looked around again, but there was no Jack. For a brief moment, Kat was concerned.

Suddenly, Jack's head popped up from the middle of the watering hole. He began swimming toward Kat, who stood on the shoreline. "Now that was refreshing," Jack said as he slowly rose out of the water. His body glistened with the many water beads clinging to it.

Kat gasped. He had on no clothes. Her first instinct was to turn away, but she knew that's what a woman would do. She had to fight the urge and look straight at him as if he weren't completely naked. "Wh-where are your clothes?"

"They're drying on that rock over there. Don't worry, I brought dry clothes in my roll. I wouldn't walk back into camp like this. I'd make all the ladies faint," Jack said with that sly grin. His teeth were really white. Kat found it funny that she noticed his teeth at this point. She forced herself to look at his face. He walked over to his roll and squatted down to retrieve his clean clothes. Now that he wasn't looking at her, she let her eyes roam. His body was amazing. Muscles, rock-hard muscles that moved in perfect rhythm with each other. Two big flat muscles made up his chest. His stomach had three, no, four ripples that tapered down to his slim hips. She hadn't noticed his hips were that slim when he had on pants. Those thighs. Lean, muscular, beautiful. Even his feet were a work of art. Curved and strong. She looked at the area below his stomach. She had never before seen this on a man. He had black curly hair, and his "thing" curved out of it. Perfectly. She thought she would be repulsed by it, like she was when she saw it on animals. Of course, he wasn't licking his, and maybe that made the difference. It was amazing. It made her feel kind of funny. He now had his back to her again as he pulled his pants on. She stared at the beautiful muscles of his back and his buttocks. She wanted to go up and feel them. The entire time he talked to her, she had to make certain she responded to him in a way that seemed normal. She had to make certain this moment didn't become awkward for him, because she intended to watch him bathe every night if she could.

"So, what did you and Laura talk about today?" Jack asked.

"She wants me to teach her how to throw a knife and shoot a pistol," Kat replied while soaking in every inch of his skin with her eyes. "I agreed to do it."

"I think that's a good idea. Make sure you teach her how to be safe with weapons. Don't need her unnecessarily shooting herself or anyone else. Does she want to learn because she truly wants to know how to defend herself, or do you think she just wants some attention from you?"

"No, she really wants to learn. She said some other things that made me sure of it," Kat replied. She was feeling disappointment because, except for his head and feet, he was completely covered up.

"Being alone with you will just be a bonus for her," Jack teased.

"It's strictly business," Kat said.

"What's the matter? Not interested in finding yourself a girlfriend right now? You got some wild oats to sow?"

"Yeah…no. I'm just not interested in settling down, and she's…she's just not my type," Kat sputtered.

"So what is your type, kid? Blonde? Redhead?"

"I don't categorize women by the color of their hair. That's just stupid."

"You know, kid, you're right. That's just male talk. It goes a lot deeper than the color of their hair.

"Well, you're quite a philosopher," Kat exclaimed. "Never would have guessed that."

"Well, kid, you hurt my feelings. I'm a very sensitive guy, you know. I just mask it with my charming good looks and quick sense of humor." Jack smiled again with those beautiful white teeth.

"So, what's Jack Parker's type?"

"My type? My type of woman would have to be beautiful, smart, strong, capable, and happy…and it goes without saying, she'd have to adore me. She'd have to want to live on a ranch and help me raise horses, cattle and chickens because I love my eggs, and she'd have to love dogs."

"What about cats?"

"Yeah, cats are fine. And she has to like lots and lots of sex," he finished.

Kat wondered if she had ever heard anyone say the word "sex" to her like that before. She knew what it was, but it had always been used in ways like, "What sex are the kittens?" It threw her somewhat.

"What's the matter, kid? Cat got your tongue?"

"No, I'm just tired. Ready to hit the hay, I guess."

"Let's head back to camp. We'll get some supper and some shut-eye. You'll have to take a turn as watchman, but not tonight. I'm taking the second shift. Appleton's got first watch and Clem Sichter will relieve me."

After a delicious supper of quail and rattlesnake, Kat rolled out her bed. Jack walked by and tapped Kat in the butt with his boot. "Sleep tight, kid. Enjoy dreaming about your perfect woman."

Kat did have dreams, but they certainly weren't about a woman.

CHAPTER 6

Kat woke early the next morning and walked up stream for some private time. She wandered into the water with her clothes on and took a bar of soap. Once under the water she removed her clothes and scrubbed them and herself. When she crawled out she quickly wrapped a blanket around her body and pulled on dry clothes with the blanket still on her back. It was tricky getting the cloth that bound her breasts to fit right, but finally she managed and then headed back to camp.

People were just beginning to stir. Kat had grabbed a net from Cook's wagon on the way to the stream. She had caught several fish and brought them back to camp. She, Cook, and some of the other men quickly cleaned the fish and they enjoyed them fried for breakfast. The travelers were all grateful for the delicious treat. Kat smiled broadly. Cook said to Kat, "Normally, I'd paddle anyone who took my stuff without asking, but I'll let it slide this time."

"Oh, Cook, I would have asked, but you were sleeping like a baby. You looked so sweet and peaceful I just couldn't wake you," Kat replied.

"Ah, kid, just for that I think I will paddle you," he said in his gruff voice as he waved a large spoon in the air. The entire camp laughed at the exchange between the old man and the kid. They made a great pair. The kid was resourceful and had so far found plenty of food. The old man had the magic touch and could make anything taste good.

After breakfast, Kat and Laura stood at the end of a wagon. Kat showed Laura a pistol. She demonstrated each part and described how it contributed to the whole mechanism. Laura was to repeat after her so she would be certain to learn. Kat also showed her the bullets and how to load the gun: always pointing it away from you or anyone else and toward the ground. Then Kat showed her the safe way to carry a gun and how to holster it so one could get to it quickly.

"Holstering a gun doesn't always mean having it on a belt at your waist," Kat told her. "You may want to have an extra fold in the back of your dress and tuck it securely in there. Or you can secure it inside of your coat. In the home, I always like to have a gun in the kitchen. Make sure if you have children in the house they can't get to it. But once they are old enough to handle a gun, teach them how to use it. That's it for now. Looks like we're getting ready to pull out."

Laura looked a little disappointed.

"Have patience, Laura. You'll get to shoot it next time." Kat smiled. "You have to walk before you can run."

It was early and the sun was already hot. "It's gonna be another scorcher," Jack said as he pulled up alongside Kat. Jack's horse was sure acting up. He was a stallion, and Kat was riding a mare. "Settle down, Bullet. We've got a long, hot day ahead of us, and you'll need your energy." Kat's horse flattened back her ears and nipped at Bullet. Bullet bared his teeth and tried to nip back. Jack yanked his head back with the reigns.

"You'd better teach Bullet some manners. I don't want him marking up Ginger," Kat said.

"She is a beautiful horse. Have you had her long?"

"No, not really. I did some, ah, work for my neighbor, and in exchange he said I could pick a horse from his herd. I picked Ginger because she's strong and really smart for a horse. She always keeps her cool—except when pushy stallions are around."

Jack looked Ginger up and down. "You certainly picked well. If you plan on breeding her later, let me know. I think she and Bullet could produce some great offspring."

"Sure." Kat liked that idea, but the statement made her a bit sad. She realized there was something called the future. She would have to come out of her disguise at some point, but it sure couldn't be around these people or during this trip. She imagined one day talking with Jack, Laura, and the others on the wagon train, like normal, and the next day having to disappear, never to see them again.

At this point she wasn't sure how that would happen. It took all her concentration to keep up this charade.

Today, Kat had great luck hunting. Rabbits. Lots of them. She also found raspberry bushes. The berries were delicious. She spent an entire hour picking as many as she could, as quickly as she could. There was enough for everyone to have some. She caught up with the train at about noon. She gave the berries to Cook, who was very impressed. He even had a little sugar to put on the berries to sweeten them up for the folks. Lunch consisted again of beans and cornbread, but the berries provided a welcome treat for the grateful folks. They all applauded when Cook brought them out. Kat felt herself flush.

After lunch, Kat worked with Laura. She showed her the knife she liked to throw, taught her the grip, and even let her throw it a few times. Not bad for a beginner, but she still had a long way to go. Kat told her if she wanted to be truly good with a knife she must throw whenever she had a spare moment.

Laura nodded her head in agreement. "When will I get to shoot?" she asked.

"I was thinking about that," Kat replied. "Since I already have enough food for the evening meal, I want you to ride out with me today and we'll find a place to practice. We'll have Jack ride ahead and make sure there are no Indians around. We don't need to draw extra attention to ourselves."

Kat and Laura rode ahead of the wagon train after the midday meal. Kat could see she needed to give Laura some riding tips as well. The good thing was, Laura listened well and learned quickly. It was as if she really felt it was a life-or-death situation. Kat was glad about that. Laura took to shooting like a duck to water. Some folks had natural talent with a gun, and Laura was one of them. Kat told her so and Laura beamed.

"What we're going to work on with you is the mental part of shooting," Kat told her. "When you use a gun, it may be because you are in a stressful situation. You may be excited because there is an entire herd of deer in front of you. Or, you may be scared because you just heard a cougar screech and he is up on a ledge, ready to pounce. If you panic, if you lose your control, you can lose your life. You must force yourself out of panic and into cool, calm focus. You won't understand until it happens to you."

Laura's knife throwing took a bit more work. Kat was constantly asking her how much practice she was getting in each day. Laura was a good student. She rode out with Kat and Jack every afternoon and sometimes in the morning. She was actually becoming a big help to Kat with the hunting. Laura shot her first deer a week later. The first shot took the animal down. Laura quickly got off another shot and impressed Kat and Jack by downing a second animal that was really moving. Most folks on the wagon train were very impressed with Laura's newfound talent and the fact that the kid and Jack were helping her hone her skills. A few, like Mr. and Mrs. Dickerson, thought it was horrible that a young girl like Laura would ride off with two men for hours at a time.

Horrible that Laura had taken to wearing pants when she would go off hunting, and horrible that she practiced every waking moment with that knife. If she kept it up, no man would want to marry her.

Kat really worked with Laura on her knife throwing. She needed to get that down before she could work a whip, Kat told her. "Now, look again at how my fingers grip the blade. Yes, you have to be cautious—after all, it is a knife—but you act as if you're uncomfortable with it."

"It just doesn't feel natural to me," Laura complained. "Your fingers seem to be made for it. They are so slender, and your arm just whips out so gracefully. I feel awkward when I do it."

"Just keep practicing, Laura. One day you'll do it perfectly, and your body will just know how. That's how it was with me."

"Really, you haven't always been able to throw like this?" Laura asked with excitement.

"Hell, no." (Kat had decided to start swearing a little. It was a manly thing to do.) "It took me a long time. One day I just started getting it right, and I still practice daily."

"John, I don't know how I'll ever be able to repay you and Jack for helping me, but somehow I'll find a way."

"Laura, I don't ever want you to mention that again. There is no need to 'repay' me. If everyone in this world would do a little to help someone else, mankind would be so much better off. Just help someone else someday who needs it. That's how you can 'repay' me."

"Well, you don't have to get mad at me for it," Laura said.

"I'm not mad at you. I'm just upset that people spend more time making trouble for others rather than helping them," Kat said in a softer tone. "Let's get back. It's time for supper, and I'm starving."

The venison was delicious, and most of the folks had high praise for Laura. Kat watched her student with pride. Laura had much more confidence, and it seemed to grow on a daily basis. She now had a twinkle in her eye and her face shone. To Kat, she seemed much different than when she had first met Laura. She didn't seem to be a "victim" anymore.

Jack watched the kid and was very proud of him. He was doing a great job teaching Laura. Jack wasn't stepping in on this one. He saw that Laura was being taught so much more than the mechanics of how to shoot a gun and throw a knife. John was doing it right. The kid was really something else. Jack felt this was the beginning of a long relationship with this kid. They were definitely cut from the same cloth. He would have a talk with the kid, see what his plans were for the future. John was young, but age didn't matter. It was about the person. This kid would make a great partner for the ranching operation he intended to start, once he felt it was safe to settle down somewhere. Heck, even if Laura remained in the picture she'd be a great asset, although the kid didn't really display any feelings of romance toward her. He was young. Maybe those feelings hadn't kicked in yet. How old did he say he was again? That was odd. Jack couldn't remember, and he always prided himself on having a great memory. Maybe old age? Twenty-six wasn't old enough to start losing your memory, was it?

That night, Kat had first watch. It was still hot, even though the sun had already melted into the horizon. Kat and Ginger circled the wagon and kept an eye out for trouble. All she heard were the night insects and an occasional hoot owl. Kat could understand the appeal of living on the prairie for some folks. The tall swaying grasses and wide-open spaces made her feel in touch with a higher power. She had never really gone to church. Boris wasn't what you'd call a man of God, but Kat definitely felt there was something out there. One look at nature told her it was true. The prairies did lack trees and Kat wondered if she would tire of it if she lived out here. Where she grew up, there were almost too many trees. It tended to make her feel closed in. Kat looked up to the twinkling stars and wondered if there was a place with both rolling prairies and forests. Now that would be ideal Kat thought as she painted the picture in her mind.

Jack showed up an hour early for his watch. "Hey, kid, I thought I would ride out and have a look before I sent you off to bed, since the moon is full tonight."

"That's fine. I'm actually wide awake," Kat said.

"Have a smoke with me then," Jack said. "Hey, kid. How old are you? I was trying to remember that earlier today."

"Well, you thought I looked fifteen."

"You're fifteen then?" Jack asked.

"My parents never really felt it was important to mark down birthdays, so I'm not really sure. I think you're about right."

"Where are your parents now, kid?"

"You sure are full of questions," Kat said. Jack waited. Kat continued, "They are dead. My father died when I was very young and my mother died a few years ago. I don't have any real brothers or sisters. Nothing to keep me where I was, so I thought I would head west. Seems to be the thing to do these days."

"What are you going to do when you get to where you're going?" Jack asked.

"I don't know. I'm still trying to figure that out."

"A talented young fellow like yourself—the sky's the limit. You can do whatever you want."

Kat snorted, "Oh, I don't think it's quite that simple."

Jack flicked out his cigarette and headed out for a quick patrol. Tonight's moon lit the whole sky. The stars paled in comparison. Jack was thankful for the natural light, which allowed him to see a long distance. Bullet's hooves on the hard packed soil seemed to be the only sound for miles. Jack was eerily away of how quiet it was on the prairie. The entire world seemed extra still as if waiting for something to happen. He felt as though he were the only being on earth. Normally, he enjoyed the feeling of being alone but lately he longed for something else. What that was he wasn't sure. Maybe he was getting bored with traveling. Often his mind would wander to the ranch he was building in his mind. Jack shook his head, daydreaming could get you killed. He cleared his mind and turned Bullet around. Tonight, he felt the urge to head south.

After riding for some time, his nose told him his feeling of isolation was over. It was the tangy smoke of a dying campfire that caught his attention, and he headed in its direction. When he was close enough, Jack dismounted and left Bullet staked a safe distance from the camp. Bullet's presence often spooked other horses, and he did not need to draw attention to himself.

Jack crawled to the top of small knoll a short distance from the camp to get a really good look. It was the posse, as he suspected. Jack's eyes narrowed as he wondered what they were doing still so close to the wagon train? They should have been long gone by now if they thought their fugitive was somewhere else. Did they have another motive? This was very odd. All the men were asleep, including the one who was supposed to be on watch. There was no reason they should still be hanging around. Jack was concerned but could do nothing about it tonight. He took no chances. Even though every man looked to be completely passed out, Jack slowly turned and crawled away without making a sound. Thankfully, he found Bullet staked where he had left him. Although Bullet had a tendency to misbehave he had not failed Jack yet. Jack led him further from the posse's campsite before mounting him and heading back to the wagon train. Tomorrow could prove to be an interesting day.

After Jack had come back from patrol and relieved Kat, she headed for the stream to bathe. She dawdled a bit because she could. It was eerie and beautiful with the full moon above her. It always felt so good to remove the cloth that bound her breasts. She let the water caress her skin as she relaxed and turned back into a woman for a few moments. The thought of someone coming upon her brought he back to reality and she decided to get to work. Kat scrubbed herself and her clothes. She felt her hair and thought it might be time to cut it again. Rather than mess with that, she had opted to tie the small ponytail back with a leather strap. She left the water and crawled up the embankment. After putting on her clothes, she headed back to the camp to sleep the rest of the night away.

Kat woke refreshed and ready for another day. She had finally started to relax, convinced she had the folks fooled and satisfied because they seemed to appreciate her contribution so much.

Jack didn't bother to sleep all night.

CHAPTER 7

Jack, Kat, and Laura rode out after breakfast. Jack seemed distant. Kat decided he must be tired. He rode off for a while. Kat could tell he was making a wide circle to the south. It was hot, and he seemed to be pushing Bullet hard. Kat and Laura stop for some lessons in knife throwing. They'd had little luck finding game that morning but did happen to come upon some quail eggs. Cook would appreciate the eggs very much. Kat had brought the packhorse along this particular morning. She went through her duffle and found a blanket to wrap the eggs in for safekeeping. She and Laura were not far from the wagon train, so Kat decided it would be best to get the eggs back to Cook before any broke. Where had Jack gone? Kat wondered. He'd been gone longer than usual.

It bothered her when she realized how often her mind turned to thoughts of Jack. Kat realized she had very strong feelings for him. She enjoyed their conversations and admired his talents. He always seemed so sure of himself. To top it off, Kat loved to look at him. Those compelling blue eyes and his boldly handsome face would be etched in her mind forever. Kat never dreamt there were men like Jack in the world. She knew he liked John Deer, and because of that she felt guilt, guilt for keeping such a huge secret from him. And there was doubt—would they have liked each other if she had met him as a woman? And finally there was sadness. She could not imagine not having him in her life but knew she would never have the courage to reveal herself to him. How would he react? Probably with anger, confusion, or disgust. She would have to slip out of his life quietly someday. There was a fleeting glimmer of hope she could re-enter his life a woman and start over. No, she thought. She couldn't go on without confessing who she had been.

"Why are you shaking your head?" Laura asked.

"Oh, was I? I was just thinking, that's all," Kat replied without looking up.

"Thinking about what? Your perfect mate?" Laura teased.

Kat did look up now.

"I'm very, very intuitive," Laura said, and she smiled.

"What the hell did she mean?" Kat thought. She suddenly understood why men became frustrated with women.

Just then, Jack rode up. He had a disturbing announcement: "A group of men just rode into camp. Looks like it could be that posse again. Why don't you two ride into camp, and if it looks like trouble, fire a shot to signal me and I'll storm them."

"You'll storm them? You? One person?" Kat said sarcastically. She turned to Laura. "Laura, why don't you ride back to camp? If it looks like trouble, fire a shot and Jack and I will storm from two different directions. If it's nothing, just ride back out after they've gone and tell us what they wanted. Don't let them know we are out here, just in case. Even if they seem harmless, it's better to play it safe. And, Laura, don't break the eggs."

"Yes, that is a better idea. Go ahead, Laura. We'll wait here," Jack said.

Laura confidently rode back to the wagon train. Kat was very proud of her. She turned to Jack. "Is that why you were gone so long? Do you think it's that same posse, the one that was after the girl?"

Jack looked at Kat for a moment without saying a word. For a moment it made Kat uncomfortable. "Yes, I do think it was them, but I don't know why they would be back."

Kat and Jack took turns watching through Jack's telescope. It was the posse. Kat studied the group hard. It was an almost exact repeat of the last meeting. The group talked with Appleton. Clay ogled Laura when she rode into camp, and Trevor rode up and down the train, looking into wagons and looking the horses up and down. After some time the men rode away. They had not gone far when Kat noticed Trevor turn his horse back toward the train. He got Appleton's attention and seemed to say one more thing. He then turned and rode off.

Kat's heart was beating hard.

When Jack spoke it actually startled her. "So, what did you see? You sure hogged the glass."

"Oh, sorry. I just wanted to make sure they weren't just posing as a posse and actually here to make trouble. You know, letting us get out on the prairie a ways and then coming back to rob us. I was thinking that's what they might be up to. It's very odd. We'll have to see what Laura says when she gets back."

Twenty minutes later, Jack and Kat watched Laura approach. Kat studied her face hard for a reaction. There was none. Laura pulled up her horse and dismounted.

"It was the posse again," Laura said. "They're still looking for the woman who murdered the nice farmer. Oh, and the man who killed the drifters. But they were more interested in the woman."

"Why?" Kat asked a little too quickly.

"Yes, why did they come here again? Did they forget they had already talked to us? Do they have some reason to be talking to us again? Seems to me they are wasting their time out here," Jack said.

"I don't know. If they had a reason, they didn't offer one. They left behind another picture of the woman, but they don't have a good description of the man. I don't know how they think they'll catch him. One posse member has seen the man, so he could identify him. I think that's their only chance. Well, anyhow, they're gone now. I truly think they're just a posse and not out to rob us. I can't imagine they'd be back," Laura said.

"Let's hope not," Kat and Jack said in unison. They looked at each other and laughed.

"Look at us. We must be spending too much time together. We're even starting to talk alike," Kat giggled.

"Yeah, we're like an old married couple," Jack said.

"You two are very odd," Laura said, shaking her head. "Shall we go kill something, John?"

"Yes, let's," Kat replied.

The days went on much as they had that first week. They scouted, hunted, ate, slept, and kept watch. Kat really enjoyed watching and studying the people heading west. It seemed to her some people were heading toward a new life and the others were running away from an old one. The Shafer family was comprised of a mother and father and two girls with reddish-blond hair. They were all very happy. As Kat talked with them, she learned they had decided to head west due to a series of tragedies. First, all their livestock took ill and died. Then, the oldest son and youngest daughters fell ill and died of scarlet fever. To top it all off, their house burned down. Kat felt like crying when she heard their story. Yet they all had such positive attitudes. The girls had great imaginations, and although they had no toys, they seemed to find ways to play. The entire family worked as a team so no one person was overworked. The parents looked the children in the eye when they talked to them; they spoke encouraging words and never yelled at one another. Kat made mental notes for the day when she would have a family—if that day ever came.

Then there were the Dickersons. Mr. Dickerson always looked mad. A permanent scowl autographed his face. Kat wondered if he had been born that way or did all his years of being mad make his face look like that? His wife looked haggard and worn. She didn't seem much happier than her husband. The children also wore scowls Kat was sure they'd take into their adulthood. It was rumored they had plenty of money. They had a nice wagon and good-looking livestock. Contrary to the way the Shafers acted, the Dickersons always spoke as if they were mad at each other, never looked at one another, and rarely smiled.

Kat had made a hobby of observing others' behavior. She found it interesting and educational. Kat studied the way men acted so she could copy their behavior and families so maybe someday she could apply the knowledge she gained to her own life. She even studied animals, because they never lied. You always knew if an animal was mad, sad, or nervous. If an animal didn't like someone, you knew it. They didn't pretend to like you. Animals never judged you for your station in life, how you looked, or how much you owned. They knew things before humans did and it always paid to trust their instincts, especially in the wilderness.

Animal instincts came into play for her and Jack one day on the prairie. Luckily, Laura had ridden out in the morning but stayed with the train for the afternoon. It was hot, really hot. The air felt thick as pea soup. Kat and Jack were dripping with sweat. Kat was annoyed as she felt water droplets running down her back and between her breasts. She couldn't even scratch. The only good part about it was that Kat could watch the muscles on Jack's back as his shirt clung to his body. She could actually see his back muscles moving through the wet fabric. Why it was so appealing when he removed his hat to run his fingers through his hair was confusing to her.

There was no breeze to relieve them. The horses plodded along without energy, their heads hanging toward the ground. Bullet wasn't even up to bothering Ginger.

Kat scratched her head as if she were half asleep. "There's just nothing out on this prairie to shoot today," she complained. "It's as if all the animals have disappeared into thin air." Just then, both horses stopped dead in their tracks and snapped their heads up. Kat felt Ginger tense. She could feel the energy well up in the powerful animal. As if on cue, both horses simultaneously spun around and broke into a dead run in the direction opposite the one that they had been heading.

Kat and Jack were caught completely off guard. They hung on for dear life. Just moments after the horses had turned tail and run, the strongest wind Kat had ever felt slapped her in the back. The force of it picked up dirt and drove it into her skin. The sun disappeared and the sky was now a strange black-green color. Stinging rain began to pelt them. She turned her head to see the blur that was Jack and Bullet riding hard next to her. Ginger's powerful body ate up the ground beneath them. All around her was a confusing, roaring noise, and the whirling rain and dirt were blinding. Kat felt an overpowering urge to look behind her. When she did, the sight filled her with awe and terror. It was a twister, a huge one. She'd never seen one before, and it looked to be as wide as a barn. Even in the confusion she knew Jack saw it, too. He was trying to turn Bullet toward the north. It finally worked and to Kat's relief Ginger followed Bullet's lead.

That was the last thing Kat remembered. Something flew in front of Ginger's legs. The horse went down and Kat with her. They both slammed hard into the ground. Everything went black.

Jack saw it out of the corner of his eye. It looked bad. The horse actually rolled over the kid. Amazingly, Ginger got up and continued to run. Jack could not get Bullet to stop. He pulled hard, and finally Bullet sat down on his haunches. Jack jumped off Bullet's back and darted for the kid. The wind made it almost impossible to make his way back. Finally, he made it to John's side. He lay motionless. Jack grabbed him, threw him over his shoulder, and ran as fast as he could.

The horses were long gone. Jack had seen twisters before but never one as big and terrifying as this. He knew he couldn't outrun it. Instead, Jack ran toward the river. He slid down a big embankment. In the blinding wind, his eyes searched up and down the riverbank. He spotted a rock formation jutting out of the bank and hanging over the river. Jack headed for it and wedged himself and the kid underneath it. It just might work if they didn't get sucked up in the twister or drown from the river water that seemed to be going in every direction at once. Was the kid even alive? He didn't have time to check. He felt himself being lifted out of the water and pulled tight against the rock overhang. It was the most powerful force he had ever felt. It sucked the air out of him and seemed to last forever. In reality, it was over in a matter of minutes.

The unearthly force then released him and the kid, and they dropped down into the water. He came back up and noticed he still had a hold of the kid, who was coughing and sputtering now. Jack stood in the chest-deep water holding the kid's head above the surface and watched in amazement as the tornado swept across the prairie. "I think it went right over our heads. That's the strangest thing that's ever happened to me."

"So you saved my life?" Kat had come-to.

"I guess I did. There. Now we're even. You saved me from a rattlesnake and I saved you from a twister."

"True, but I didn't risk my life to kill the rattler. Thank you."

"Now, don't get all mushy on me, kid. We'd better get back to the wagon train and see how they fared. I think the twister missed them, but I bet they have some wind damage," Jack said. Jack noticed the kid wasn't putting any weight on one leg. "Let me have a look at your leg. Take your trousers off, if it's not too painful."

"No, really. It's just my ankle and foot. Let me slip off my boot." The boot came off with great difficulty due to the swelling and the water. Jack could tell it hurt and that the kid was close to tears. He was proud of his attempt to be brave. Jack had become very fond of him. The kid had a great heart and was strong and capable despite his slight build. Jack often noticed him just watching and learning. He sensed the kid was hiding something, though, something to do with his past maybe? He seemed to avoid any questions about his family. Jack could respect that. It's not like he wanted to offer a lot of information about his past, either.

"Well, I'm not a doctor," Jack said, "but I don't see any bones jutting out. That's a good sign. My guess is you have a severe sprain. You also have a huge bump on your head."

"That explains the huge headache I have. Where are the horses?"

"Your guess is as good as mine. After Ginger squashed you, she got up and took off with Bullet. I'm hoping they made it."

"I could sure use a horse about now," Kat said. "I don't think I can walk."

"How about if I carry you? You're amazingly light for someone who eats as much as you do." Jack said in an attempt to lighten the situation.

"Are you sure?"

"Yes, I'm not leaving you out here for the vultures to pick at, and we're not that far from camp. Let's see, I think piggy-back style would work best."

As carefully as he could, Jack hoisted the kid on his back. He'd only gone a few feet when he heard the kid let out a little painful laugh.

"What's so funny?" Jack asked.

"Just this. I was comparing you to Ginger."

"Yeah, I bet we are a sight.

Appleton and Mr. Shafer's eyes scoured the prairie. Appleton was on horseback and Shafer drove a buckboard. The entire wagon train felt their hearts sink as Ginger and Bullet entered camp alone. Ginger was quite cut up and limped slightly. It was not a good sign. Twisters did strange things. They had all heard the stories of people being driven right through trees or lifted off their horses and found broken and dead ten miles away.

"Let's split up, Shafer. If they're still alive they could be severely injured, and the quicker we find them the better chance they'll have."

"Wait a minute, Appleton. What's that up ahead?"

Appleton squinted. "It looks like one of them, but I can't tell which one. Let's go."

As they approached, they discovered it was not one but both of the missing men.

"Parker! Deer! Are you okay?"

Jack was the first to speak. "Deer's okay. I, on the other hand, have a broken back from this extra burden I've been carrying for about a mile now. What took you guys so long?" Jack carefully set his load down on the back of the buckboard and frowned as the kid winced in pain.

"Well, we had to stay and comfort the women for awhile," Mr. Shafer offered. "They were afraid the two best-looking men on the wagon train had blown away. Did you fellers get a look at that twister? That's the biggest one I've ever seen in my life. I was praying it wouldn't turn our way. We would have been done for if it had. There's nowhere to take cover out here."

"Deer, you gonna be okay on that buckboard?" Appleton asked as he noticed discomfort on the kid's face. "You look a little green."

"I'm just starting to realize how much I hurt all over, that's all."

"Like where, kid?" Jack asked, seriously for once.

"My head, my ankle, my foot, my butt, my ribs, my chest, my arms, and my neck. That about covers it."

"You gonna be okay?" Jack whispered, serious again.

"I don't know. It's the first time I've ever been rolled on by a horse during a twister. Let's just get back to camp." To the men the kid was looking greener by the minute. They had to stop once so he could throw up on the way back to camp. They were all anxious to get the kid back where he could lie down and just be still for a while.

Back at camp, Laura rushed to their side. Kat heard Jack quickly recounting the story to Laura and the others who were all gathered around listening. Kat wanted to get off the buckboard but couldn't move. "Get him in the back of my wagon," Laura commanded. "I helped my father all the time with his patients. I need some water and a lantern." Kat heard all this but felt like she was in a different world. She did not want to pass out. She was scared, so scared about revealing her identity. She was aware when Jack laid her in the back of the wagon. She saw Cook placed a pail of water at her side. Someone else brought a lantern. Things were beginning to get hazy.

"Oh, shit," Kat whispered. She felt herself drifting into unconsciousness. She pushed Laura's hands away when Laura started to loosen her shirt. Laura stood up and closed the curtain to the front and back of the wagon.

Kat wasn't sure what happened next. She thought she heard Laura whisper, "Don't worry. I'll take care of you. I won't let anyone in here."

CHAPTER 8

"More cool water," Laura commanded as she poked her head out through the curtain of the wagon. Someone immediately brought her a pail. To Laura's dismay, her patient was running a fever now, and Laura was frightened about internal bleeding. The people of the wagon train waited and worried. They had all grown fond of the kid that was so capable of keeping them fed.

Several hours later, Laura emerged from the wagon. All eyes turned to her as she reported what she knew.

"He's resting now. I'm trying to keep the fever down. There seems to be quite a bit of pain in the middle section, so I expect either broken or cracked ribs and maybe even internal bleeding. If there is bleeding internally, I have no way to stop it. One thing's certain: he can't take any movement right now, so we are stuck here for a couple days."

"Laura, can I take a look at the kid. See if there's anything I can do?"

"No, there's nothing you can do, Jack. He needs uninterrupted rest. If people are poking their heads in, even with good intentions, it can only do more harm."

Laura went back into the wagon to look after her patient. After her parents died so suddenly, she had been lost, sad, and scared. She didn't know how she would ever make her way in the world. It seemed she made one mistake after another at first. She felt that she was worthless. That was, until "John Deer" came along. Laura never dreamt someone would help her learn the things she really needed to know. Learning how to shoot, throw a knife, hunt for food, and ride a horse had given her the courage she needed to go on. It was all due to this person, who lay before her, struggling for life.

"You will live," Laura whispered to Kat as she laid damp rags on her head. "And I will find a way to repay you for all you've given me."

Laura kept watch all night and through the rest of the next day. She dozed now and then but mostly she kept watch and prayed. At the end of the second day, as Laura dozed, she heard her name whispered. Her eyes flew opened. What joy she felt to see a pair of eyes looking back at her. "You're awake!" Laura smiled. "How are you feeling?" Laura felt Kat's forehead. It was sweaty and cooler. "Your fever broke. That's a very good sign."

"I'm thirsty and I have to go," Kat struggled to say.

"Yes, yes, here's some water and here's a chamber pot. Can you manage with the pot?" Laura asked as Kat slowly pushed herself up.

"Yes. I'd like to try," Kat said.

"Okay, I'll give you some privacy and go tell the folks you've finally decided to wake up from your nap." Laura disappeared through the tent flap.

Kat was very stiff and sore. As the memories of the last couple of days rushed back, so did a million thoughts and questions. How long had she slept? How many on the wagon train now knew her secret? After all, she was undressed and wrapped in just a blanket. Kat would have been more terrified, but she was too tired and too sore. She remained on the edge of the bed and waited for whatever happened next.

Finally, Laura entered the wagon. She smiled. "Everyone is so happy to hear you are back with us. I can't tell you how wonderful everyone has been. They know you can't hunt right now, but that's okay. Jack's been taking care of that. The people would like to know if they can start moving again. After all, we've been in the same spot for the past two days," Laura rambled on.

Kat had taken in everything Laura had said, but the big question still lingered in her mind. "Laura, I need to know. What…who…"

"Only me. I wouldn't let anyone in the tent. I know your secret. At least I think I do. Unless you're just a crazy person. Oh, I'm sorry. I mean—"

"Laura," Kat whispered. She was exhausted and still not thinking clearly. "So you've seen me without clothes and you know I am really a woman. Right?"

"Yes," came Laura's short reply.

"Why didn't you tell anyone? What did you think? What are you thinking now?"

"Listen," Laura said, leaning in toward Kat. "Whoever you are. Whatever you are. You've done more for me in a few weeks than anyone has ever done for me in my life—and at a time when, God knows, I needed it more than ever. I needed it to live. I can't even begin to tell you what I was thinking." Laura's voice lowered to a whisper. "I even considered killing myself."

Kat frowned yet could understand.

Laura continued with tears welling in her eyes. "Am I curious as to what's going on? Yes. Will I understand if you don't want to tell me? Yes. Do I still want to be around you? The answer is, again, yes. I believe you are an exceptionally good person who was sent into my life for a reason. I am loyal to you and will stick by you, no matter what. That's really all I can think to tell you. The rest is up to you. Except for…" She smiled and the tears stopped for a second. "I'm really glad you didn't die, because I owe you my life."

Kat just sat. She sat and soaked it in, realizing how lucky she was to have met this girl…this young woman. In a rush, she felt what Laura might have been feeling these past several weeks. Losing her parents had had a stronger effect than Kat had ever realized. Kat had been too wrapped up in her own life. Laura had been through hell. Now that Laura knew her secret, Kat actually felt a huge relief. But now what? Kat's eyes rose to meet Laura's, who was patiently waiting for whatever Kat would offer.

Kat began, "Laura, I am a woman. I am not some sick, crazy person. I am just in disguise."

Laura relaxed and smiled. "I'm glad to know that, but please, continue."

"I am here because I got into some trouble back in Missouri. Laura, please hang in with me while I finish this entire story."

"I will on one condition. Please tell me your name. I don't know how to address you right now, and to say 'John' just doesn't feel right," Laura said calmly.

"My name's Katherine. People call me Kat."

Laura smiled and nodded so Kat would finish.

"This may come as a shock to you. That posse is looking for me. But Laura," Kat said with tears in her eyes now, "it's not like they said." Kat's voice lowered to a whisper. "I did kill him, but he was not a nice farmer. He was…he was…a pig, an animal. Laura, he tried to rape me. It was self-defense. I've tried so hard not to think about it. Now I'm in big trouble. I didn't know what to do, so this is what I did. I just wanted to get out and head west. I wanted to put as much distance between me and my shitty family, who 'arranged' this." Kat was really sobbing now, which she never did. "I just wanted to get out west, far away, then figure out what to do."

Kat was quiet then. She couldn't believe all that had come out of her mouth. Had she made a big mistake? Laura was quite religious. Murder was wrong.

Would she turn her in, let everyone know about this crazy life she had been living? Kat was suddenly ashamed. What kind of a woman was she to carry on like a man, thinking she could fool these people? Thinking she could get away with murder? She slowly lifted her head to see Laura's face.

Laura had a huge smile on her face. "I knew it!" Laura said. "I was suspicious about you."

Kat knew at that point Laura wouldn't turn her in. She was too thrilled with all the facts surrounding the crazy situation. Kat was beginning to feel horror that everyone secretly knew.

"Oh," Laura whispered. "Don't worry. I can guarantee you no one suspects a thing. When I saw the picture the posse handed out, there was something familiar about it, but trust me, no one else knows. Whatever you had to do, I believe you had good reason, Kat," Laura said, taking Kat's hand in hers. "Your secret is safe with me. I will help you, because you've helped me so much."

Kat was satisfied with all Laura had told her. She wanted to get out of the wagon for a while and get some fresh air. Laura took the cloth that bound her breasts and wrapped it around Kat's rib cage and then helped her get dressed. Now the cloth served a dual purpose. Laura had told Kat she suspected she had cracked ribs. Cook had brought his cane to the wagon earlier when he heard Kat had a bad sprain. It came in handy now. Kat eased her way out of the wagon and limped a couple of steps.

"Glad to see you're back on your feet. Or should I say, foot?" Appleton said with a big grin.

Everyone else had kind words of encouragement. Kat was somewhat worried they'd be upset about having to sit in one place so long. That wasn't the case. She was deeply moved by their words and concern. But where was Jack? He was the one she wanted to see. Not wanting to come right out and ask about Jack, Kat inquired, "Is everyone all right? I've been asleep so long I feel like I'm behind on the news."

"Yes, we're all fine. The rest did us good. We've been pushing awfully hard the past week in this hot weather," Mr. Shafer offered. "We're just so glad you're okay. Aren't we, Dickerson?"

Mr. Dickerson just scowled. Kat got a big kick out of the way Mr. Shafer liked to pick on Dickerson. He was such a sourpuss.

About that time, Jack rode up with several rabbits. Kat thought it made sense for him to take over the hunting while she was laid up. A feeling of relief swept over Kat to discover Jack was alive and well.

"Hey, kid. You're up and at 'em," Jack said, the concern apparent in his voice.

"Well, I'm up, but I wouldn't say I'm at 'em yet," Kat replied. "Thanks for taking over the hunting while I was out."

"You're welcome."

"Here you go, Cook. I'm looking forward to your delicious rabbit stew," Jack said.

Kat was spent. She headed back to the wagon for her bedroll. Rather than sleep inside, she rolled her bedding out beside the wagon. Fresh air sure beat the musty wagon she'd been cooped up in the past few days. Laura brought her some broth and a plate of beans and insisted Kat eat it to help build her strength. Kat ate a little and then decided she should go to the bathroom before she went to bed. Laura helped her over a knoll and down to the stream.

After Kat relieved herself, Laura helped her wash up while keeping a watchful eye. Kat felt like a new person. She hadn't had a chance to bathe since before the twister. Laura washed her hair, combed it, and pulled it back with a leather strap. Laura washed Kat's clothes and laid them out on the rocks to dry. It was a real relief, not to mention a necessity, that Laura now knew her secret. Kat would have had a tough time pulling this off without her help. She imagined what the people on the wagon train must have thought. A young girl tending to a young "man's" needs like Laura was doing practically meant they were married. The people of the wagon train seemed to accept it, as if it were meant to be.

The two of them slowly headed back to the camp. Kat hobbled with her cane and Laura carried her wet clothes and the basket of soaps and rags. Jack met them at the edge of camp. "Need any help?"

"No thanks, Jack," Laura said. "I've got it under control."

"I can see that, but if you do need something, let me know."

"Thanks again, Jack, for taking over the hunting the past couple days. I'm thinking I'll need help for just another day, and then I can get back to my duties," Kat said.

"Kid, it's gonna be more than a day. You just take your time. I've seen too many people try to rush back to work before they've fully recovered. You're just asking for a setback. Laura and I will have the final say as to when you're back on the trail again."

Kat glanced at Laura and saw her beaming with pride to discover Jack would give her the responsibility of determining when it was best for her patient to go back to work. For this reason, Kat did not fight the decision. Jack was probably right anyhow. She had already noticed that she had felt better and then worse several times in just the two short hours she had been up. It's just that she felt so worthless not being able to contribute and having people wait on her hand and foot. She'd never make it as one of those high-society women she'd read about that spent most of their days just sitting there looking pretty while others waited on them.

Laura helped Kat to her bedroll. As she eased down and got comfortable, Laura told her, "I'll be in the wagon right above you. Just call my name if you need anything." She lowered herself to her ear and whispered, "Goodnight, Kat."

It was strange to hear her name. Kat hadn't heard anyone say it in such a long time. She went to sleep almost immediately. It was a deep sleep filled with strange dreams. Her body was healing, which probably contributed to her jumbled thoughts and dreams. Nothing really made sense—it was a collage of her mother gently swinging with her on a porch swing and then telling her to go hunt some antelope for the evening meal. The antelope she hunted all had normal bodies, but their heads were Harley Sneed's. Hundreds of the antelope appeared before her. She shot them, but more and more kept appearing. Finally, she decided to head back to camp, but she'd taken so long trying to kill all the antelope the train had left with out her. She rode and rode, trying to catch up to them. Then she was out in the middle of nowhere when a huge twister came out of the sky and began chasing her. She rode as fast as she could and finally caught up to the wagon train. No one would believe her when she told them a twister was on its way. They just kept going about their chores, blind to the imminent danger. Kat was frantic in her dream to find Jack. He'd believe her and make the people listen. She pulled back the curtain on a wagon and there were Laura, Jack, and Trevor, all looking at her as though she were a stranger. To Kat's horror, Jack was holding and stroking Flex, her cat from the farm.

"You know, don't you?" Kat asked Jack in her dream. He wouldn't answer her. He just kept staring at her. "You know, admit it. Admit it!" she cried out.

"Hey, hey," Jack said to her. He had dropped Flex, who went to Trevor's lap and let him stroke her.

"What are you doing here?" Kat asked Trevor in her dream.

"I came to find my cat," Trevor replied while stroking Flex. "I knew she was here."

"She's not your cat! She doesn't belong to anyone or need anyone. She can take care of herself!"

"She needs love. She needs a home. I'm taking her home," Trevor insisted.

"Kat, I told them," Laura confessed in the dream. "I thought they should know."

"You told them! You told them! No!" Kat cried.

"Hey, hey," Jack spoke again.

Kat's dream dissolved as Jack's face came in to view. "Hey, kid. You're dreaming. You were yelling and thrashing around. I was afraid you would hurt yourself," Jack was bent over her. "Do you want me to get Laura?"

"No. I'm okay." She attempted to push herself up. "Why are you still up? Did I wake you?"

"Here, kid, let me help you." Jack gently pulled her up to a sitting position. "No, you didn't wake me. I was on watch. That was quite a dream you were having. You seemed pretty pissed off."

"What time is it?" Kat asked, partly to give herself a minute to think. What had she said? It was all disappearing from her mind.

"It's after midnight. You should go back to sleep."

Kat snorted, "I've been sleeping for two days. Besides, I have to go."

"Need help?"

"No, I can manage," Kat said. She grabbed her gun and began to hobble off into the dark. Kat made sure Jack didn't follow her. She just wanted to get better so life could get back to normal. Whatever that was. She didn't think she'd ever really know what normal was. Kat was still feeling strange about her dream. Sitting there with her mother had been really wonderful. It seemed very real and comforting. The part about Trevor, Laura, and Jack disturbed her. And Flex. Where did that part come from? A smile came to her lips as she thought about Flex.

Kat did her thing and headed back to camp. Thankfully she didn't feel exhausted as she had earlier when she'd been up and moving around. She was still stiff and sore; however, the more she moved around the more she was able to limber up. It was a good sign, she thought, to feel improvement. Ah, her bedroll. Kat thought she was wide awake but was able to fall fast asleep the moment her head hit the pillow.

Jack checked on the kid frequently during the night. That had been quite a scare. First, the narrow escape from the tornado and then the kid's turn for the worse. Jack remembered his heart pounding as the kid began to fade. If Laura hadn't taken over, Jack wasn't sure what might have happened. He was grateful to Laura. She was doing such a great job of taking care of him. If it weren't for her, Jack really wondered if the kid would be alive at all? Jack didn't understand why he had grown so fond of John, but he had. He felt a connection and a need to watch out for him and protect him. Why? Maybe by protecting John, he was protecting his younger brother, Sam. Jack suspected that wasn't it. John and Sam weren't really alike. Jack just shook his head and finally headed off to catch a few hours of sleep before sun-up.

A few short hours later the sun was up and camp was beginning to stir. Cook had some oatmeal going. Laura brought Kat a bowl with a double dose of molasses and a sprinkling of raisins, courtesy of Cook. The plan was for Kat to ride in the back of the Shafers' wagon that day. She was beginning to get very bored and the little Shafer girls took turns reading to her to liven her spirits. Holly wanted to teach her how to knit even though she was a boy. Kat pretended not to know how, and little Holly was thrilled when "John" picked it up so quickly.

"You girls stop pestering John and let him rest," Mrs. Shafer warned from the front of the wagon.

"Oh, Mrs. Shafer, it's really no bother. I'm bored, and they are entertaining me. If I need to rest I'll let them know."

The day wore on and Kat moved about as much as possible whenever the train stopped. She was determined to speed up her recovery. Cook made her a special herbal concoction he told her helped heal injuries. Even though it tasted horrible, Kat drank it out of respect and appreciation for Cook—and because she half-believed him.

By evening, Kat was feeling stronger yet. She and Laura walked to a nearby stream to bathe. Kat was pleased to see Laura had taken a rifle and her knife along. She was becoming very trail savvy. The girls enjoyed the cool water. A good washing after being on the trail for a while was a real treat. They laughed and talked and took their time lounging in the water. The relief of sharing her secret with another person was something Kat appreciated more than she realized. Laura helped Kat wash her clothes and hair and helped her get dressed, all the while keeping a watchful eye for anyone who might come from the direction of the wagon train.

CHAPTER 9

The following day, Kat insisted on attempting to ride her own horse. Ginger, thankfully, had made it through the tornado relatively injury-free. She had several cuts and scrapes but nothing that would really slow her down. It felt good to be on horseback again. She and Laura rode a short distance from the wagon train, each sporting a gun and knife. Kat was pleased to see she instinctively carried weapons with her at all times.

Kat and Laura stopped for a rest. They found a green patch of grass that the horses thoroughly enjoyed. It had rained in this part of the country recently, bringing color back to the prairie and lifting the moods of the animals and the girls. Kat found she needed to walk frequently to prevent cramping up. So that's what they did. They walked and talked. It was like having a new friend now that Laura shared her secret. Kat openly answered Laura's unending questions about her past, how she came up with the idea for her disguise and why she decided to head west. Kat could tell Laura was truly a curious soul.

Kat answered the questions and in turn learned that Laura had lived most of her life in Tennessee. Her father had been a doctor and Laura was their only child. Her father had always wanted a son to teach his medicine to, but he only had a girl. So Laura spent many hours in her father's office, learning by listening and observing. Her father put little effort into teaching her, but thanks to Laura's persistent curiosity and the many questions she asked, she managed to learn a lot. She spoke enthusiastically about all she had learned watching her father and attending school. Kat realized Laura was really quite smart. Funny how her opinion of Laura had changed. When she first met her, she thought she was a stupid girl. Kat told her this, and Laura smiled and said, "Well, I guess first impressions can be deceiving." They laughed.

"What do you think of Jack?" Laura asked.

Kat turned her head sharply toward her. "What do you mean, what do I think of Jack?"

"What do you think of him? I can't really figure him out. At times he seems so relaxed and happy, joking around with everyone, and then it's as if he remembers he shouldn't behave like that and becomes serious and guarded again. It's like he is hiding something—except when he is around you. He enjoys picking on you."

"One thing I've discovered on this trip is that everyone seems to be hiding something," Kat observed. "I think it's because the world is not set up to allow us to be our true selves. Maybe that will change over time. Probably not in my lifetime."

Kat thought Laura was smart and Laura thought Kat was very observant and people-smart. Despite all Kat was hiding, she seemed comfortable with people and people seemed to like her. Laura wondered if that would be the case if they knew she was really a woman.

"So, how long are you planning to keep up your disguise?"

Kat shook her head. "That's my problem. I don't plan. I got this far by making it up as I went along. Someday I'll have to 'turn back into a woman,' but I haven't figured out how to do that. When I get to California, I'll come up with something. Until then, I'll stick with being *John;* it has worked out pretty well."

Laura studied Kat's disguise. Before she knew her secret, Laura had thought "John" was a handsome boy, with his black hair and deep green eyes. Laura smiled as she remembered thinking what nice skin he had and how, if he ever filled out, he would make a very stunning-looking man. She had always thought "John" looked too skinny and attributed it to the fact that he was still a growing boy.

"What is it you want, Kat?" Laura asked.

"A family, someday. Even though the family I came from was pretty horrible, I know they can also be wonderful. My mother loved my real father very much—I knew by the way she talked about him—and she loved me very much. The years with my mother were very special, although I was always worried about her." Kat told Laura how her mother had married Boris after her father's death and how Boris had worked her to death. "One lesson I learned from my mother is not to marry the wrong man. She went from happy, beautiful, and peaceful to sad, tired, and an early grave, all because of the man in her life. I will not marry the wrong man. I will choose very carefully or I will choose to be alone."

Laura told her she hoped she could stick to that plan. After her parents died Laura felt the pressure to find someone to marry, someone to take care of her. The thought at the time made her very sad. Deep down she realized rushing into marriage probably meant marrying someone she didn't love. Her dream was to meet a man she could talk to and who would listen to her. A man who would see she had something to offer. Since meeting Kat and learning how to be self-sufficient, her dream had now been rekindled and she would never consider marrying for anything other than love. Laura wondered who she and Kat would end up marrying someday. She knew how beautiful Kat was underneath her disguise. Kat had a wealth of dark hair and deep green eyes. She was thin and strong and would look very feminine in women's clothes. It amazed her she had pulled off being a man so well but also realized there was more to the costume than her external appearance. Kat had learned how to walk like a man, talk, sit, and mount and ride a horse like a man. Laura asked her about it, and Kat told her she had to think about it every minute of the day. Laura couldn't imagine changing all the mannerisms that come naturally to you every moment of the day! Now that Laura knew, she was aware of Kat's slip-ups. She would see a movement that was just a bit too graceful or Kat would make a facial expression or a noise that was too feminine. The disguise still worked though, because people thought she was a boy.

Laura and Kat saw Jack approaching from the north. He had ridden far today and they both wondered what was up. Did he suspect trouble of some kind?

Jack had ridden out ahead and circled the train several times. He felt edgy today. Several things could prove dangerous to the wagon train, such as animals, Indians, bandits, and obviously bad weather. The sky was clear blue with just a few white clouds and the temperature had moderated. Maybe he was just feeling overprotective since the kid was back out on the trail, or possibly he was reacting to all that had happened in the past few days. Still, he felt something was out there.

"Hi, Jack," Laura greeted cheerfully. "Did you see anything unusual out there?"

"No, everything appears to be normal, but I still think we should keep our guard up. We are moving into rougher country now. Hey, kid, how are you feeling?"

"Actually, very good. As long as I take little breaks now and then I do okay. Laura's been a big help. I see you've found some quail for dinner. They are so tasty, but Cook hates cleaning them. How about if you and I head back early, Laura, and round up some help cleaning them?"

"That's a good idea. I don't want Cook mad at me," Jack replied. He handed the birds over to Laura and Kat. "I'm heading back out for a look. If there's any trouble, fire off three quick shots and I'll be back in a flash."

Jack rode on and thought about what was making him so uneasy. He had a gut feeling it had to do with the posse that kept showing up. It wasn't right. Why would they keep following the wagon train? Jack mentally ran through the men and women of the wagon train to determine whom they might suspect. He came up empty every time. None of the women came close to looking like the beautiful woman in the picture. If they were after the man, that didn't add up for Jack either. They had only a verbal description of him and not a good one at that. It just didn't make sense. None of the men came close to matching the description except for Jack, and he had not let them see him. He had always been out when they made their visits. Out with the kid.

Jack yanked Bullet to a stop so hard that the huge horse almost sat down on his haunches. The image of the kid's face came full into his mind. He remembered bits and pieces of conversations. No one knew it, but he had put the drawing of the woman in his pocket. He pulled it out and stared at it.

"Damn," Jack whispered. He turned Bullet around and headed back to camp.

CHAPTER 10

The wagon train was buzzing with activity as it always was in preparation for the evening meal. The birds had been cleaned and families were moving around, working, talking, and laughing. Everything appeared normal. He didn't see them at first. They had become thick as thieves, as if they shared a special bond. Finally, he spotted them. Laura and the kid stepped out from behind a wagon. They were carrying canteens.

Jack approached them. "What are you two up to?"

"Hi, Jack," Laura smiled cheerfully. "We thought we'd ride out and fill the canteens at the lake up ahead. We're running low on water. Mr. Appleton asked us if we'd go get some. He said that would get us through until tomorrow, when the train passes by the lake and they can fill the water barrels."

"Good idea. Laura, how about you let the kid and me ride out there after the evening meal. We haven't had a chance to chat in a while, and I'd like to have a man-to-man talk with him."

"That's fine with me," Laura said.

Kat had barely swallowed the last bite of her evening meal when Jack approached her. "Laura will be staying here and I'm going to go with you for water. Are you ready to go?"

"Sure. I was going to have seconds but I guess I can do without."

Jack watched every move the kid made. They grabbed the canteens and rode off toward the lake. Jack was quiet for a long while.

"What's up, Jack? Are you expecting trouble?"

"I'm always expecting trouble," Jack answered shortly. "Let's get to the lake and we'll talk more then. I want to keep alert while we are on the trail."

They arrived at the lake in no time. It was beautiful, surrounded with greenery, flowers, and rock formations. It looked like a painting. The evening was still and the lake was like glass. They filled the canteens and then sat down to have a smoke. Jack watched intently. Every move.

The kid broke the silence. "You look so serious. What's going on? Are we heading into hostile Indian territory?"

"No, that's not it. I think that posse is still following us." Jack studied the face before him for a response.

"I don't understand. Why would they follow us?"

"I don't know? Got any ideas?"

"No, I don't"

Meanwhile, Jack continued to study the face before him. He mentally removed the hat, added longer hair, and changed the clothing to a dress. The stubble, what was that? Paint?

"What? Do I have something in my teeth?" Kat asked.

"No." He looked at the hands, the arms, and the legs. He took notice of the hips, the bottom, and the chest.

"Are your ribs still sore? Is Laura wrapping them for you?" Jack inquired.

"Yes, they are still sore and it helps to have them wrapped, although I get awfully sweaty and hot."

"Speaking of that, I think we should take a swim while we're here. We may not get a chance for a bath in the next few days," Jack said as he began to unbutton his shirt.

"Oh no, the pressure of the water really hurts my ribs. I can't breathe very well in the water."

"Well don't go all the way in then. Here's some soap." Jack handed off the bar of soap.

Thanks, I think I'll just wash up my hands, feet, and face. I don't want to rewrap my ribs and I would need to for the long ride back."

"Suit yourself," Jack said. "I think I'll enjoy a nice long bath."

He took his time undressing, all the while talking so the kid would have to watch. Jack noticed the kid working hard to keep a steady gaze, and he watched for facial expressions as he talked. Every once in a while he turned away to grab something then tried to catch a reaction when he quickly turned back around. The kid was playing it well.

Kat was incredibly uncomfortable. It wasn't the first time she'd been in this situation. After a few moments she gave in and decided to take advantage of the scenery. Kat drank in the sight of him. His body was covered in lean muscles. Kat imagined if she touched them they would be as hard as rock. He was perfectly proportioned. Every thing about his body looked long. Did all men look like this? She couldn't imagine that they did. It made Kat sad to think that some day another woman would have him. Why that thought entered her head, she wasn't sure. She decided to dismiss the thought and get back to enjoying the view. It was strange but even his face looked different when he was naked. Kat openly admitted to herself that she thought he was devastatingly handsome. Imagine what he would do if he could read her mind, she thought. She bet he didn't have a clue that all she wanted to do was run her fingers through his beautiful tousled black hair. It set off those intense, blue eyes wonderfully. His shoulders and chest were broad and strong. There was not one bit of fat on his mid section. Kat remembered how grotesque Boris looked without his shirt on. Kat quickly dismissed that image. Jack's thighs were like a work of art, long and muscular, and the thing in between made Kat feel funny. She only took a quick glance but would have looked longer if she could have.

Jack thought he could sense some unease. He mentioned that maybe the posse was really out to rob the train. It was rumored that the Dickersons were traveling with quite a bit of cash.

"Maybe," Kat replied. Her responses were short.

"Well, I have an idea," Jack said, as he nonchalantly stood naked in front of her. "I think I should remain out of sight. Do you realize they haven't seen either one of us? You could go talk to them next time and really feel them out. Ask some questions. See if you can get an idea of what they're up to. I'll remain hidden in case we need to surprise them. That's what we should do." Jack stopped and waited for her reaction.

"I have a better idea. I think we should both stay hidden and have Laura talk to them. We'll tell her what we suspect. If we need to surprise them, two will be better than one."

"Can Laura do that?" Jack asked. "What if she's too nervous or doesn't think to ask the right questions—after all, she is only a woman."

"Only a woman?" Jack thought he could sense a bit of a bite in the reply. "How do you think Laura would feel to know you said that about her? She respects you and admires the fact that you don't treat her differently because she's female."

"Well, come on," Jack egged, "you can't tell me you wouldn't worry that a woman would mess this up. It's a man's job. Now, don't get me wrong. I understand why you taught her to shoot and throw a knife. After all, she was totally helpless. But I've got to say, it makes me nervous riding next to a female with a gun."

"Why would that make you nervous?" Again, he sensed the bite.

"Because everyone knows they aren't as strong physically or mentally as men. They get scared easily; they can't handle their emotions or think under pressure. That's why they are only good for household chores, like doing laundry, cleaning, cooking, and of course, bearing children."

"I still think having Laura talk to them is the best option. I think she will do just fine." The reply seemed to come through gritted teeth.

Jack realized he had pushed it too far and would not get the reaction he had hoped for, but it had been fun. He tried a new angle as he walked into the water. "Oh, I get it. You're sweet on her. She nursed you back to health and now you're in love with her. Have you kissed her? What was it like?"

"No, it's not like that," the kid broke in, but Jack kept talking as he swam out deeper.

"Hey, kid, have you ever had sex?"

"No, I haven't. Why don't you give me some pointers? That is, unless you're still a virgin. Or maybe unable to perform because of all the time in the saddle."

Jack wasn't ready for that retort. A sly smile lifted the corner of his mouth. "Of course I'm not a virgin. I've got lots of advice to give in that area. I'd be happy to give you a few pointers. First, I recommend you try the merchandise before you buy." Although it was starting to get dark out, he was sure he saw steam coming out of those tiny ears. "Here's what to do. Get her in a quiet romantic place. Tell her she means everything to you. You don't have to actually mean the things you say, because—trust me—women fall for it every time. Then tell her once you get enough money you are going to ask her to marry you. That's important, because they've got to think you intend to marry them to give up the goods. Then start slow. Just a few kisses and caresses in non-threatening areas. Talk to her while you're doing this. Let it heat up a bit. Tell her no woman has ever made you feel like this and that you want her so badly it actually hurts. Make sure to caress her in all the right places, if you know what I mean. That gets women really heated up. Try removing her clothes without her noticing. If she begins to protest, tell her you just want to see her breasts—after all, you're as good as married. She'll do it. Women aren't the smartest creatures—"

"You know, Jack," came the interruption. "I wasn't serious when I said I wanted some pointers. I'm going around the bend to see if I can catch some fish for breakfast."

"Okay, take your time. I'm going to take a nice long bath and enjoy this cool water." Jack smiled up to the sky as he took long smooth backstrokes through the water.

Kat climbed to the top of the rock. She still had the bar of soap in her hand. Boy, was she mad. How could Jack say those things? It was quite an eye-opening experience, being in a man's world. Kat looked behind her and saw that Jack was still swimming and diving in the lake. Could she sneak in a quick bath? It sounded heavenly, and it could be a while before she had another opportunity. Jack was far away. He would still have to dry off, put on his clothes, and walk to the top of the rock. She had time. She took one last glance to make sure Jack was still swimming and then shimmied down the rock embankment. She felt she deserved it and she really needed to cool off.

This little section of the lake provided perfect privacy for her. She could quickly undress, soap up, rinse off, and get dressed again in no time. She wouldn't even take the time to wash her clothes.

Jack watched and the second the kid began the descent, Jack dove under water and swam toward the rocky curve of the lake. He came up by a ledge that provided great cover. Slowly he eased himself around the rock, careful not to make any splashing noises.

He had the perfect view.

Jack watched from his vantage point as the hair was unbound and shook free. He felt bad about all he had said, but he hadn't known what else to do. It wasn't like he could just come right out and ask, "Hey, are you really a woman in disguise because you are wanted for murder?" No, he needed time to think about how to handle this if it were true.

Jack realized he was holding his breath. He cursed the dimming light and strained his eyes to see the proof. Off came the shirt. Slowly, the cloth began to unwind. It seemed to take forever. Finally, the last strip fell to the ground and Kat's breasts were exposed. Somehow, Jack was still surprise, but now he had his proof, he should have swum back to shore and put his clothes back on. But he didn't. He couldn't take his eyes off her. He watched as she rubbed her breasts, which were beautiful, firm and round. She rubbed her stomach and her back. Jack took in every movement in awe. It was a scene he would replay several times in his mind in the coming days. She sat on a rock and pulled her boots off. Jack realized he was holding his breath again, and the thought ran through his mind a second time that he'd seen enough and should get back. He didn't move a muscle.

Kat unbuttoned her pants and eased them down. She wasn't wearing any undergarment, which for some reason was a huge turn-on for Jack. God, she was beautiful. Creamy white skin covered her beautiful body. Long, perfectly-shaped legs led up to the area where she wasn't wearing any undergarments. Her stomach was flat and her tiny waist accented her breasts perfectly. Jack was certain he didn't even blink as he watched her body disappear inch-by-inch as she entered the water. Jack was beside himself. He wasn't really prepared to see all that, and he was a man of strong urges. He told himself the only reason he didn't go back now was because he wanted to make sure she didn't drown.

She washed quickly and came back out of the water. Jack was glad he stayed. Finally, he swam back to his area when she began pulling her boots on. He decided to stay true to his word and take a long time in the water. Beside, he had to after seeing that.

Jack had a million thoughts in his head. He had to make sure he didn't act differently now that he knew.

She came down the rock formation on Jack's side of the shoreline.

"So, how was the fishing? Any luck?" Jack asked from the water.

"No, so I went ahead and took a quick dip," she replied.

"Damn," Jack thought. He suddenly realized he would have to get out of the water naked in front of her. Even though he'd been naked in front of her, even when he suspected, it bothered him this time. Mostly because he would need to control himself. Thankfully, she had her back to him, digging around in her saddlebag. Jack came out of the water and quickly pulled on his pants and boots.

"What are you looking for?" Jack asked hoarsely.

"A leather thong to tie my hair back. It's hard to get a decent haircut and shave out on the trail, so I've opted to let my hair grow until I can find a decent barber," she replied just as she found it and quickly yanked it out of her saddle-bag, sending it flying through the air and landing at Jack's feet. He bent over and picked it up.

"Here you go," he quietly said as he handed it to her. Jack was surprised to feel tingles as her hand lightly touched his.

"Thanks."

They filled the canteens and mounted the horses. Kat and Jack rode back in silence for a while. It was Jack who finally broke the silence.

"Kid, I've been thinking about what you said. I think it is a good idea to have Laura talk to the posse if they show up. I hope you're not mad at me for what I said about Laura. I was just trying to wind you up because I know you like her."

Jack thought she actually looked a little relieved as she smartly answered, "Why would I be mad."

It was quite dark by now and peaceful. Jack broke the silence again. "So, kid? What do you want to do when you get out west?"

He really was wondering. How long was she going to carry on with this charade? What were her plans for the future? What was her name again? Once he was alone he would pull out the picture and look at it for the hundredth time.

"I don't know yet. I'm making this up as I go," she replied.

Jack believed her.

They continued on toward camp, speaking very little, each lost in their own thoughts.

CHAPTER 11

Back at camp, most of the people had settled down for the night. Appleton, Shafer, and Dickerson were still up discussing night-watch plans. Jack made a point of speaking to them about the posse. He told them how he suspected the posse was still in the area and that the reason they were there was to rob them.

He turned to Dickerson. "Rumor has it you're carrying a lot of cash."

This made Dickerson furious. He thought that was a secret and wondered if his big-mouthed wife had told another big-mouthed woman who then spread it all over the countryside. It also made him mad at Jack. He didn't like him.

"It's not true!" Dickerson snapped.

"It doesn't matter whether it's true or not. If they suspect it and are up to no good, we're still in danger. Here's my plan…"

Jack told them how he and "John Deer" had already discussed keeping their distance from the wagon train. The posse hadn't spotted them yet, and in the event of trouble, Jack and John could ride in and take them by surprise.

The men's opinion of the posse had been slowly deteriorating. Normally, they respected lawmen, but they had begun to doubt this posse's intentions. The men of the wagon train did respect Jack and John. They discussed the plan Jack had proposed and voted in favor of it. Feeling they had come up with a solution, they could now go to bed.

Jack had the night off from watch duty. He lay on his roll. Finally, he had a moment to himself to think about all that had happened. How all the pieces had begun to fit together while he was out on the prairie earlier in the day. Once it had all come together he had to get his proof, and he did with their trip to the lake. What a great job she had done keeping a poker face as he tried to rile her up. He pulled out the paper and read her name: *Katherine*. What had she been through? Why had she killed the farmer? Was the posse really after her? How had she learned to throw knives, hunt, shoot a gun, and ride so well? Where Jack came from, women couldn't do things like that. They had to rely on men for food, shelter, and, Lord knows, protection. He had never imagined a woman could do the things Katherine could. Not that he thought they couldn't; it had just never crossed his mind before. The more he found out about her, the more he wanted to know. Jack definitely had more questions than answers.

Before drifting completely off to sleep, Jack's mind went back to the lake, and the part he was saving until last to recreate in his mind. He smiled as he revisited Katherine undressing by the lake…

The wagon train pulled out early the next morning. They were getting into a real routine now; packing up and moving out went smoother and more quickly each day. Getting an early start in the cool mornings allowed for longer breaks during the heat of the day, when the animals and people really needed the rest.

Jack had gotten up before dawn, saddled Bullet, and rode out on an early-morning scouting mission. He had much on his mind: the posse, Katherine, Laura, and Dickerson. He couldn't imagine the posse was actually still snooping around because of Katherine. Her disguise was so good. No one on the train knew except for Jack, and possibly Laura. Jack was almost sure Laura knew. That's why the two had become so close. However, Jack wasn't sure exactly when Laura had found out. Had she always known? Had Katherine confided in her? Or had Laura made the discovery when she was nursing her back to health? That had to be it. Her behavior did seem to change toward Katherine at that time. They seemed to grow closer, but in a friendly sort of way. Jack could see how Laura would be compelled to keep Katherine's disguise a secret. Laura had once been in deep trouble, too, and Katherine had helped her get back on her feet and was the reason she was now safely making her way west. Katherine must have had an explanation for Laura as to the reasoning behind her disguise. Had she told the truth about killing the farmer, or had Katherine merely told her disguise was the only way a woman could safely travel alone? Jack didn't know, but he wanted to find out. He had a compelling need to understand why she had killed the farmer and taken his money.

As these questions ran through Jack's mind, his thoughts returned to the first time he laid eyes on "her" that day on the boardwalk. He shook his head as he remembered how she was actually going to take on two men who were after a young girl. She was definitely brave. He also thought back to their early conversations about Katherine's family and about how old she was. How much of it was true? Parts of it must have been for her to reply as quickly as she did. Jack's mind then wandered to the sight of her by the lake. He said to himself with a smile, "You're definitely not fifteen."

Jack was about an hour into his early-morning scouting mission when he came across a recently abandoned campsite. It had to have been the posse. There were six or eight horses, no wagon or buckboard, and empty whiskey bottles around the campfire. Again, they were riding parallel to the train, which led Jack to the only conclusion possible: they were following them and must strongly suspect the person they were after was still with the wagon train. Either that or they intended to rob them. But what were they waiting for? Were they waiting for them to get deeper into no man's land or possibly closer to a fort so they could haul them in to the authorities? Perhaps they had simply felt the timing wasn't right or didn't have the proof they needed. He decided his first step would be to work on Laura.

That evening, Jack had his chance. Katherine was occupied talking with Cook. Laura was standing alone at the edge of the wagon. She was practicing throwing her knife into targets she had made.

"Good evening, Laura," Jack began. "How was the hunt today?"

"Oh, hello, Jack. It went well. John's teaching me how to find game when it is scarce. You know, I think I've learned more in the past several weeks than I have in my entire lifetime. How was *your* hunt today? Did you see any sign of the posse?"

"Actually, I did. I'm not sure I think they're trying to rob us anymore. If that were their intention, you'd think they would have done it by now. I think they're just trying to catch up to the woman who killed that farmer. After all, she must be awfully dangerous if she'd kill a nice old innocent man, don't you think, Laura?"

"Oh, I don't know. There must be more to the story than what we've heard. Did you see her picture? She didn't look dangerous to me," Laura replied, looking directly at Jack.

"It's a very strange story. I just can't understand why she would kill that nice old man for no reason," Jack said, trying to sound as if he were making casual conversation.

"Women don't kill, Jack. She must have had a reason."

"What kind of a reason could she have possibly had?"

"Maybe she was trying to prevent something horrible from happening to her," Laura spouted out a little too quickly.

"Oh," was Jack's only reply.

Now it made perfect sense. Jack became angry as he pictured some crusty old man trying to hurt Katherine. If men aren't there to protect them, women and children's only choices are to get hurt or take the steps to protect themselves. Judging by Katherine's skill and independence, she had probably spent her entire life protecting herself, he figured.

During supper, Jack watched her from afar. He felt she was a stranger he had to get to know all over again. He wasn't sure how to act around her now. His behavior shouldn't change, but he knew it would. Eventually, she would need to know he knew. How to get to that point was the question. Laura knowing was one thing. She most likely found out when Katherine was in a weakened state. Not to mention that Laura was a woman. Jack believed it would be harder for Katherine to trust a man with her secret. He would have to get her to trust him enough to tell him. But how?

While Jack watched Katherine, Dickerson watched Jack. Some people didn't even need a good reason to hate. Often, they just needed to begin with another emotion and let that emotion fester. For Dickerson, it had begun as jealousy and resentment. Dickerson resented Jack for being younger than him and unattached. Dickerson hated that he had to be married and have all those damn kids. If he were free like Jack, all his money would belong only to him. He wouldn't have some nagging wife who wanted to spend it on furnishings and clothes for her and the kids. Oh, to be free again, to hang out in saloons and whorehouses. To spend his money on the things he wanted to spend it on.

Jack saw Katherine walking away from Cook. He headed toward her without a notion of what he was going to say. "Hey, kid. How are your ribs and ankle doing?"

"I'm almost one hundred percent. Everyday they feel better," she replied. She seemed in high spirits. Jack was glad she was feeling better. He knew that talking with Cook always brightened her mood.

"Are you still wrapping those ribs?"

"Yes, but it's really more of a precaution. I still have a little bit of pain, and I don't want any setbacks. Laura recommends I continue to use the wrap."

Jack thought for a minute. This wasn't getting him anywhere. "That Laura, she's a hell of a gal. What do you think she's going to do out west? Has she mentioned anything to you?"

"We have talked about it, now that you ask. There are really a lot of things I think she can do. She's very smart and wouldn't have a problem teaching. I could see her pursuing nursing or even becoming a doctor. She made mention she'd like to get her hands on some new medical journals. During her parent's accident, her father's medical journals were swept away. Cook told me folks out west don't hold women back so much. He's heard of women practicing medicine and owning businesses. They have more of a fifty-fifty partnership with their husbands on the ranches. That's probably hard for you to fathom," she ended with a bite.

It didn't go unnoticed. "No, it's not hard for me. I think women should be given more rights. They have more abilities than they're given credit for," Jack continued, wanting to plant the seed that would hopefully grow into the trust he needed. "I've heard that too, about the western territories being more open to women. I think it's because people have to be more honest to make a go of it out west. That's part of the appeal to me." He noticed she was looking at him with disbelief. Likely an after-effect of the conversation he had with her previously about "what women are good for." "Why are you looking at me like that?"

"I just thought you thought differently about women, that's all," she replied with narrowed, disbelieving eyes.

"Because of what I said earlier? Kid, I was just trying to see if I could fool you into telling me if you had feelings for Laura. I didn't think you'd just come out and tell me if I asked. Plus, I was trying to see if you had messed-up ideas about a woman's 'place.' So I laid it on thick. It doesn't sound like you've had a lot of female influence in your life. Boys who grow up with too much male influence often get the wrong idea about women and don't know how to treat them; they think of them as second rate. I was just trying to find out how you really saw them. Laura's a great gal who has been through a lot. If your idea of women is like so many other men's, I wanted to find out and figure out a way to set you straight. Sorry I wasn't honest with you, kid. From now on, I'll be straightforward and honest with you and you can be straightforward and honest with me. Deal?" Jack asked as he extended a hand.

Her voice sounded weak as she replied, "Deal." She extended her hand and they shook on it.

"Kid, I think it would be a good idea if you and I vowed to watch over Laura until she gets settled. She's still young and hasn't been on her own for long. What do you think?" Jack asked in an attempt to discover Katherine's plans for the future.

"Laura turns seventeen next week. She is getting all grown up. I would actu-ally like her to learn to be self-sufficient. There are no guarantees I will be around to watch out for her," Kat replied.

"Hey, I've got first watch tonight. Want to ride out and have a look around before sunset?" Jack asked, not sure why he did. He was just so curious. He wanted to stare at her, yet he felt conspicuous when he did. "I want to ride up to a high spot and get a good look at things before night falls."

"Sure, I'll go," she replied.

Jack secretly scolded himself for looking forward to it so much.

CHAPTER 12

Kat was in high spirits. Life was good. Her body was regaining its strength. For the first time in her life she had a real female friend. Laura knew more about her than anyone in her life ever had, with the exception of her mother. Being with Jack also lifted Kat's spirits. She always enjoyed her time with him. It felt good to know Jack respected her, and Kat knew he cared about her. That, of course, added to her guilt. She felt she was lying to him. Lying wasn't the real word, Kat thought. Deceiving, that was a more accurate description. If she had a choice, she wouldn't deceive him, but the way she saw it she had no choice. What would Jack do if he found out? Surely he would hate her or think she was deranged.

"What's on your mind, kid?" Jack broke into Kat's thoughts. "You must be thinking about me," he teased.

"Yes, I was thinking of you. After all, you are the center of my life," Kat teased back.

Jack smiled broadly.

"There's flat rock. You can see for miles from this spot. Come on up and take a look." Jack said as he dismounted and grabbed some items from his saddlebag.

Kat and Jack crawled up on the rock. It was perfectly smooth and flat, slanting up at a slight angle and keeping them hidden from anything in front of them. They lay belly-down on the rock and looked out for miles and miles in all directions. Jack pulled out his telescope and scoured the landscape. "What do you see?" Kat asked.

"I see something hairy with long ears and a twitchy nose."

"Very nice, a rabbit. Do you see anything else?" Kat asked impatiently. She loved peering through Jack's telescope.

Jack knew once he turned it over to her he wouldn't get it back for a while. "I see...whoa!"

"What is it? What is it?" she asked rather impatiently.

"That's the biggest pile of dung I've ever seen!"

She punched him on the shoulder. "Here, see for your self," Jack said as he offered her the telescope.

She grabbed the instrument and peered through the eyepiece. Jack sat up and lit a cigarette. This was his opportunity to stare at her close-up while she was completely occupied with something else.

"So, what do you see?" Jack asked as his eyes roamed over her face and hair. She had removed her hat. He looked at the back of her neck and her shoulders, at her back and waist. He then looked at her small, firm bottom and long legs. Interesting how a woman with the right clothing could pass as a man. It was more than that though, Jack thought as he took a long drag on his cigarette, it was the way she talked and moved. If you didn't know, and not too many people did, you could see how she managed to pull this off. It still amazed him.

"I see the dung pile, and...a lot of torn up ground. Buffalo must have made a mad dash through here not too long ago. Probably explains the huge dung pile. And I see what looks like an abandoned campsite."

"You do?" Jack asked in surprise. "I didn't see that."

"Guess that makes me the better scout," she teased.

Jack grabbed the scope and took a look. "I think you're right. Shall we ride down there and have a look?"

"You think I am a better scout?" she asked with a smile. Jack noticed how beautiful she was when she smiled.

"No. I think you're right about an abandoned campsite." Jack and Kat walked back and mounted the horses. They cautiously rode out to have a look.

The campsite looked to be about two days old. From the horse prints they counted six riders. "Do you think it was the posse?" she asked seriously.

"The empty whiskey bottles are their trademark," Jack replied. "They must still be trailing us and I don't know why. Do you?"

"No, I can't understand why they would still trail us after they learned the people they're looking for are definitely not on the train."

"Maybe they're not convinced of that," Jack replied, feeling he might be tipping his hand. "Or maybe they think someone on the train knows something.

Or, possibly, they are out to rob us. Some of those fellows looked a little shady to me." Jack watched her carefully for a reaction, but her poker face held firm.

Jack was concerned. He knew he needed to stay one step ahead of this posse. It was very likely they were after Katherine, but how could they possibly know? He was catching on to their pattern. They stayed about a day and a half in front of the train. He would ride ahead and spy on them. Once they slowed down to wait for the train, he would get Katherine and get out of there. Vigilant, he had to stay vigilant.

"Well, it appears they've gone on ahead for now. Let's circle toward the south east and then head back to camp," Jack offered. He knew if the posse would be anywhere close it would be in the other direction. He had no intention of leading Katherine into harm's way.

Kat knew she couldn't continue to ignore the posse. Now that she saw the evidence for herself, it was more real than ever. They were hunting her down and not giving up. She would need to come up with a plan. She would not be caught.

People were getting anxious to get to their destination and start their new lives. Trail life was exciting at first but quickly became monotonous, and most had been on the trail even longer than Kat had. The weather had been good—they had that to be thankful for—and they had not run into any hostile Indians. Since the tragic river crossing, and the tornado, no one else had suffered any life-threatening injuries or illnesses. All in all, Kat felt things had gone quite well for the entire group.

Kat and Laura rode with the train until they were within a half-mile of flat rock. They then each took one of the little Shafer girls and rode to the rock to show them. Jack lent his telescope to Kat for the special trip.

The little girls adored Laura and "John" and were thrilled to go on an excursion beyond their wagon. Mr. and Mrs. Shafer were thankful, too. They knew the girls were getting bored. Laura and Kat took the girls to the base of the rock and let them climb on the unusually flat stone. They then lay flat on their stomachs, just as Jack and Kat had the night before, and looked out across the prairie. What a special treat, since today there was actually a small herd of buffalo grazing in the distance. Kat and Laura looked at each other with raised eyebrows. Downing a buffalo would keep the train fed for days, but there was plenty of time for that later. The little girls were very patient and each let the other have a turn looking through Jack's scope. They were so cute and so considerate of each other. Kat felt a little left out, since she had never had a sibling around to play with and talk to. Trevor had been the closest thing to a real sibling, she guessed, but he had been gone so much while she was growing up. She couldn't blame him. Trevor didn't quite fit in with Clay, Henry, and Boris. What Kat could blame him for was hunting her down like a mad dog. Her fond feelings for Trevor quickly vanished as she thought about how he had turned on her when it mattered most.

Kat turned her attention once again to the little girls. She would love to have a couple of her own, and maybe a boy or two, someday. Her children would be nurtured and loved, and their mother wouldn't die on them, leaving them to fend for themselves. Both the boys and girls would be taught useful skills. Her boys and girls would learn to ride, hunt, and fish, and both would learn to cook, wash, and mend. Kat didn't care what her husband had to say about that; it was just the way it was going to be. Kat shook her head. There she went again, getting way ahead of herself. After all, she might never even get married or have children. Especially looking the way she did now.

Kat popped out of her daydream when Holly, the younger Shafer girl, asked, "John, do you have family, or were they killed, like Laura's?"

Rachel, the other little girl, quickly admonished her sister for saying something so insensitive. "Oh, Laura, I'm sorry. Did I make you sad?" Holly looked truly concerned.

"That's perfectly okay, Holly, people sometimes lose their loved ones. It's all right to talk about it," Laura said gently as she hid any hurt she might have been feeling.

"My brother died, and my sister," Holly offered. "I felt so bad, and so did Ma and Pa, but I'm really glad they're not dead—and neither is Rachel. I'm also glad that you're not dead, John. I prayed really hard when you were sick. I told God I would try not to be mad at him anymore for taking my brother and sister if he would just give Laura the power to heal you. He did and I'm very happy now. I even feel better about my brother and sister. Ma said God may take something away, but you can't blame him for it. He'll always replace the loss later, maybe in another way. I think at least for a while you and Laura are the replacement."

Kat and Laura looked at each other and smiled. Little Holly sure had a way of seeing through people and situations. "Well, those are some awfully big shoes to fill," Kat said. "Now you've got me thinking I have to start acting better. No more talking with my mouth full. No more forgetting to say my prayers and forgetting to say excuse me after I burp."

The little girls laughed. "Sometimes we're naughty, too. We stuck cockle-burs in Mr. Dickerson's boots because he said that you and Laura were sinners," Rachel said. She was very proud of herself when she said it.

Holly chimed in, "He even said Laura was a whore!"

Kat looked at Laura and could tell she was appalled. Kat calmly smiled. "Girls, I know you know Laura is a very respectable young lady, and we should all be proud of what she has learned to do over the past several weeks. Does anyone else on the train say bad things like that?" Kat asked.

"No," Holly, the more outspoken one, replied. "They all tell Mr. Dickerson to shut up!"

"Good," Laura replied, the hurt lifting from her face, "and you know, girls, that you shouldn't say things like 'whore' or 'shut up.'"

"Yes, we know," the girls said in unison, but with a slightly naughty smile on their lips.

"Let's get these little ladies back, Laura, so we can get to our hunting," Kat said.

Laura and Kat returned the girls to their parents. Mr. and Mrs. Shafer thanked them. "Did they behave?" Mrs. Shafer asked.

"They were little angels," Laura said as she looked sideways at the girls and winked at them.

"Thank you so much for all you two do for this wagon train," Mr. Shafer said. "It's great having capable people who can put food on the table each night so I can concentrate on my family's safety—" Mr. Shafer then turned to Laura "—and it is very reassuring to know there is someone around who has medical knowledge."

Laura blushed brightly. Kat knew how she felt. It meant so much to be appreciated for what you contributed. Kat had received her fair share of compliments about her hunting, but Laura had never felt as appreciated as she did just then. Kat was thrilled to have witnessed Laura's moment.

Kat and Laura rode on ahead of the train once again. Kat wanted to speak to Jack and get his advice on shooting buffalo. She wondered if buffalo easily stampeded, knowing that could be very dangerous. She had her chance when the train had stopped for the midday meal and Jack rode into camp. He looked hot and dusty from a long morning of hard scouting. Kat shook her head as she realized that was even appealing to her.

"Hi, Jack. Did you see anything out there?" Kat asked. She knew he would know she was asking about the posse.

"Yes. I spotted the posse about six miles ahead of the train," Jack replied in a serious tone. "That seems to be their pattern."

"I'd like to get a closer look at them, Jack. Could we ride out tonight?"

"No!" Jack's reply was short. "It's too dangerous."

"No, it's not!" Kat replied, angry that Jack's answer had been so curt. "I have just as much right as you do to see what danger lies ahead. Just because you're the 'scout' doesn't mean you're the only one interested in protecting these people."

"I'm sorry, kid," Jack replied, "but my answer is still no. Those men are definitely up to something, and there are six of them. We can't risk getting caught spying on them. Even though some of them seem to drink a lot, they are still on high alert for Indians, wild animals, and outlaws. It would be too risky for you."

Kat just looked at him. She didn't push the issue because she could tell he had made up his mind. "Fine. I wanted to talk to you about hunting buffalo. Laura and I spotted a small herd, but I don't want to cause a stampede."

"That's smart, kid," Jack said. "Not only that, the buffalo holds a special place in the hearts of the Indians. They don't like the white man to come along and senselessly kill them."

Kat didn't attempt to hide her disappointment. She really wanted to hunt a buffalo. Jack smiled and continued, "On the other hand, buffalo meat is delicious, and their hides are very useful."

"What about the Indians?" Kat asked.

"I said they don't like *senseless* killing. If we just shoot one and use the entire animal as they would, they will not be offended," Jack said with his beautiful smile. "They may stampede, but if we position ourselves between the wagon train and the buffalo, they should run away from the train, not towards it."

"Great!" Katherine said. "You're sure they'll run away?"

"I better come with you just to make sure," Jack said.

It was early afternoon. Kat, Laura, and Jack positioned themselves between the wagon train and the buffalo. Kat, they had decided, would get to take the first shot. Hopefully, one shot would be sufficient to take down a buffalo.

Kat's heart was beating fast in anticipation. Jack and Laura were right next to her as she took aim. They didn't want to miss a moment of it. Kat took a deep breath and let it out slowly as her finger pulled the trigger. The entire herd yanked their heads up from their grazing position and took off in a stampede…away from the wagon train.

The animal Kat had shot lay still on the ground. She was elate and Laura was so excited she was jumping up and down.

Jack just stood and smiled at her. He wanted to hug her but instead laid his hand on her shoulder and said, "Good job, kid. You did it in one shot."

Now the work began. Mr. Shafer and Appleton brought up a buckboard and the group began to work on the animal. It was hard work but well worth it. The one buffalo would feed the wagon train for several days. The evening meal was delicious. Everyone congratulated Kat and the others on the hunt. Cook told Kat that of all wagon trains he'd been on, this one was definitely the best fed. Between Kat's hunting and his cooking, they could convince the entire East Coast to go west. Cook always had a way with words. The entire wagon train laughed, all except Dickerson, who merely grunted and turned his back.

Jack had first watch that night. He rode out early to get a good look at the posse before they settled down for the night. Jack was beat tired. For the past several nights he'd had very little sleep. Keeping track of this posse had cut in to his routine. Along the way, Jack thought about Katherine. He was so proud of the way she had brought down the buffalo. The look in her eyes when she turned to Jack for approval was one he'd never forget. Jack felt anguish as he wondered how he could ever get her to tell him the truth about herself. He didn't have an answer, and he hated that. Eventually, one would come to him, but until then he'd have to be patient.

Jack found the posse's trail and followed it until he was about a mile from their camp. He then left Bullet and approached on foot. The group had camped just over a small embankment and Jack crawled up the embankment where he was within earshot. Gun drawn, he lay in the grass just a few yards from the campfire and listened…

"Clay, shut your mouth. You get louder and louder every time you tip that bottle! We are in Indian territory. Are you trying to get us all scalped?"

Jack mentally made note of the members of the party.

"You shut up, little brother," the one called Clay replied in a slurred voice. "You always were a pussy. I'd kill those red bastards with this pistol before they'd get near me with a knife."

"Clay—" a different male voice now "—put that pistol down before you accidentally shoot someone. You're drunk, and your brother's right. We've got to be careful. We are so close now. Think about the reward money."

"Hee! Hee!" Clay was chuckling now. "Who would have thought my own sister would make me rich! She doesn't have a clue I'm about to haul her sorry ass to jail to collect my reward. I'll be buying me the finest whiskey for the trip home."

"She's not your real sister, dumbass."

"Shut up, Trevor. I've had enough of your bratty mouth. I'm five years older than you and you have to listen to me," Clay replied. "I know she's not my real sister. That's why I'm thinking we should teach her a thing or two before we turn her in. She needs to be put in her place."

Trevor was the name of the other brother, Jack concluded. It sounded like he did not get along with Clay. Or maybe weeks of traveling with him had taken a toll on their brotherly relationship. Clay was trouble. He sickened Jack. It would be over his dead body that he'd ever get his hands on Katherine.

"Clay, go to bed, or you won't have to worry about Indians because I'll kill you myself," Trevor snarled.

Jack was furious. Her own brothers, or whatever they were to Katherine, were after her. Jack knew Clay's kind: loud, obnoxious, and dangerous to be around because of his own stupidity. What kind of a worm would turn against a person like Katherine? Jack listened a while longer. Clay spouted off a few more stupid comments, but as the rest of the group ignored him, he lost some steam.

Jack decided he'd better get out of there. He imagined Clay stumbling over the embankment to urinate and discovering Jack spying on them. His only choice then would be to shoot Clay. Jack enjoyed the thought of shooting Clay for a moment and then realized it wasn't practical. Another time perhaps. Jack made his way back to his mount and rode north, keenly surveying the landscape.

Jack figured they had about five days before they entered Wyoming Territory, and another five-day ride before they hit Fort Laramie. That's where the posse would likely take their "prisoner" to collect the reward money. There wasn't much time, but there would be enough. Now he had to formulate the plan.

Back at camp, Kat dozed. She awoke fully when Jack made his way back to camp shortly after midnight. She feigned sleep as Jack walked by. He stopped for a few moments and Kat could feel him looking at her. Finally, he went to his bedroll to lie down. Kat waited another twenty minutes before she eased herself up. She looked over at Jack and could tell by his steady breathing that he was asleep.

As stealthily as a cat, she made her way to Ginger and carefully turned her toward the darkness of the night. She was far more concerned about making it past Jack, who was asleep, than past Mr. Dickerson, who was on guard duty, and probably also asleep.

She headed out in the direction she had seen Jack go earlier in the night. The moon was bright and she was able to follow his trail somewhat, at least enough to get her where she wanted to go.

It was the same embankment Jack had hid behind. By now, all but two of the men were asleep. Trevor sat with his rifle across his knees, looking out onto the prairie. Another man sat next to him talking. They kept their voices low, but Kat was still able to make out what they said.

"That brother of yours is a loose cannon, Trevor. He's putting us all in danger," the man said with conviction. "You know, if you hadn't decided at the last minute to come with us, one of these men would have shot him by now. The only reason they haven't is out of respect for you. We have less than two weeks left of this journey. It's your job to keep Clay under control. Once we nab 'em we'll give Clay his cut of the money, but he's not welcome to ride with us anymore. He can find his own way back."

"I understand," Trevor replied. "The only reason I came on this excursion in the first place was because Clay wanted to go so badly and I knew he'd be trouble."

Kat felt a little better. Hunting her down wasn't his priority. He was here because of Clay. The fact remained, however, that Trevor would collect the reward money! She held her resolve to not forgive him.

"Nab 'em?" the phrase returned to Kat's mind. "Did they mean nab him or nab them?" she wondered frantically. Either way, they must have had reason to think the man who brutally slew the drifters was traveling somewhere out here. Kat suddenly realized she needed to be on the lookout for him. A young *boy* like herself would look like an easy target to him. She decided to be extra careful on the way back.

Kat stayed a while longer. The other man left Trevor to his watch and went back to his bedroll. From her vantage point Kat could see Trevor. She reminisced about the good times she'd had with him. Just then, Trevor looked into the darkness directly at the spot where Kat lay. She froze for what seemed like an eternity. It was really only a few moments before Trevor's gaze drifted off in another direction.

Kat waited a few minutes longer before slipping back to where she had left Ginger. She mounted and rode back toward the wagon train, keeping a watchful eye in all directions.

Relief swept over her as she saw the outline of the wagons in the moonlight. "That was really stupid," she scolded herself. Out of pure curiosity she had gone within a few yards of the men who wanted to capture her. Not to mention a brutal killer was likely roaming the prairie, and there she was, out by herself in the middle of the night.

The thought had barely finished forming in her mind when he appeared out of nowhere and pulled her off her horse. She was caught totally off guard and he had her pinned in no time. She couldn't pull her knife, as he had her arms under his knees, and she couldn't scream, as his hand was clamped down over her mouth.

He bent his head down and said in an angry voice, "See what happens when you ride around in the middle of the night by yourself? What the hell were you thinking?" It was Jack and he was mad. She couldn't answer because he was still covering her mouth.

He took his hand off her mouth but she still didn't answer, mostly because she knew he was right and also because she was so relieved it was Jack. Thinking about the brutal killer being out there on the dark prairie at the same time she had been had her all worked up. She was actually fighting tears. "Sorry I scared you, kid, but you can't take stupid chances. You went to find the posse, didn't you?"

Kat could only nod her head, yes. She was still too upset to speak. Jack rolled off her and sat on the ground. He reached into his shirt pocket and pulled out a cigarette, lit it, and handed it to Kat. She took it with shaking hands. After a few drags, she calmed down enough to talk.

"Yes, I went to see the posse. I followed your tracks and snuck up on them. I listened to them talk a while and then headed back. As I listened, I realized how stupid it was that I was out there riding around on the prairie alone this time of night. I was just getting myself all worked up over the possible dangers, including the man they talked about who brutally killed the drifters, when you tackled me and scared the shit out of me!"

"What did they say about the man who killed the drifters?"

Kat tried to remember. "I really don't think they actually mentioned him. They just said something about nabbing 'him' or 'nabbing them,' collecting the reward and heading home. They must think they're around here."

After saying that, Kat thought it was a good time for her to shut up. She was shaken up and didn't want to risk saying too much.

"What do you think?" Jack asked her.

"I don't have a clue. What do you think?"

"I think you should promise me you won't ride out alone like that again. Just because you haven't seen anything and nothing's happened to you—well, other than being tackled by a tornado—doesn't mean there's not a lot of danger out there. In fact, I think from now on you should stay close to the train during the day. We have plenty of food, and if we need a little more, I can do some hunting."

"No," Kat protested, "and I don't get it. Why are you being so protective of me?"

Jack paused for a long time. Kat could tell he was about to tell her something important. She waited until he was ready. "I told you I have a younger brother about your age that I left back in Missouri. Maybe by protecting you I feel like I'm protecting him."

"If he's my age he must know how to handle himself," Kat replied, still not fully understanding; but then again, Jack hadn't told her everything.

He continued, "Sam is capable, but he's the only sibling I have left. My sister, Sarah, was raped and killed by some men passing through a few months back. I wasn't there to protect her. Sam and I rode off to look at some horses in a neighboring town. I've learned you can never let your guard down, because there are bad people everywhere. They like to take advantage of those they consider weaker than they are, usually females, children, or old people. And I learned you must always look out for your loved ones."

Kat was trembling now. She wanted to cry as she imagined the pain Jack was feeling. Not only had his sister been brutally killed, but Jack also felt it was his fault for not being there to protect her.

"I'm so sorry, Jack. I didn't..." was all she could manage. She swallowed hard and spoke again. "Where is Sam now? And your parents?"

"My parents died about three years ago. They both came down with fever. Once I got word I headed back home, but they were too far gone by the time I arrived. After we buried them, I stayed and worked the farm and looked after Sam and Sarah. When Sarah was killed, I sold the farm, crops, and livestock to my aunt and uncle. Sam is staying with them and growing up a little more. When he's older, I'll invite him to come out west and live with me on the ranch I'm going to build. I've always preferred raising livestock to raising crops."

Kat was stunned. She had wondered about Jack's past, but she just figured he had a perfect family life. He seemed so together. She wanted to hug him but knew she couldn't.

"I have a feeling something's going to happen. I need to keep an eye out for trouble, and I can't do that when I have to worry that you're out gallivanting around the countryside," Jack said.

Normally, Kat would have protested. How could she after hearing that? She told Jack what he wanted to hear because she couldn't bear to cause him any more worry. She said she'd stay in camp, all the while thinking perhaps she would just slip out some night. Maybe leave a note that Laura could give him so he wouldn't worry.

Jack seemed satisfied with her reply.

They headed back to camp in silence. Kat was spent. She was ready to lie down and sleep. When she did, her sleep was not peaceful. Kat dreamt of brutal killers on the loose. Then her dream morphed into an even more horrible picture, of a run-in between Jack and the posse. Jack was trying to protect her in the dream, and all the while Kat wanted to protect Jack from the posse. But it was as if she were stone. She could see Jack needed help, but she couldn't get to him. She felt helpless. Jack was blocking the posse from getting to her. The posse pulled their guns and took aim at Jack. "Bang!"

Kat bolted straight out of her bedroll. Cook laughed at her. He was holding a pan and a big spoon that he had clanged together. "I thought that'd get you out of bed, kid. You're usually the first one up."

Kat took a look around and saw that half the train was already up and starting their morning chores. "Thanks a lot, Cook," Kat grumbled.

She was tired. The events of last night had taken a toll on her. She got up and immediately looked around for Jack. He was already up and packing his saddlebag with supplies for the day's ride. Kat bet he hadn't gotten much sleep last night either.

Kat was feeling dusty and dirty. She helped herself to a pail of water, a sponge, and soap and headed for cover behind a group of rocks a short distance from camp. Jack watched her go. He continued to work but kept a worried eye out for her until she returned.

Behind the rock, Kat scrubbed down as best she could. She wished for a stream to fully immerse in, but there weren't any nearby. Better yet, she wished for a hot bath with scented water and scented soaps like she would sometimes treat herself to back on the farm. Someday. For now, the pail of water would have to suffice.

When Kat returned to camp Laura cheerfully greeted her, "Good morning, sleepyhead. Are you ready for some breakfast and a great day of hunting?"

"We are not going hunting today, Laura," Kat replied. She could see Laura was disappointed but smart enough to not protest.

Kat told her about going to see the posse the night before. How she had gotten close enough to hear that they were still probably after her and the killer, who was likely wandering in the nearby countryside.

"Kat, I don't know what you looked like before, but do you really think your brothers would recognize you now if they saw you?" Laura asked.

"I honestly don't know. Clay might not. He's dumb as a post; but Trevor, he got all the other boys' brains. He may figure it out.

"Well, we just have to make sure they don't see you," Laura replied with her there's-a-solution-for-everything tone.

"Laura, I think they are planning to storm the wagon train to find me."

Laura gave her a horrified look.

"Don't worry, I've come up with a plan. I'm going to have to leave soon. I thought I'd wait a few days until we were deeper into Wyoming. I've heard there are several abandoned homesteads there, and I plan on finding one to hide out in for a while. You ride on to South Passe and stay there. After about a month I'll come and find you there." Laura smiled, and so did Kat. "From there, I think we should ride on to Salt Lake City. I'll make my 'transformation' back into a woman before we get to Salt Lake City and we can winter there. Come spring, we'll decide if we want to stay there or head on to California."

"Oh, Kat!" Laura exclaimed.

"Shhh," Kat admonished.

"I'm sorry." Laura's eyes filled with tears. "I'm just so glad you're my friend and you've included me in your future. Frankly, I didn't know what I was going to do. I was actually dreading the end of this trail ride, if you can believe that."

"I can believe it, because I've felt the same way. I've really enjoyed this little deviation from reality. But sooner or later the future will be here and we'll have to be ready for it."

Laura smiled. "I am so thankful I met you. How am I going to ever repay you?"

It was Kat's turn to smile. "What? Saving my life once wasn't enough?"

The two headed to Cook's wagon for breakfast. As Kat ate she looked around at the people of the wagon train. She was really going to miss them. Many had become her friends and she hoped the best for them as they began their new lives out west. Maybe someday she'd run into them again, she hoped, as she watched the little Shafer girls playing together beside the wagon. Kat imagined what they would look like when they grew up. Real beauties, she imagined—and what personalities they had. Kat truly hoped she'd someday learn how they turned out. And Cook. Kat smiled as she looked at him fondly. He had become like a lovable grandfather to her. Her hope was that Cook would always be happy and never alone. She worried about who would take care of him in his old age.

Mr. Appleton. Kat was impressed with his ability to lead people and still be a nice person. He was due much credit for getting this wagon train across the prairie with such little incident. She made a note to tell him so before she left. Kat knew how good it made her feel when she received praise. Mr. Appleton sure did deserve some.

Her eyes then drifted over to Mr. Dickerson. Her hope was that she never had to see him again. Kat had a bad feeling about him, and she'd learned to trust her instincts. She didn't even attempt to summon up a good thought when it came to Dickerson.

As Kat picked up her water cup, her eyes met Jack's from across the campsite. Jack then turned away as Appleton called his name and began speaking with him about the day's business.

The thought of never seeing Jack weighed on her like a pile of bricks. She had never wanted to be with someone as much as she wanted to be with Jack. Every day she looked forward to whatever time they had together. Every one of their conversations had meant so much to her. Working with him to keep the train fed and protected was the most fulfilling thing she'd ever done. She even enjoyed the way her stomach did little flip-flops every time he rode back into camp in the evening. He was the first person she looked for when her eyes opened in the morning. Kat then let her mind drift to the more intimate moments. Well, to him they weren't intimate, Kat thought, but to her they meant everything. When he put a hand on her shoulder to congratulate her on a great shot. Or their fingers accidentally touching when he handed her something. Kat's mind drifted further as she thought back to the day she saw him bathing. The scene was crystal clear in her mind and she became completely lost in her thoughts.

"Kid!" Cook was hollering at her. "Have you gone deaf? I asked if you wanted the last of the mush."

"Oh, sorry, Cook. I guess I was daydreaming. Yeah, I'll take it."

Jack was looking at her and smiling; she knew it amused him at how much she could eat. Imagine if he knew she was a woman, Kat thought, he'd think she was a pig! Kat would miss that smile.

The wagon train pulled out. The people who had seemed so tired a week ago now rode with new vigor. They became excited the closer they got to their destinations. Many planned on ranching in Wyoming Territory. Several would winter at the forts or in one of the small towns before deciding what they would do for a living. All of them would be thrilled that they no longer had to ride in a wagon on a dusty trail all day long.

Kat didn't know how these people did it. Just plodding along for hours. Kat found it incredibly boring to stay with the train all day. She was getting fidgety in the saddle after just a few hours. Laura leaned over and said, "See why I get ornery when you won't let me go hunting with you?"

Kat nodded. She and Laura couldn't really carry on a conversation. What would they talk about that was acceptable for other's ears? At least she had her thoughts and plans to keep her company. Kat was excited about her future, now that she finally had one. What would she and Laura end up doing, she wondered? They'd find a way to make a living, she supposed, and find a nice place to live. Harley's stash of money would make starting a new life a little easier.

Finally, it was time to stop for the midday meal.

Jack rode into camp and talked with the men about the trail up ahead. The weather was holding, and they were making good time. Jack and Mr. Appleton looked at the maps. They figured they'd be in Wyoming by late the next evening. Mr. Appleton was obviously pleased about that but to Jack, it just meant one day closer to trouble. He wondered if Katherine realized the posse could storm the train at any time to find her. Maybe she thought they were just out there to find the man who had killed the drifter. Jack didn't know what was going on in her head, but one thing was sure: he'd have to get her out of here soon. Tomorrow night, that's when they would disappear.

Jack saw Katherine and approached her. "How was your morning with the wagon train?" he asked. He was anxious to see her after thinking about her all morning.

"Long and boring," Kat replied. "I'm not cut out for monotony."

"Well, you won't have to put up with it for long. We are actually ahead of schedule and should hit Wyoming by tomorrow evening."

Jack thought that bit of information made her a bit sad.

"Where do you think you'll end up, Jack?" she asked him.

"I honestly don't know. I was planning all along on ranching in California. I don't think that's going to work for me after all. I might continue riding north to Oregon and see what I can find, or I may head south to Mexico."

"Why? I thought you wanted to build a ranch and eventually have Sam come live with you."

"I've got some unfinished business I really should attend to before I start my life," Jack said.

She wrinkled her brows together.

Jack smiled. "What's that look all about?"

"I just don't understand why you've decided this now. What about your dream to build a ranch, and what about Sam? He's been through a lot, too. How is he going to feel if you just wander around for a few years?" To Jack her tone sounded a bit desperate. It gave him a glimmer of hope about her feelings for him. He never imagined she would have feelings for him. Oh, he knew she looked at him as a friend, but he thought that was it. Then again, maybe she had thought about his earlier offer to be a part of his ranch and had considered taking him up on the offer. Either way, it gave him a bit of hope that she wanted to be with him at some level.

"Sam will be fine, and I'll invite him to come live with me once I get settled."

Kat could tell she was out of the picture—not that she was ever really in the picture. "I was just worried about him, that's all," Kat muttered. She was ready to put an end to the horrible conversation. Kat felt as if there were a rock in the pit of her stomach. Life without Jack was just something she would have to get use to. Although, ever since she had made her plan with Laura, she thought in the back of her mind that maybe she'd run into him again. What she'd do then she didn't know. Not that it mattered. She'd been making this up as she went anyway.

One of the men called Jack over. Kat sat in the shade of a wagon with her plate of food. For once she wasn't hungry, but ate anyway, knowing she'd need her strength over the next several days.

The afternoon ride was more tedious and long than the morning one had been. Kat couldn't even muster up happy thoughts to keep her mind occupied. By the late-afternoon break she was really feeling down.

"Staying with the wagon train all day really puts you in a sour mood, doesn't it?" Laura smiled at Kat.

"Yeah, it's not the thing for me," Kat replied. She couldn't even summon a smile.

"Kat, I could stay with you in the wilderness. I'd keep you company."

Kat did smile then. "No. I need you to get a life started for us. Don't worry about me. I'll be just fine."

But Kat was feeling very despondent by the time they started moving again. Jack hadn't stopped back for the afternoon break. As they plodded along, Kat began to think. She thought about her past and how empty it seemed. There had been no one to love her back at Boris's farm and she had survived. At least she had Laura and was in a position to make her own decisions now. Back on the farm she had practically been forced to marry Harley. Imagine a life with him! She scolded herself for being such a baby about Jack. It didn't remove the hurt, but it did put things back into perspective.

That evening, Kat made an effort to talk with Laura. She didn't want Laura worrying. She also occupied her time by playing with the Shafer girls. They pretended to be horses, and Kat sat on the ground and lassoed them as they ran around her. The girls laughed and laughed. Their mother looked on in appreciation. Finally, Mrs. Shafer called them away as people began to quiet down for the night. Kat looked around, but there was no sign of Jack. Just as she began to feel panic, she saw him in the distance. He pulled Bullet up next to the cook wagon but didn't remove the saddle and bridle. Instead he walked right up to Kat and leaned next to her.

"Saddle up Ginger and come with me," he said in a low tone.

Kat thought she could sense urgency in his voice. She obeyed, but before they both mounted, she asked, "Is it the posse?"

"No. They're camping south of here. I think they're in for a long night of drinking. I can tell they are getting excited because they're nearing the end of their journey. Just get on your horse and come with me." He smiled.

They rode north and west about five miles. Kat noticed the scenery was beginning to change. She saw more trees, and the land wasn't so flat. They came to a grove of trees and Jack put his fingers to his lips to signal for her to be quiet. Bullet and Ginger were left to munch grass as Jack and Kat made their way through the grove of trees. Jack put his hand against Kat's middle to make her stop. His touch sent waves of sensation through her body. Jack leaned over and whispered in her ear. "Be very quiet and go look around that rock into the valley."

Kat followed his instructions, and it was well worth it. When she looked below, she laid eyes on a herd of beautiful wild horses. She gasped. For the longest time, Kat couldn't take her eyes off them. They looked different than regular horses. They seemed to know they were free. She watched for several minutes, actually forgetting about Jack for the moment. When she did turn and looked at him, she wanted nothing more than to kiss him. She almost laughed, imagining his reaction if she did. She wondered if he suspected something because he was looking at her so strangely.

Finally Kat spoke in a low voice. Jack had to lean in to hear her as she whispered. "I have never seen wild horses. Are there a lot of them out here?"

Jack whispered back, "I've heard there are." They both enjoyed the intimate moment, and Kat was so thankful he had shared it with her. She didn't know how to express her thanks without sounding too feminine.

"See—" Kat turned to him as if that moment would convince him to stay and build a ranching operation, "—the best horses in the world are right here."

"I think you're right."

They stayed longer than they had to, each enjoying the other's company in silence. It was late when they headed back. Jack mentioned he wanted to ride south before he went to sleep, just to make sure the posse was behaving. As they came to the top of the knoll, Jack stopped Bullet abruptly. He grabbed Ginger's reigns and backed her down the hill. Kat was surprised by the action.

"What's going on?" Kat asked.

"There are strangers in the camp," Jack said as he dismounted. He pulled his telescope out of his bag. Kat didn't even bother him to have a look. Jack continued, "Guess who?"

"The posse. What's happening?" Kat's heart was beating wildly.

"One of them is talking to Appleton. The others are snooping around. Appleton is shaking his head 'no' and pointing. I can tell he's trying to get them to leave. The big dumb-looking one is sticking his head in wagons. Laura's scolding him now. Oh, no," Jack said, "he grabbed her and is...wait, wait. The younger guy just came over and broke it up. He and the dumb one are arguing now."

Clay and Trevor. Kat was sure of it. Trevor was always trying to clean up Clay's messes.

"Now the young guy is walking around the back of the wagons. He's all alone and he is looking your packhorse over," Jack said.

Kat was staving off panic. What if the men rode toward them? They were trapped just on the opposite side of the knoll. Kat had no intention of letting them see her. She didn't know what to do. Jack would think something were up if she just got on Ginger and rode back to the grove of trees.

Maybe she should run on foot. She was frozen with fear.

"I can tell the people aren't welcoming them. Appleton is trying to get them to leave. The men are mounting their horses now and heading off...south again."

Kat was relieved. That was too close for comfort. Someone up there must be watching out for her. What were the chances she'd be out of camp at this time of night? They stayed put until the posse was well out of sight.

Kat knew she had to leave immediately. It had become too risky. Neither Jack nor Kat spoke for a while. Jack put the glass back up to his eye. "Laura's coming this direction."

Thank, God! Kat thought.

It didn't take Laura long to find them, "Did you see the posse?"

"Yes, that's why we stayed out here. What did they want?" Kat asked.

"They think we are hiding someone. I could tell they really thought they would find something tonight. Some of them are very obnoxious," Laura said with disgust. "They asked Mr. Appleton if there was anyone else traveling with us. He lied and said no. Then some of them started nosing around."

"Laura, do you think they'll be back tonight?" Jack asked.

"I don't know if it will be tonight, but I know they'll be back. They weren't satisfied with Mr. Appleton's answer."

"Well, they're gone for now," Jack said. "Let's head back to camp."

As Kat headed back to camp, a plan began to formulate in her mind. Once Jack left to do his scouting, she would get up, grab the things she needed, and ride off. If she rode all night and into the next day, she would have a good head start on the posse. She was sure she could lose them once she hit more wooded areas.

Back at camp, most people had settled down for the night. Mr. Appleton cornered Jack to speak with him about the posse. Mr. Dickerson sat on the back of his wagon and watched.

Kat pretended to get ready for bed. She laid on her bedroll in the shadow of a wagon and watched Jack ride off to the west. Kat wondered if he would circle to the south and confront the posse. Was he going to talk to them? That could be dangerous. She didn't want Jack to be in any danger because of her. It was best that she left.

Kat lay there, still as a mouse. She had to be certain everyone was in a deep sleep before she headed out. Just when she was ready to make a move she saw a shadow behind one of the wagons. A figure mounted a horse and rode in the direction of the posse. It was Mr. Dickerson. What was he up to?

She couldn't stick around to find out. After crawling out of her bedroll as quietly as she could manage, Kat made her way to Ginger. She glanced over at Laura, who was lying in her bedroll under a wagon. Her eyes were wide open and she slightly moved her hand to let Kat know she understood now was the time. Kat walked Ginger and the packhorse quietly away from the camp. When she felt she was a safe distance to the north, she mounted Ginger and rode. Luck was on her side. It was a clear night and she rode hard, using the stars as a guide. It was eerie to be out in the wild countryside alone. She tried hard not to think that a brutal killer could be waiting in the dark shadows.

Color had begun to touch the sky just before dawn, when she stopped at a stream to fill her canteens. This country was foreign to her and she didn't know how long she would ride without coming across water. She wished it would rain and cover up her trail. Looking up, she saw there wasn't a cloud in the sky. Fatigue was beginning to cloud her thoughts as she continued to ride west. She would need a good lead before she could even consider stopping. Kat took a break at noon to let the horses graze and rest. They'd been on the trail for several weeks and didn't have the stamina they had on her first flight after the "incident." Kat didn't let that stop her. She rode all afternoon, dozing off a couple times in the saddle. Ginger was beginning to stumble and Kat knew it was time to stop.

It was early evening when Kat came upon a series of three little abandon cabins right next to each other. She couldn't believe her luck. There was even a small shed for the horses. Kat tied the animals outside to graze and sat in an old chair on the porch of the cabin. Again she dozed off, she figured for about an hour.

When she woke, she led the horses into the shed and bedded them down for the night. Once the horses were taken care of, Kat headed inside the cabin, rolled out her blanket, and lay down on the floor. She was fast asleep in seconds.

CHAPTER 13

Jack had watched her while she was dozing on the porch. What a brave soul she was to head off alone. Brave and stupid. Why didn't she come to him for help? Didn't she trust him? Or was she just that scared? He followed her immediately after she snuck off that night. Jack pretended to go find the posse but ended up circling back. He knew she'd leave.

She had ridden hard for almost an entire day. He saw her nod off in the saddle a few times and thought about making his presence known. His concern was that she would run from him. He still thought it would be best if she decided to tell him her secret on her own. The problem was he had no idea how to get her to do that. The other problem was the posse. They just weren't giving up. And if they didn't get them to give up, they could never live in peace. Jack was tired, too. After Kat went in to the cabin for the night, he sat in a chair on the porch with his rifle across his knees and went to sleep.

Jack woke to the sound of a cocking gun.

There she was, looking tired and angry, with her pistol pointing at his temple. "Jack Parker, what are you up to?"

"I have every right to ask you the same question," he retorted without moving a muscle, since she still had the gun pointed at his head.

"And I have every right not to tell you. It's a free country. Maybe I just decided it was time for me to leave. Why did you follow me?" She was really suspicious of him now. Did he intend to take her back to the wagon train?

"Put down the gun. You're making me nervous. You're tired and jumpy," Jack said with authority.

"First, tell me why you followed me," Kat said with determination.

"Why don't you tell me why you left?" Jack said with as much determination.

"I believe I'm the one with the upper hand here. Or should I say the gun?" Kat said. She wasn't about to show her hand until she had a better understanding of the situation.

The argument ended as they both heard the sound of thundering hooves approaching. It was Laura, and she was approaching fast. Something was definitely wrong.

"The posse's coming. We've got to leave, fast."

Kat thought quickly. "Jack, you and Laura stay here. I've got to leave, and don't follow me this time. It's me they're after." She thought that was a foolproof plan and headed for the door.

Jack grabbed her arm as she rushed past. "Katherine," he said softly.

She looked at him in shock. "You know!" It was more than she could comprehend. How did he know? Was he here to turn her in for the reward money?

"Katherine," he said again in a low, soft voice. "They're after me, too."

It only took a moment before it sunk in. "You killed the drifters?" Katherine asked in astonishment. Jack wasn't a killer. She looked into his eyes and she knew. "They killed Sarah, didn't they?"

Jack nodded. In an instant, the dam of secrets broke and the truths had come pouring out. Jack knew about her and didn't think she was a maniac. Jack had confessed his crime and she understood. They both turned and looked at Laura to see her reaction.

"Well, we are in quite a pickle. We don't have time to run, and Dickerson told the posse he thought Jack was their man. One of the men knows what you look like and said he could identify you if he saw you, Jack. He saw you riding out of town with the drifters that night..." Laura said, and her voice drifted off. She seemed a bit uncomfortable speaking about it.

"How do you know Dickerson told them?" Jack asked. He still wasn't completely putting the puzzle pieces together.

"The posse rode into camp shortly after everyone got up. They thought for sure you'd be back from your night watch and that they could catch you off guard. They were hollering at Dickerson, saying things like, "Where is he, Dickerson? You promised he'd be here.""

Laura continued with her incredible story, "Dickerson, that weasel, was saying, 'He was here last night. He couldn't have gotten far. I'm still entitled to that reward money when you catch him!' The posse then began to look for you, Kat. They tore every wagon apart and dragged every female in front of

Trevor and Clay to see if she was their renegade sister. In the ruckus, I slipped out of camp and stood just in the shadow of the woods, listening to it all. Then, in the confusion, Mrs. Shafer asked, "Where's Laura?" That made the men of the posse stop in their tracks. They all had the same thought, I could tell." Laura paused for a moment. "They thought Katherine Yelta was posing as a women named Laura who had magically disappeared from the wagon train at the same time their other suspect had…"

"I thought that would be a great time to leave and look for you two. I rode fast but my horse quickly tired and developed a limp. The posse gained on me, and now they're right behind me."

"Let me get this straight," Jack said. "They are looking for a man fitting my description and a nineteen-year-old woman they have a picture of…and we have no chance to out run them?"

Laura threw Jack a desperate look. The situation did seem hopeless.

"Jack!" Kat said with new clarity. "They aren't going to find what they're looking for when they open this door. I've got an idea…"

They worked fast and with precision. Less than twenty minutes went by before the posse was pulling up to the series of cabins. The next few minutes seemed like an eternity. The posse proceeded with caution now. They split up, and by twos the six men entered the cabins simultaneously.

The leader and his cousin entered the first cabin and proceeded to tear it apart, finding nothing.

Clay and Trevor split up to enter the second and third cabins, each going with another man in the party.

Clay wanted to find her. He couldn't wait to see her surprised face when she realized he had her. She thought she was something special, better than him and his brothers, just because she wasn't their blood. He'd finally show her who was better.

Trevor wanted to find her. It was just a game of odds. There were three cabins, and they had to be hiding out in one of them. If Clay found her first, Trevor could picture her going for her gun. Clay would try to shoot her. He'd probably miss, and she'd kill him. Then she'd be wanted for two murders. Trevor's partner was the man who could identify the drifters' killer by sight. Trevor had chosen him to partner with on purpose. He wanted to know if this crazed killer was holding Kat hostage. What Kat did might have been wrong, but he wasn't going to let some crazy killer get her.

Clay busted through his door at the same time Trevor busted through his.

Kat looked up at her stepbrother. The three of them sat huddled in the corner. Kat was in the middle with her arms protectively around Laura and Jack, who sat on either side of her.

The two intruders had their guns drawn and pointed at the three huddled on the floor. In an instant, the plan came together in his mind. "Is that our man?" Trevor asked his partner as he pointed to the 'boy' in the middle of the two women.

"No, that's not him. Either of those two women your sister?" His partner inquired.

"No," Trevor replied truthfully.

"Sorry to bother you folks. I'm sure we scared the dickens out of you. Have you seen anyone else around these parts?" Trevor asked the three, his eyes on the 'boy' in the middle the entire time.

Laura was the one who stood slowly. "Yes, we crossed a man and a woman heading back east about a day ago."

"What did they look like?" the other man asked.

Laura continued, "The man was in his mid-twenties. He was tall, with black hair and blue eyes. The woman looked to be about twenty. She was real pretty with long black hair and green eyes. We were scared of them, but they seemed to be in a really big hurry and just asked us for a canteen of water. We gave it to them."

"About a day ago you say?" the man with Trevor said with disappointment. "Trevor, we'd better hightail it back. They've got a good head start on us."

"You're right. Daylight's burning," Trevor said. His eyes went from the pretty woman who spoke to the boy in the middle with a protective arm around the big homely woman.

"Our apologies again, folks. Come on, Trevor," the other man said as he exited the cabin.

Kat had kept her head down to avoid eye contact with Trevor. She was almost home free. Obviously, he hadn't recognized her, but he still hadn't left the cabin. That's when it happened. As if drawn by a force she couldn't control, Kat looked up and her eyes met Trevor's. One more step and he would have been out the cabin door. Terror gripped her as she saw recognition in Trevor's face. Then something happened she would never forget. Trevor winked at her, turned, and was gone. Only Kat had seen the small gesture. It had been so quick and meant only for her.

After they heard the posse gathering outside and mounting their horses, the three went to the dirty window and peered out at them.

Trevor and his partner told the others what they had found. The others told how they had also had no luck in their cabins. They mounted their horses and headed east. Kat, Jack, and Laura watched in motionless silence for several minutes after they left.

Laura finally broke the silence. "I can't believe that worked!" Laura exclaimed, hugging Kat. They turned, looked at Jack, and broke out in excited, uncontrollable laughter.

"Ha, ha. Alright, you two got me in to this get up, now get me out," Jack said, his expression indicating that he was not as amused.

"No," Kat said, trying to be serious. "You better stay like that in case the posse comes back." Kat and Laura broke in to fits of laughter again.

Jack looked at Kat and smiled. He never would have imagined anyone could talk him into wearing a dress. Then again there was really no time to protest. Kat had come up with the plan and put everyone to work. The two followed her instructions without question. First, Jack had to shave. Kat pulled the one dress, petticoat, and pair of stockings she had brought with her from her saddlebag. The dress was wrinkled, but that didn't matter. It was quite a challenge fitting Jack into it. After he put on the stockings and petticoat, Kat and Laura attempted to pull the dress up Jack's arms. Kat pulled out her knife and popped a few stitches so it would go all they way up to his shoulders. It was far from fastening in the back, so Laura and Kat took a piece of rawhide string and strung it through a hook and eye on the back of the dress. There was about a seven-inch gap, so Jack would have to keep his back to the wall. This gave the girls plenty of room to create some big breasts for him. They figured if Jack's breast were big enough, they would keep the men's eyes off Jack's face. The final touch was Laura's bonnet. They fastened it on Jack's head and tied it under his chin. The three of them hurried to huddle together in the corner. Just seconds before the door opened, Kat leaned over to Jack and whispered, *"You look pretty enough to kiss."*

Finally, Laura was able to speak. "Well," she said, quite out of breath from laughing so hard. "If you'll excuse me, I need to make a little trip outside after all that. Kat, I think we've tortured Jack long enough. Help him get out of that thing. I'll be back in a little bit in case you need help."

Laura left. Kat stood and looked at Jack, who was removing his bonnet. So much had happened in the last hour. She had discovered that he knew who she was. How long had he known? And what must he think of her? She had learned he was the brutal killer and it didn't bother her in the least. Finally, they had confronted and 'defeated' the posse that had been tailing them for weeks. It was all quite a relief, and she suddenly felt quite awkward.

Jack turned his back to her and looked at her over his shoulder. "Could you help me out of my dress. I feel as if I could faint!" It was the best impersonation he could muster of a southern belle. Kat stepped forward and began to untie the rawhide. The knot was impossible to work. The dress had been so tight. Jack enjoyed the feeling of Kat's fingers brushing his skin as she fought to untie it. Finally, she pulled her knife, slipped it between his back and the string, and cut it in half. Jack smiled. She was quite the little problem-solver. Jack turned to face her as she pulled the dress down his arms.

Jack watched her. Slowly, he reached up and removed her hat, tossing it to the floor. Jack then put his hand on her cheek and ran his fingers gently up through her hair. "You did good," he whispered.

If he'd thought about it he wouldn't have done it, but he didn't allow himself to think. Jack brought his hand under her chin and tilted her head up. He bent down and put his lips on hers. It was a long-awaited kiss for them both.

Jack took his time. Slowly, he pulled his head back and looked for her reaction. Her eyes stayed closed for a moment. She opened them leisurely. Jack was pleased with the reaction. "Now, are you going to finish helping me out of this dress?" he whispered.

"Yes, of course," was her hoarse reply. At that point, she wanted nothing more than to kiss him again. So much had happened and was still happening. Jack obviously didn't think she was odd. He now thought of her as a woman. Now Kat was really confused. She was unsure how to behave. Everything had changed in the course of an hour.

Kat pulled the dress down to his ankles and Jack stepped out of it. Kat looked up at him as she squatted on the floor. She couldn't help herself and burst into laughter again at the sight of Jack standing there, bare-chested with women's stockings running up his legs and a pair of petticoats on his bottom half.

He stood for a moment looking indignant, his hands on his waist. That made Kat laugh even harder. She sat down on the ground, unable to keep her balance as her body shook with laughter. Suddenly she found herself being tackled. Kat was lying flat on the ground, still laughing, while Jack lay on top of her, pinning her arms over her head.

"How am I going to get you to stop laughing at me?" Jack asked. His face was just inches from hers. They both knew the answer and welcomed it. Kat melted as Jack's lips touched hers, gently at first. She responded eagerly and his kisses deepened. She didn't want him to stop. She was feeling things she had never felt before. She loved the feeling of his body touching the length of hers. This kissing thing had her reeling. She wanted more and more. Jack's tongue traced the edge of her lips and she thought she'd go mad.

Clunk. They heard the sound of a water bucket plunk down on the porch. Laura was back and she was just outside the door. They both snapped out of it and jumped up in a flash. They waited, but Laura didn't come in. Kat dashed to the window and peered out. Laura was walking back to the horse barn with the other pail of water for the horses. Kat felt Jack standing closely behind her as she looked out the window. Jack began nibbling on her neck. Kat closed her eyes and enjoyed it for a moment before she turned around. "Jack," she whispered. "We have to stop. Laura will be coming back at any moment!"

Jack knew she was right. Besides, he needed a moment to cool down. "Okay. You're right. Um, I think it's probably best if you don't help me undress any further," he said with a smug smile that Kat enjoyed. "Why don't you go out on the porch and I'll take it from here."

Kat nodded and quickly exited the cabin.

CHAPTER 14

Laura put the pail of water in front of Ginger and let her have a good long drink before letting Bullet have his turn. She thought back to what had taken place earlier. She had been scared but also very angry. How could a brother hunt his sister down like he had? Imagine her own brother riding with a posse after someone as wonderful as Kat just to collect reward money. If she ever got her hands on him, she'd choke him. Laura realized she was gritting her teeth as she fantasized about her hands around that Trevor's neck.

After letting all the horses have a drink, Laura picked up the pail and headed toward the cabin door. She saw Kat on the front step mindlessly drawing pictures in the dirt. She seemed distracted. Laura wondered if she was feeling bad about facing her brother who had turned against her.

"Kat."

Kat snapped her head up.

"We did it. Can you believe it?" Laura was shaking her head and smiling in disbelief. She plopped down beside Kat and put an arm around her shoulder. "Are you feeling okay? You look a little rung out," Laura said with concern for her friend.

"I'm fine," Kat said with a smile. "It's been a big day. I can't believe all that's happened; I'm still trying to take it in."

Laura could tell that her friend was just fine. In fact, she seemed unbelievably happy, almost in a dreamlike state. It must have been quite a relief to feel like a free woman after being wanted for so long. "Is Jack still inside?" Laura asked.

"Yes, he's finishing up changing." Kat turned to her and looked her in the eye. "Laura, I was so proud of you today. You saved our lives, and the way you talked to that man and Trevor—even I was convinced. How did you ever come up with that story? It was amazing."

"Yeah, I guess it was," Laura said with confidence.

Laura and Kat heard the cabin door open. Jack walked out and sat down beside the two women. "Well ladies, now what?"

It was a good question.

That evening the three celebrated their freedom with a delicious meal of fried fish and raspberries. Kat thought it was one of the best meals she had ever tasted. They built a campfire outside and sat around it. After several weeks on the open prairie, none of them wanted to be cooped up in the cabin.

They all talked lightly about the future without making any definite decisions. Since Kat was now a free woman, she needed a new plan. She thought Laura would be open to anything. Kat couldn't help but wonder about Jack. Did he still plan on heading south to Mexico now that he was in the clear?

Until they were convinced the posse had headed back east, none of them would commit to a plan. For now, the feeling of freedom was enough. It was just the three of them, no longer in disguise and no longer obligated to the people of the wagon train. Jack assured Kat and Laura that the people of train would be fine on their own. They were in safer territory and had enough food to take them far beyond their destination.

Kat gorged herself on the fish while Jack enjoyed watching her. Although she still wore pants and a man's shirt, she looked different. Her shoulder-length hair now hung loose. She no longer wore the cloth around her breasts and she had dropped her male mannerisms. No longer did she walk with the stagger. Rather, she walked with a giddy freedom and a grace he had never really noticed before. She sounded different to him. Her voice had become softer and she laughed more. Laura laughed more, too. Jack knew the two women would always be good friends.

Jack stole glances at Katherine across the fire. He couldn't wait to get her alone. Not to kiss her, but to get to know her. He knew what kind of a person she was, but he didn't know about her past, her present feelings, or her plans for the future. He wanted to know what she had been like as a little girl. What she had done back on the farm. How she was dealing with the fact that she'd killed someone. For some people, once they've murdered, they are never quite the same again. What was she afraid of? What did she look like in a dress? For some reason, that was hard for him to picture. She had a head start on him. Jack had already shared many things with her. She even knew what *he* looked like in a dress. How could he get her alone without it looking suspicious to Laura? It would have to be after Laura went to bed.

Suddenly, Laura made a move. It was as if she had read his thoughts. She stood and announced, "Well, saving your lives has really taken it out of me. I'm going inside and straight to bed. Wake me up if you'd like me to take a watch tonight. Let me get a few hours of sleep first, though, or I'll be no good on watch." And with that, Laura disappeared through the cabin door.

Jack was the first to speak. "So do you feel different as a free woman?"

"I really do. Now I just need to come up with a plan for the rest of my life."

"What do you have in mind?" Jack asked. "You must have been developing some kind of plan all that time on the trail."

"My plan was to leave the train tonight and get as far away as I could. I had planned on meeting up with Laura at South Passe in about a month. We were planning to travel on, winter at Salt Lake City, and decide whether to stay there or travel on to California in the spring. I figured I would make my transformation back into a woman sometime before we hit Salt Lake City. Laura and I were going to get a little place and jobs for the winter."

Jack noticed she wasn't looking him in the eye. The whole time she just poked at the fire with a big stick. Maybe she felt awkward because of what had happened earlier in the day. "Is that still the plan?"

"Probably. Since I've 'turned back into a woman,' my options have suddenly become limited. It's not like I can buy a ranch and expect to hire a crew to run it. Also, Laura's been so great. I want to stick with her and help her any way I can. She seems very self-sufficient, but we have to remember she's still very young. This is rough country with rough people, and I want to watch out for her. When I told her about my plan I'd never seen someone look happier. So, when did you figure out I wasn't 'John'?"

Jack always enjoyed how things just came out of her mouth. No beating around the bush with her. "Laura told me."

"No she didn't." she wasn't buying that.

Jack thought he'd have a little fun with her.

"Kat. Can I call you, Kat? Anyway, the entire train knew. They were just going along with it to amuse you."

"That's not true either. Fine, I've got all night. Just keep trying to fool me until you get tired of it and want to tell me the truth," Kat replied.

"Okay, here's the truth," Jack said as he slid around the campfire next to her. "One day you were bending over the campfire and I looked at that cute little bottom of yours and said to myself, 'Now, that is not a man butt!' So I waited until you fell fast asleep and I looked down your shirt and said, 'Men don't have those.'"

Kat punched him in the arm and laughed.

"Hmm," Jack said in a softer voice as he picked up her hand and gently caressed it. "You don't believe that one either. Maybe it's because I looked at these hands and knew no man could possess something so beautiful and graceful."

Jack didn't stop. "Or maybe it was your beautiful eyes. Every chance I got I looked deep into your eyes, and then I knew." That was actually partly true.

"I don't believe you," she softly said.

"Then it was this graceful, delicate neck," he said as he stroked the soft skin of her neck, "and these perfect little ears."

She wasn't buying it but she was no longer protesting with such force. Jack knew his little game was having an effect on her.

"Then it must have been these lips. I've found them irresistible for quite some…" Jack's lips were on hers.

He could feel her giving in to the passion of the moment. Knowing she enjoyed it only heightened his passion. Suddenly, Kat pulled back. "I don't want Laura to know. She'll be worried that I'm leaving her out in the cold. She's done so much for me, and she's so young."

"Laura went to bed," Jack replied as he continued to kiss her.

"Jack, I've got to check." Jack stayed by the fire and watched Kat run up to the porch and peer in the window.

Kat returned to the campfire. "She is asleep, but Jack, I've got a problem. I lose control when you kiss me. I don't know what it is. But I think it's important that we keep our heads. We could still be in danger, and I don't want Laura to feel strange around us."

Jack burst out laughing. He loved her honesty and loved that she was so open about her feelings. He knew women often pretended to not like intimacy. He knew with her it would be much different—and he had every intention of finding out how different. Someday. Actually, she was right. He had a hard time keeping his head in her presence, and they did need to stay alert. "You're right, Kat. I've got the same problem. A posse could have walked right up to us and we wouldn't have noticed. I also don't want Laura to worry or feel uncomfortable," Jack agreed.

"So, really now, how did you find out about me?" Kat asked.

Jack told her. He told her the whole story, except for the part about seeing her naked. He didn't know if she was ready for that, and he didn't know if he could tell the story and control himself.

"Why didn't you confront me?" Kat asked.

"And what would you have done? You would have run. I was trying to get you to tell me, but you just wouldn't break," Jack said.

"That's probably true." Now that Kat thought about it, she could remember several times when Jack had tried to get her to say something. It was actually humorous now as she thought about it.

Kat and Jack talked into the night. It was a wonderful night for both of them. They told happy stories of their childhood. Kat talked about how she had spent her days roaming through the woods, teaching herself to hunt, fish, throw a knife, and ride horses.

Jack expressed concern that she'd had a lonely childhood. She reassured him it was not. "I had so many pets. They kept me company." Kat told him about Flex.

Jack told her about life with his parents and younger brother and sister. He talked about the mischief he got in to at school and how he had dreamed of building the best ranch in the west, from the land to the livestock, the corrals to the house, even the landscaping and garden.

Kat thought it was a wonderful dream. The garden back on the farm had always been her project. She loved planting it, tending it, and picking fresh vegetables. Now she could only imagine it run over with weeds.

It was well after midnight when Jack looked over and noticed Kat had fallen asleep right in the middle of one of his stories. He picked her up gently and took her inside to her bed. Jack glanced over at Laura to make sure she was fast asleep. Jack bent down and kissed Kat on the cheek. He then paused a few moments to watch her sleep.

The sun rose just enough to peek through the dirty window of the cabin. Laura's eyes popped open the minute the light touched them. She looked about to see where she was. The lump on the other side of the room that was Kat brought all the memories of the past couple days rushing back. Laura sat up and stretched her young limber body, rubbed the sleep from her eyes, and broke into a huge smile. She couldn't believe her good fortune. She had made it to Wyoming. She was traveling with two of the best people she'd ever met in her life, and she had hope.

Quietly, Laura walked out of the cabin so as not to wake Kat. As she breathed in the fresh morning air, Laura thought about how much her life had changed during this journey, and about how much she had changed. No longer was she a scared little girl. The future was something she looked forward to with excitement rather than dreaded. It amazed her how people could make such a difference in your life. Kat had given her the confidence and skills she needed to bring out what had been buried deep down—confidence and self-reliance. Laura knew Kat didn't see it that way, didn't realize the gift she'd given her. Laura did see it as a great gift. That's why she hadn't hesitated to risk her life to save Kat and Jack and why she had summoned all her courage to talk to that no-good stepbrother of Kat's when he entered the cabin. It was the greatest role she'd played to date in her life, and it worked! Believe in yourself and it will happen. That's what Kat always told her. Yesterday was proof of that. She had helped set Kat and Jack free. The posse was fooled, and now those evil bastards were long gone. Now they were free. Free to forget the past and start a new and wonderful life.

In her joy, Laura literally skipped down the steps of the cabin to the water pail—her every move witnessed by the man looking through a telescope high on the hill, deep in the forest.

CHAPTER 15

Jack had just finished feeding and watering the horses. He met Laura at the watering pail. "Good morning, Laura," Jack said as he approached. "Did you have a good night's sleep?"

"I did!" Laura replied cheerfully. "I haven't slept that soundly in a long time."

"Where's Kat? She's not still sleeping, is she?"

Laura nodded. "Yes, and I think we should let her sleep. She's been through a lot in the past few days. Now she can finally relax and get some rest."

"As long as she's up before noon. I want to hit the trail by then. Makes me nervous to sit in one place too long."

"Jack, what is your plan?" Laura looked worried.

"My plan is to travel with you two lovely young ladies until we reach our destination. I need the two of you for protection, obviously," Jack teased.

Laura was relieved. She'd suspected Jack would stick around, but you never knew with men.

"So tell me," she said, truly curious, "what is the final destination?"

"I think we'll know when we get there, and not a minute sooner," was Jack's honest reply.

Laura smiled and nodded.

Kat slept so deeply that the morning sun did not wake her as it normally would have. Instead, she was far away in dreamland. Happy dreams of freedom. In her dream, she watched Jack and Laura happily talking and drinking from the water pail, and that made her happy. But then the dream changed. Kat suddenly felt an overwhelming sense of danger. Something was out there, and she had to warn Jack and Laura. She tried to holler at them, but nothing would come out of her mouth. She tried to run to them, but her legs wouldn't move. Kat's eyes flew open. Her heart was pounding and she sat straight up. It took her a few moments before she realized it was just a dream. A terrible dream that left her with a bad feeling.

Kat got up and headed out the door. It was well past sunup. She never slept that late.

Laura looked at her and smiled. "Good morning, sleepyhead. You must finally feel relaxed if you're able to sleep this late!"

"Yeah," Kat replied, not really feeling relaxed. "Where's Jack?"

"He's getting things ready so we can move out. He said he wants to hit the trail by noon today."

"I think that's a good idea. I'm ready to get out of here."

The group packed up so fast, they were on the trail less than an hour later. They didn't even stop to eat until mid-afternoon. It was hot, and the horses needed a rest. Jack grabbed some jerky and raisins and scouted ahead.

"Why are we pushing so hard?" Laura asked. "I feel like we're running again!"

"We always push hard the first day and fall into a more comfortable pace after that," Kat replied. She wasn't lying but it was only half the truth.

"Where did Jack go? All he said was sit tight and he'd be back within the hour."

"I'm sure he just wants to see what's out there. He's the cautious type. Always on the lookout for danger." Kat smiled. She could tell Laura was suspicious and she didn't want to worry her.

Jack came back with canteens of fresh water. "Did you see anything out there?" Kat asked him under her breath.

"Things look good. Just us and the wild animals," Jack said cheerfully. "Are you two ready to ride out? We'll go until we find the best camping spot Wyoming has to offer."

The three headed out once again. Kat felt more relaxed. They enjoyed the scenery as they rode. The land was really beautiful and the air was so fresh. Wyoming looked different than the wide-open prairies. It seemed more rugged and wild. Kat was beginning to feel revived after her days of little sleep. She hoped they would camp near a stream where they could catch some fish and take a bath!

The sun was heading down when they found the perfect camping spot Jack had talked about. To Kat's delight it was near a stream with a perfect little waterfall. There was a nice rock face behind them, and they would be able to build a fire there safely. Jack took the fishing net and handed it to Kat. "Would you like to do the honors while I have a look around and gather some firewood? I'll be back just after dark."

"I'd love to," Kat happily replied. "Come on, Laura. We're going to catch some fish for supper."

Jack rode off and Kat and Laura tended the horses, set up camp, and headed off to do some fishing. They waded into the knee-deep water and enjoyed the feeling of it as it rushed past them. The water was clear and full of trout. It took Kat and Laura's combined strength to hold the net in the rushing water. It didn't take long to catch plenty of fish for the feast Kat was craving. Kat and Laura cleaned their catch and started preparing the evening meal.

Jack came back as promised, just as it was getting dark. "Mmm, that smells good enough to eat!" And eat they did. It was delicious, and such a treat after their trail meal of jerky and raisins earlier in the day. Their camping spot was perfect. It was completely secluded and very beautiful. They felt as if they were the only people on earth. Kat sat with her knees pulled up to her chest. "This land is really beautiful," she commented, as much to herself as to the others.

"It is," Jack replied, "but it can also be dangerous. This part of the country hasn't seen many white people. We must be on the alert for Indians and wild animals. There are big predators out here, and we're going to encounter more wooded areas where dangers lie. We have to stay alert at all times."

Kat turned to him and smiled. "Well, aren't you depressing?"

"I mean it, Kat. Just promise me you two will stay alert. We are out in no man's land and we always have to be cautious."

"What kind of predators, Jack?" Laura asked with concern.

"Mountain lions, wolves, and bears, to name a few. I'm not trying to scare you; I just want you to know the reality of this land. From time to time I may have to leave for a while. That's when I want the two of you to be extra cautious. Keep your guns next to you at all times. If you encounter a bear or a big cat, do not turn and run. Freeze and see if it will go away. If it doesn't, then back away slowly. However, if you see an Indian, turn, run, and yell for help."

"But Jack, what if we see an Indian and a wild animal at the same time? Then what do we do?" Kat mocked.

Jack just rolled his eyes.

Kat turned her gaze back to the stream and gasped. "Look," she whispered. Two deer stood in the middle of the stream in front of them. It was a magical sight.

Kat could feel this land was different, and she did take what Jack said seriously. She respected his opinion and trusted his instinct. If he thought they should exercise extra caution, she would do so. The deer stood looking at them with their big brown eyes for a moment. They seemed curious but not frightened. In perfect synchronicity they turned and bound off into the woods.

"Jack, Laura and I are going to head downstream and find a good spot to take a bath," Kat said as she stood up to gather her soap and clean clothes.

"No, you're not. It's too dangerous. You can bathe right here. I'll turn my back."

"Fine by me. Are you alright with that, Laura?" Kat asked.

"Sure. Jack's an honest man," Laura teased.

Kat and Laura waded into the water. Jack turned his back to the girls.

Kat couldn't help but tease. "This water sure is refreshing. My, but a bath feels great after a long day on the trail."

"I think this is the best bath I've ever had," Laura joined in.

The girls laughed as they undressed under the water and took their time splashing around. It did feel good to wash their bodies and their hair. Kat enjoyed how easy it was to wash and dry her hair now that it was shoulder length. Laura had beautiful, thick brown hair, but it took so long to wash and dry. The water was about chest deep. Kat and Laura were having a good time with the situation. Besides teasing Jack about how great the water felt, Laura would jump out from time to time, exposing her naked breasts to Jack's back. Kat thought it was hilarious.

Jack wondered what the two were up to; they were really laughing it up, and at his expense, he was certain. It was pure torture for him, knowing Kat was completely naked just a few feet away. He tried to reason through the situation, telling himself she was always naked under her clothes anyway. This shouldn't be any different. It didn't work.

From a great distance, the man with the telescope watched. He watched Jack with his back to the girls as they bathed. "Well, isn't he honorable," the man mocked under his breath. He watched the brown-haired girl jump out of the water behind the man's back. He found it quite entertaining. She had spunk.

It was time he made his move. It wasn't right for "Mr. Honorable" to travel alone with two women. The man behind the glass didn't trust him. Yes, he should make a move soon, but the timing had to be right. He would pick the right time, and then he would move in…

Jack stood first watch that night. He knew what Kat meant about this country being different. It felt different to him, too. Never had he been in a land that felt so large and wild. It was as if he'd struck gold by coming here. This was where he wanted to be. This was going to be home. Jack had heard many things about the West and about the Wyoming and Montana areas. A person had to use his common sense to separate the fact from the fiction. He'd heard tales of great animals. Beavers taller than he was. Bison that walked upright on two feet, fierce bears that stood fifteen feet tall and could outrun a horse, and goats with great horns that could walk straight up the side of a mountain. Right! He'd have to see that to believe it.

Right now, Jack's concern was winter. It was late August. He knew they were farther north than where they had started in Missouri. He just wasn't sure how much sooner winter would hit. Jack figured they'd travel until he found the perfect spot. He wanted to be near timber yet with a good stretch of open ground. Access to water was critical. When he saw it, he'd know.

Jack was building the cabin in his mind. It would start out small but be very strong. He would reinforce the walls and insulate them with brush and mud for extra warmth. He'd build a stable for the horses. He really wished he had a couple hired hands, a team of oxen or even mules. Their horses weren't built for physical labor, and the ride across the prairie had been hard on them. The prairie grass was difficult for them to chew and seemed to lack the nourishment they needed. Thankfully, the grass in this part of the country seemed to suit the horses much better.

Jack knew winter would be tough on all of them. They were strangers to the land, but they were also smart and wilderness-wise. He was inventive and had a great ability to solve problems, although he hadn't had a chance to exercise this skill on the trail, he also was quite a craftsman. He had built several additions on the farm back in Missouri and come up with ideas to make life a little easier. When he was just ten, he built a washbasin and table that stood waist high so his mother wouldn't have to bend over to do the laundry. She was so proud of him, telling him what a big difference it made. In their barn he built shoots from the haymow and let gravity do the job to deliver the nightly hay to the animals. Chore time went much quicker.

Jack was thankful he had Kat along with him. He felt so for the obvious reasons but also because she was a better hunter and tracker than any man he'd ever met. She was feminine yet very strong. She also seemed to have incredible luck. Jack's father once told him to hang around lucky people, because their luck would rub off on him. Jack thought his father was crazy at the time but now he believed it. And Laura, if she chose to stay with them, would be quite an asset. She knew medicine and had become an accomplished outdoorswoman thanks to Kat. Jack was concerned for Laura. He wondered if she'd get bored living out in the middle of nowhere with just the two of them. Laura was close to marrying age. She might have aspirations of finding a husband and settling down in a more civilized area to raise a family. It wasn't really fair for him and Kat to drag her along. Then again, he'd never asked her what she wanted. They'd been too busy running up to this point. Maybe now their running days would be over and they could get on with the rest of their lives. If only Laura had come with a big strong husband. Now that would really come in handy when it came time to build the ranch!

Jack hated to wake Kat to take second watch. He knew he must, though, or he'd be too tired to be any good to them. She looked so peaceful. He shook her shoulder and she popped up in an instant.

"What's wrong?" Kat blurted out.

"Nothing," Jack whispered, and he smiled. "I'm just waking you for your watch. Come with me. I want to show you something."

"We can't leave Laura; it's not safe," Kat replied, glancing over at Laura's sleeping form.

"We are just going to up to the top of that rock. The moon is full tonight and the view is incredible."

That was good enough for Kat. She pulled on her boots and followed Jack to the top of the rock. The climb was challenging, but finally they made it.

Kat gazed out at the sight before her. For what seemed like miles and miles across the flat land, buffalo were grazing. "Oh, Jack, I have never seen such a large herd of animals in all my life! Every buffalo alive must be in this valley!" Kat whispered, as if they would run if they heard her. "How many are there, do you think?"

"I bet there are five or ten thousand of them." Jack watched her as she stood in awe at the sight. It was incredible. Jack had never seen anything like it—the buffalo and Kat. In the moonlight she was even more beautiful than usual. He gazed at her perfect face, a face that sometimes looked like that of child and sometimes like that of woman. He devoured her light green eyes that held so much wisdom and adventure, and finally his eyes rested on her beautiful red lips.

They sat down on the rock to soak in the sight. "Kat," Jack began softly, "you are so beautiful."

She turned to look at him. "Well, when it's me or the buffalo, I bet I do look good."

"No, really you are," Jack said as he pushed a strand of hair from her face. "I'm going to have you ride behind me from now on, because you're becoming quite a distraction. Right now I should be sleeping, but I can't seem to take myself away from you."

"But if I rode behind you, then I'd be distracted."

It was the first time she had talked about her attraction to Jack. It sent him to the moon to hear it. "Well," Jack said, taking her hand, "we've got quite a problem. What are we going to do about it?" He began caressing her hand, sending waves of sensation through Kat's body.

"I don't know," Kat replied, unable to think of anything else to say.

Jack lifted her hand and kissed it, all the while looking into her eyes. Kat thought he was beautiful, too, although she would have felt strange saying so. He had intense blue eyes. His face was strong, tan, and handsome. Kat had never seen a more handsome man and doubted she ever would. Looking at his shoulders, her mind drifted back to the day she saw him bathing. She remembered how he had looked coming out of the water, her mind recalling ever detail.

Jack pulled her to him. Although he intended to kiss her tenderly, his hunger for her overwhelmed him, and his kiss became ravenous. He had been able to suppress it all day, but the minute he got close to her his passion came to the surface. Jack's tongue traced the outline of her lips and Kat responded with a low moan. He had to get closer. As if they'd done this a thousand times, Kat threw her arms around his neck while he grabbed her thigh and pulled her astraddle across his lap. She came to him willingly. Only their clothes kept them apart, and they were barely doing that. Jack ran his hands down the length of her back to her buttocks. He stopped there to enjoy her firm roundness before moving on slowly to caress the backs of her thighs. His hands were big and strong and her thighs so small. He never realized how feminine and petite she was.

His touch sent Kat reeling. She wanted more but didn't really know what that was. Although she'd never done this before, her instincts served her well. She pressed her firm young body into Jack's and rubbed against his manly part. To her surprise, she felt his hardness against her. So that's how it worked.

He grabbed her buttocks and pulled her tightly to him, all the while kissing her with the hunger of a starving man. Jack knew he was losing control. He was trying to be rational. He couldn't make love to her yet. They had too much hard work ahead of them. If she were to get pregnant, her life and the baby's life would be in great danger. He couldn't do that to her. Now was not the time. Just a few more kisses and then he'd stop. Jack didn't know who was in control of his hands. His mind was saying one thing and his body was acting otherwise. She was so irresistible. His hands were discovering her body as his lips and tongue explored her mouth. He felt the sides of her waist and his hands nearly spanned the smallness of it. How he loved her little waist. He rubbed her flat, strong stomach through her shirt. He needed to be closer. Jack pulled her shirt out of her pants.

Kat felt the heat of his hands touching her bare skin. Slowly, his hands traveled down until they brushed her hair down there. Kat instinctively pulled her stomach in to give him better access as she continued to kiss him. To Kat's disappointment, Jack stopped there. But then his hands began to move even more slowly upward, not missing an inch of her skin. He stopped just below her breasts. Kat ached for him to touch her there. He didn't disappoint her. Slowly, his hands cupped her breasts and held them as if they were gold. Kat gasped in between kisses. How he could be so gentle, Kat didn't know, but she sure enjoyed it. He softly and sweetly caressed the roundness of her breasts. When his thumbs dragged across her nipples, she threw her head back and gasped.

Jack's rational mind ceased to function at that point. He pulled open her shirt and exposed her beautiful naked breasts in the moonlight. Jack pulled her up toward him. He had to taste her. His lips encircled one breast while his hand caressed the other. Kat was completely gone now. She didn't care what happened next, as long as he kept touching her.

As if pricked with a pin, Jack abruptly stopped. It was one of the hardest things he'd ever done in his life.

"Kat, honey, I want to make love to you so badly it's killing me. But we can't."

Kat was disappointed. A million possible reasons went through her mind. Was he married? Did he not intend to be with her for a long time? Had she done something he didn't like?

"Why not?" she asked in a small voice, like a child's.

"Because," he said as he slid her off his lap, "we have a hard trail ahead of us. In fact, we don't know what lies ahead. You can't get pregnant right now. It would put you at risk—and our baby."

Kat liked that he said *our*. "You're right," Kat agreed reluctantly. She was disappointed yet impressed that he was so considerate. It meant more to her than if he had made passionate love to her all night.

Jack said, "Um, I'm going back to camp to take a cold dip in the stream, and then I'm going to get a little shut eye."

"Are you hot?" Kat asked naively. "I think the temperature is rather nice tonight."

"Yes, I am," Jack answered as he stood and extended a hand to help her up. They took one last look at the buffalo and headed back to camp. Laura was still sound asleep. Kat grabbed her gun and headed to the rock to take her turn at watch.

Jack headed for the stream.

She wanted more than anything to join him but knew he was right. Who knew what they had ahead of them.

As the sun came up, the little camp packed up their gear and prepared to move out.

That day they traveled over rolling plains, across several streams, and over rocky terrain. Jack was steering them further north and figured they were into Montana Territory by now.

At night they ate their evening meal by the campfire, wondered at the beautiful land, and learned about each other.

One night, Jack asked Laura if she'd thought about her future.

Laura replied, "My future's somewhere up ahead. I feel like we are getting close."

"Laura," Jack replied seriously. "This land is very remote. We haven't seen anyone for days. You won't have much of a social life out here. You two will need to decide if you want to find a place to spend the winter with me here in Montana, or if you would like me to ride south with the two of you toward a warmer climate before winter hits. The decision needs to be made soon. I believe we are safe from the posse now, so we could head south if you want."

"Absolutely not," Laura replied. Obviously she didn't need time to think. "I love this country and I'm planning to live here."

Kat clapped her hands together in delight. "Oh, Laura, I'm so glad. I've been worried about dragging you across this remote land against your will."

"Against my will? This land is beautiful; and after all you've taught me I don't think you could drag me anywhere against my will," Laura teased.

Kat was so thrilled she hopped up and hugged Laura.

"Jack?" Laura turned to him. "What about you? You don't need a couple of women to worry about. Well, especially me. We all know Kat can fend for herself, but I—"

"Laura," Jack cut her off. "The more the better. We need as many hands as possible to get through this. Let's not fool ourselves. We're pretty far north, and I'm sure you've both heard about the harshness of northern winters. And it's not like you're some weak little high-society woman. Laura, you're a real frontiers woman. It's a big relief to me you said 'yes.' If Kat or I get sick we are going to need your expertise. You know things Kat and I don't.

Kat could see Laura beaming with pride. She was so proud of Jack for making Laura feel worthwhile. Although Kat had told her that a thousand times, it meant so much coming from him. Kat did worry about Laura being lonely, though. That's why she felt the need to keep what went on between her and Jack quiet for now.

Each day they traveled deeper into Montana Territory they saw new things: new types of rocks, new vegetation, new trees and animals. They looked the land over thoroughly wherever they went and felt a little guilty about 'passing up' certain locations that might have suited them. They just hadn't found the perfect spot yet. After all, they could always come back. In the meantime, they could enjoy several different camping spots along the way.

The man with the telescope was getting impatient. It was time he made his move. He couldn't let this go on. This man was taking them deeper and deeper into the wilderness. It wasn't right. Those women didn't know what they were in for. He must be telling them they were headed toward gold or that California was just over the horizon. He would put a stop to it, and it would happen tomorrow. He just needed tonight to perfect his plan.

As they ate trout and berries and camped by another beautiful stream, Jack commented to the girls, "This land is so rich in water. It's essential for a good ranching operation."

"So, this is good ranching land, Jack?" Laura asked.

"It most certainly is," Jack replied between bites. Kat liked how his eyes lit up when he talked about his ranch. "There are plains areas with good grass for the animals to eat and plenty of water. Just look at all the wildlife here. This land is perfect for raising animals. We are seeing more and more timber, too. Eventually, we'll be able to build a big house and plenty of stables and corrals. They only thing missing now is the cattle. I haven't yet figured out how to get the cattle here."

"Isn't that kind of important?" Kat asked.

"Sure it is, but I'll figure it out eventually."

Kat and Laura didn't doubt that.

"You know, I'm surprised we haven't seen any Indians," Laura said.

"Oh, they're around. I've seen plenty of them," Jack mentioned nonchalantly.

Both girls looked up in surprise. "You have?"

"Yes, they're keeping an eye on us. They're just curious, not hostile. The only white men through these parts up till now have been Lewis and Clark. They don't see us as a threat and don't intend to harm us."

Kat and Laura were dumbfounded. "Why didn't you tell us?" Kat asked.

"I didn't want you to worry until I was sure. I've seen enough of them now to know. They are just watching us out of curiosity."

"I'm a little nervous knowing we are being watched," Kat said.

"They only watch us from a distance to get a feel for what we are up to. It's not as if they have a telescope like I do," Jack reassured her.

"Well, if they're watching us, I'd like to get a look at one of them. I've never seen an Indian," Kat replied excitedly.

"I'm sure you'll have your chance soon," Jack said.

Laura looked a little pale. Having not seen any Indians, she had convinced herself they weren't any.

That evening, Kat and Laura wanted to take a bath in the stream but were afraid Indians might be watching them.

Jack assured them they were not. "In fact, I'll ride out and circle camp. I'd like to get a look around anyway. If I find any Indians watching you, I'll tell them to behave like gentlemen and close their eyes. Go ahead and bathe. No one's watching except maybe a couple of squirrels."

"I don't know," Laura said reluctantly. "I'll take a bath, but I'm going to make it a quick one."

"Not me," Kat replied. "I don't care who's looking. When I take a bath, I like to take my time."

As promised, Jack rode out to survey the area. The plains seemed to stretch quite a ways, but off in the distance he saw some rocky terrain. It looked crossable.

Jack headed back. He felt he'd been gone a long time. As he neared camp, he pulled out his telescope. Kat was still taking a bath. Laura was out and dressed. She was even rolling out her bedroll and preparing to lie down for the night. Jack couldn't ride in to camp with Kat still swimming around naked. That would be too awkward. He didn't put down the telescope either. He was mesmerized watching Kat swim around in the water. In fact, he longed to be there with her. At that moment, Kat decided her bath was over and rose out of the water. Jack could see her perfectly in the moonlight. Kat's slim, firm body glistened from the water and the light of the moon. God, she was beautiful. Jack could have looked at her forever. She was like art. He knew even after years with her he'd never tire of looking at her beautiful body.

Jack waited until she was dressed and then rode into camp. Kat walked up to help him unsaddle Bullet.

"You're back," Kat said softly. Jack had purposely tried not to be alone with her. Now he was, and he'd have to practice restraint.

"Bullet is such a beautiful horse," Kat continued.

"Yes, he's a great horse. The best I've ever had," Jack replied, trying to make normal conversation.

Kat removed the saddle and set it down. She turned and looked at Jack. There was a scratch on his forehead and it was bleeding a little. Reaching up to touch it, she asked with concern, "What did you do to your head?"

The one touch was all it took. Jack grabbed her and pulled her close to him. "It's just a scratch from a branch. You should know better than to touch me," Jack whispered. He pulled her close and kissed her deeply. She smelled so good. Like fresh air mixed with the slight sent of soap. The image of her standing naked in the moonlight kept floating through his mind as he kissed her. He pulled away before it got to deep.

"Well, if that's all it takes, I would have touched you hours ago," Kat teased.

"Honey, it's not just when you touch me. It's when you look at me or say my name or ride your horse in front of me. Tonight, when you licked your fingers after your meal, I almost dove across the campfire and attacked you. I figured Laura would think I'd gone mad and try to shoot me. It's every move you make, Kat. You drive me crazy."

He actually seemed in pain. She stood up on the tips of her toes and kissed the end of his nose. The tender gesture pleased Jack very much.

"Jack, I don't mean to cause you pain." She was actually concerned.

He stiffened. "Don't worry, I can resist you," Jack said with a little too much confidence.

Kat took it as a challenge. "Oh, you can? Even when I do this?" She nibbled kisses along his neck.

"Yes," Jack lied. "That doesn't bother me in the least."

"How about when I do this?" She reached up and softly kissed his lips. He played it to the hilt, pretending to be unaffected. They were both enjoying the game. She continued kissing him while she reached up to unbutton his shirt. Slowly, she put her hands inside his shirt and began caressing his bare chest.

"Nope…don't feel a thing," he muttered unconvincingly.

She slid her hands down toward his beltline and began tracing his lips with her tongue. That did it. He pulled her to him and began kissing her passionately. She felt victorious. They had both forgotten about Bullet until he headbutted Jack in the arm. It nearly knocked him down. Kat and Jack laughed. "I think Bullet is getting back at me for not letting him near Ginger. I guess I deserved that." Jack gave her a last quick kiss and spanked her on the bottom. "Now, get to bed and quit teasing me."

They got an early start the next morning. Jack told Kat and Laura they had a wide stretch of flatland to cross and would camp somewhere in the rocky terrain on the other side. The going was slow and rough. It was obvious a large buffalo herd had moved through this stretch of land. It was hard to fathom so many had moved through this valley, where now not a one was in sight.

"They sure tore the ground to pieces," Jack muttered. "Don't push the horses. The last thing we need is an injured animal. I don't care if it takes us all day to make it across this stretch."

It did take all day, and it was hot. They traveled the entire way without finding one bit of shade from the intense August sun. The horses were tired and ornery from tripping their way through the day over the rough terrain. Laura, Jack, and Kat felt the same way. They'd had to concentrate while riding that day in order to ensure the horses traveled along the safest and easiest path.

As evening approached, clouds began to build. It started to rain softly as they set up camp. "Sure, now it rains," Jack complained. "If it had rained during the day it would have softened up the ground and made it easier on the horses."

The man following them was thankful for the rain. He had to keep quite a distance behind the three so as not to be spotted. This rain would allow him to pick up the pace and surprise them sometime in the middle of the night. He could just barely see through his telescope before the rain started that they were camping at the mouth of a cave. They likely would sleep inside to escape the rain.

Jack had fashioned a torch and checked out the inside of the cave before moving the women inside for the night. "Looks safe to me, no bears or snakes or cats bigger than you and me in there. We'll keep a low fire burning at the mouth of the cave. It's going to be pitch black in there, especially if this rain keeps up. I don't want anything coming out of the rain to snuggle up with us tonight."

"How's Ginger's leg, Jack? Did you get a chance to look at it?" Kat inquired. Ginger had begun to limp a little at the end of the day.

"I don't think it's serious. There's no swelling as far as I could tell. Just a little strain; we'll have to see how she's doing tomorrow. We may have to wait here for a day or so if she needs some recovery time," Jack told her. He could see the disappointment in her face even in the dark.

"What's the matter?" Jack teased. "Don't you like cave living?"

"No, I really don't. It's dark and creepy in here. I feel like my back's against a wall."

"Well, at least our backs are dry," Laura piped in.

Jack understood what Kat meant about having her back against a wall. They were in foreign territory and didn't know what to expect. Jack didn't feel he knew the behavior of the animals in this part of the country well enough to be certain a little fire at the mouth of the cave would keep them out. It was what his instincts had told him to do, and he always followed his instincts. Those instincts included keeping a couple of loaded weapons at your sides at all times.

Jack took the first watch that dark and rainy night. It was hard to stay awake just staring out into the rain. He had learned keeping his mind active kept him awake. So Jack thought about Kat and the life he planned to build with her. For the hundredth time, he built the cabin and barns in his mind. He wanted to build an elaborate corral or fence system to work the animals and tie the ranch together. He thought up ways to make chores efficient and easier, how he could feed and water the livestock in both good weather and bad. He concocted plans to get cattle up to Montana so he could build the ranching operation he dreamed of, and he thought about having Sam come live with him in a few years. Sam was a good person. Jack knew he'd love it out here, but it was too soon. Sam needed to grow up a bit and become his own man first.

Soon three hours had passed and it was time for Jack to wake Laura for her turn at watch. As Laura took her turn on the rock Jack lay down on the other side of the cave from Kat. He wanted nothing more than to lie down next to her and hold her. That wasn't going to happen tonight, he told himself.

The cave was dark and cool. Kat had no problem sleeping in its calm interior. Jack quickly fell asleep as well. The comfort of the cave and the rain falling softly lulled him into a deep sleep. It had done the same for Laura. Kat and Jack knew Laura needed her *beauty rest,* as they often teased her. She was always the first one to bed and the last one awake in the morning. Several times she would doze off on her horse and surprisingly not fall off. Kat and Jack often pointed at her and giggled as she sat asleep in the saddle in the middle of the day.

"She's still a growing girl," Kat would point out to Jack when this happened. "I was like that a few years ago. I had to drag myself out of bed in the morning. Some days I felt like I could sleep until noon. I think it's something you out-grow."

Laura didn't have to wait to outgrow it, because after that night she would never fall asleep on watch again. Jack heard Bullet squeal out a warning, but it was too late. The fire had gone out, leaving Jack disoriented in the blackness of the cave.

The man's voice was very calm as he spoke. "I've got a gun to her head."

It was obvious that Laura was scared out of her wits. Jack could hear her trying to suck in air as fast as her lungs would work. The man had her by the throat and had a gun to her head. "I won't kill her if you talk to me. All I want to know is who you are, where you're heading with these women, and why."

Jack thought it was the oddest request. He was trying to make sense of it so he could figure out what his next move would be. What was his motivation? Where was he? Where were Laura and Kat? It was so dark.

Jack decided to play his game. "We're heading west. Why do you want to know? Why do you care?"

"You're taking them deeper into the wilderness—what are your intentions?" the man asked. "Are you planning to kill them? Just like you did the drifters? Maybe I'll spare your life if you let them go now."

"You've got it wrong. I'm not holding them hostage. They're free to—"

Suddenly there was a thud and a crash. Laura and the stranger went tumbling to the ground. It was chaos. Jack still couldn't see anything. He jumped on the dark pile of bodies and grabbed the man, dragging him to the mouth of the cave, where there was some light from the moon. Kat rode on top of the man as Jack dragged him out. She was punching and kicking him all the way.

"Jesus, Kat, stop it!" the man cried.

"Trevor!" She pulled the knife out of the scabbard tied to her thigh and held it to Trevor's neck. He didn't move a muscle. "What are you doing here?" she snarled between gritted teeth.

Jack just stood and watched. The man no longer had a gun. It had been knocked free during the scuffle. Kat seemed to have the upper hand at the moment.

"I've come to rescue you from him." Trevor pointed up at Jack, who was standing over the scene. "He's a cold-blooded killer."

"If you hurt one hair on his head, I'll make you suffer until your dying day!" Kat growled.

"But he's a killer, Kat. You're not safe, and neither is the other girl. Now put the knife away."

"He's not a killer, Trevor, and I'm going to keep this knife against your throat until I convince you of it."

That's when Trevor made a dumb move. He grabbed Kat's arm and attempted to wrestle the knife from her. In one fell swoop, Jack jumped on him, flipped him over onto his stomach, and bent his arms awkwardly behind his back. "Kat, grab the rope out of my saddle bag," Jack commanded.

Kat did as he said and in no time Trevor was hog-tied and propped up against the side of the cave. It wasn't until then they noticed Laura. She was gasping. It was as if she couldn't get air into her lungs. Jack ran to her and put his hand over her nose and mouth. Finally, Laura's breathing slowed and she was able to breathe normally again. She broke into tears, a result of her fright from being attacked, the panic of hyperventilating, and the shame of falling asleep on watch. Kat ran over and rubbed her back to try and make her feel better. It wasn't working. Laura was hysterical.

Jack didn't know how to comfort Laura so he got up and went over to the dying fire. Form the remaining burning embers, he fashioned a torch and approached Trevor, who was lying against the wall of the cave, tightly bound.

"Kat!" Jack hollered back to her, all the while keeping his eyes on Trevor. "Is this one of your no-good stepbrothers?"

"Yes, he's one of them," Kat answered.

Kat left Laura's side and stood by Jack. She began interrogating Trevor. "Are you alone?" she asked.

Trevor nodded his head.

She pulled out her knife and held it tightly to his neck. "Are you lying?"

"No, I've been alone for days. The posse headed back toward Missouri. I left them and told them I was heading to California."

"Keep talking," Kat snarled.

"I knew it was you in the cabin and I knew it would be dangerous for three women in the wilderness alone. I decided to leave the posse and come back to help. That's when I saw you were traveling with him. I figured he was the ugly woman from the cabin."

Kat turned and looked up at Jack. Jack raised his eyebrows.

Trevor continued. "He matched the description of the killer, and I was afraid he was going to take you deep into the wilderness and do something horrible to you and the other girl."

"How do I know you're telling the truth?" Kat asked.

"I guess you're just going to have to decide if you believe me," Trevor said, looking her straight in the eye. "I'm telling the truth. Do you really think I'd make up that story?"

"Maybe you're just after us for the reward," Kat offered.

"Kat, you and I both know there's no way I'm going to single-handedly drag you back to Missouri for a reward. You'd kill me first. I don't care about the money anyway. Why is it so hard to believe I was worried about you?"

"Maybe because you formed a posse to hunt me down for money!"

Trevor rolled his eyes. "Kat, I didn't form the posse. It was already formed! I came along to keep them away from you. I was so scared the day we tracked you down in the cabins. It was pure luck that I entered the cabin you were in. You are so lucky! Don't you see? I knew it was you and I let you go."

Kat knew he was telling the truth. She just didn't know if she was ready to give in.

"Don't believe him, Kat! He's lying. Look at him. He tracked you across the country and he attacked me," Laura sobbed.

Kat couldn't understand why Laura was so upset. More so than she needed to be, Kat thought. Trevor must have really scared her.

"Come on outside, Laura. Let's get some fresh air. He's not going anywhere," Kat said as she tossed her head Trevor's way.

The three of them walked a distance from the cave and sat down on some rocks. Kat could tell Jack didn't know what to say to Laura. She was so mad or scared or both. He turned to Kat. "You know your brother. Is he telling the truth?"

"I really think he is, Jack," Kat replied in a low tone. "I thought he recognized me that day at the cabin, and it's been bothering me ever since. Here I thought he was hunting me down, and then he winked at me before he left the cabin like it was our little secret. His story makes sense. He never was like the other boys, but then again, he wasn't around much either. If he's riding alone like he says he is, I don't know what harm he could do to us."

"I think you're right. I'm not one to trust people, but I do think he's telling the truth. Let's talk with him a bit more to make sure he is definitely alone and then send him on his way."

"Let's just kill him now!" Laura hissed.

"Laura, we can't do that, and you know it," Kat said in a calm voice. "Don't worry, we'll get all the information we need out of him and then we'll send him on his way. Besides, we've got time to kill while we give Ginger's leg a little rest. It might be fun."

"Well, you go ahead and have the fun. I'm going to find a place to relieve myself," Laura muttered as she made her way down the slope. "I practically relieved myself in my pants because of the asshole."

Jack and Kat exchanged glances while holding back smiles. They'd never witnessed Laura so agitated. "We'd better keep her away from Trevor. She's liable to kill him."

Kat began to head back into the cave to question Trevor when Jack grabbed her arm and pulled her back to him. He whispered in her ear, "Thanks for offering to make him suffer until his dying day if he hurt one hair on my head. That was sweet."

"Anytime," Kat answered before heading back to the cave.

CHAPTER 16

Kat entered the cave and looked at Trevor. Trevor looked back, not knowing what was going to happen. Finally he spoke. "Kat, I don't know what else to say. I've told you the truth. It's up to you if you want to believe me."

"Why did you bring Clay along?" Kat asked with narrowed eyes.

"I didn't. It was his idea to come first. In fact, he helped form the posse." Trevor glanced at her to see if that bit of information hurt her feelings. It didn't appear to, so he continued. "Kat, Clay has always had it in for you. He's jealous of you. He doesn't want to give you any credit. Your very existence pisses him off. You should have heard the things he said about you over the years when he was drunk…Actually, I'm glad you didn't. Clay is bad through and through. He wanted to catch you, do bad things to you, and then turn you in for the reward money. I just kept my mouth shut and pretended to go along with it so I could figure out what to do when they found you. What I didn't know was that you were in disguise." Trevor smiled broadly. "It was a good disguise. Kat, what about this man you're traveling with? He's the one who killed those drifters, isn't he? A man like that can't be safe to travel with. Has he hurt you?"

Kat wasn't ready to show her hand. Instead, she posed a question back at Trevor. "Do you think I killed Harley?"

"I'm sure you did, and I'm sure he deserved it. Harley was a snake, and I bet Boris had a hand in whatever happened…" Trevor said, and his voice trailed off. He could only imagine what had happened. He had questioned Boris about it, and the way he had stumbled through his denial convinced Trevor he had planned something with Harley.

The fact that Trevor was now referring to his father by his first name did not escape Kat. "Well, there you have it, Trevor. Sometimes people have a very good reason for killing." It was the only answer Kat offered, but it went a long way toward convincing Trevor. If Kat thought that man wasn't dangerous, he probably wasn't. Still, Trevor intended to hang around a bit so he could see for himself.

"So, Kat, do you believe me at all, or are you just trying to figure out how to kill me?" Trevor asked.

"I don't know, Trevor. I'm concerned you're going to try to hurt Jack. I can't untie you yet. Besides, you don't have to worry about me killing you. I think Laura will do it first."

"I'm sorry. I didn't mean to scare her. Is she all right?"

"She'll be fine eventually. But you did scare the hell out of her. She's not your biggest advocate right now."

What Trevor said made sense. If he was lying, it was the best lie he'd ever told in his life. Had it just been her, she would have untied him, but she was still worried about Jack. Kat bent down and grabbed the ropes on Trevor's wrist.

"Thank God," Trevor said with relief.

"I'm not untying you. I'm making sure you won't get away." Kat secured the ropes even tighter and walked out of the cave.

Jack was sitting outside on a rock. Laura hadn't come back yet. She was still off composing herself. Kat thought how handsome Jack looked as she approached him on the rock.

"Well, you're in charge here, Kat. Is he lying or telling the truth?"

Kat sat next to him and Jack tenderly rubbed her shoulders. "I really think he's telling the truth. I'm just not sure what to do with him now. My concern is he'll try to hurt you if I untie him."

"Well, we don't want that now do we? Let's leave him tied up for a bit. Maybe if he spends the day with us—tied up, that is—he'll see what a nice fella I am and calm down. I mean, don't you agree, Kat? One day with me and he'll love me," Jack teased.

"It might take more than a day," Kat replied. They turned as they heard Laura making her way back to the cave.

"So, when do we kill him?" Laura spat, in a voice loud enough for Trevor to hear.

"Laura, we are not going to kill him. I think he's telling the truth. We are just going to leave him tied up awhile so we can be certain," Kat replied.

"Let's bring him out under this tree so we can keep an eye on him. I need to check Ginger's leg and do a little scouting," Jack announced. "I'd also like to gather some food, seeing as how we are stranded for a day or so."

They pulled Trevor out under the tree and set him in front of the fire. Laura glared at him the entire time.

"Laura, is it? I'm sorry I scared you," Trevor said.

"Shut up!" Laura snapped back. "Prisoners aren't allowed to talk."

Trevor wisely obeyed.

"Laura, will you keep watch over our prisoner while Jack and I find some food and some more fuel for the fire? Trevor, I'll be taking your horse; mine has a sore leg."

"I'd love to!" Laura snapped. "Give me a loaded gun."

"Remember, if you need us, just fire a shot and we'll be back in no time," Kat told her as she handed her the gun.

"I'll fire two if I need you. If you just hear one it's because our prisoner got out of line and I had to shoot him. That's not worth coming back to camp early for," Laura said in a tone that almost convinced Kat she actually meant it. Kat knew Laura was really angry and wanted to worry Trevor. It was working.

Kat and Jack rode off on their task. "Maybe I'll see you later and maybe I won't," Kat called back to Trevor. "I recommend you don't piss off Laura."

"Is she safe with him?" Trevor asked Laura, who sat glaring at him.

"Safer than you are with me," Laura replied threateningly.

"Laura, I'm not here to hurt you. I followed you because I wanted to protect you."

"Shut up, prisoner," Laura replied. She was playing it extra tough. After last night, Laura vowed she would never let her guard down again. It had almost got them killed. Kat and Jack would have never fallen asleep on watch. And then, when he grabbed her, she reacted by panicking! After Kat had told her so often: Don't let yourself panic when you're in a dangerous situation. Use your mind to calm yourself down and find a way out of the danger. Laura hadn't done that at all. Instead she'd hyperventilated. She'd read about it in her father's medical books. She had been the weak damsel in distress, and she'd never forgive this man for putting her in that position. She could have believed him, but her days of being nice were over. Instead, she decided to be mean. That was the safest choice.

"Do you think Laura will be okay with him?" Jack asked Kat.

"Yes, she's so mad right now she'd do a better job than you or me at watching him," Kat said.

They rode through the little mountain range to see what the next few days' travel would bring. It was another stretch of flat lands, with streams cutting through it. "Can I look through your telescope?" Kat asked.

Jack handed it to her. He loved her curiosity. "Oh, I see dinner! Those are some big rabbits, Jack, the biggest I've ever seen." She handed the glass back and rode toward her prey. Jack followed. Kat took aim and the rabbit fell. It was big and had huge feet.

"Everything seems bigger in this country," Kat said, smiling. Jack smiled, too.

On the way back, Jack stopped and dismounted. "Hop down, honey. It's time to collect fuel for our fire."

Kat just looked at him. She knew what he meant. They were standing in a field of hardened buffalo dung. "The timber back at camp is too green and wet from last night's rain to burn. But the buffalo have left us these treasures to keep our fire burning all night long." Jack smiled at her. They filled two cloth bags with buffalo dung and headed back to camp to see how Laura was doing with the prisoner.

"Yuck, I stink!" Kat complained. "I should have just held the bag and let you do the collecting."

"Oh, come on now, honey, you enjoyed it as much as I did. Besides, there's a little pond up ahead. We'll wash up before we head back to camp."

They steered the horses toward the pond. It was a beautiful little spot surrounded by pines. They dismounted and Jack pulled a bar of soap from his saddlebag, "I came prepared for dung handling." He handed the soap to Kat. Kat rolled up her sleeves and bent down at the edge of the pond to scrub her hands. When she was done she handed the bar to Jack, and he did the same. As he squatted at the edge of the pool, Kat just couldn't resist. She tapped his bottom with her boot as if she would push him all the way in. He turned his head and looked at her with admonishment. "If I go in you're coming with me," Jack warned.

Kat took it as a challenge. Jack turned his head and finished his scrubbing, periodically glancing back to see if she was behaving herself. He finished and began to rise. Kat saw her opportunity. Her boot landed on his backside and she gave him a shove. Jack spun around quickly as he fell backwards and grabbed her leg, taking her with him, just as he promised.

Kat was surprised. She didn't know he could move that fast. The water was cold as she and Jack plunged under but also refreshing. When their heads popped back out of the water, Jack announced happily, "Look, I saved the soap!" Kat thought he looked rather boyish with his head sopping wet and his look of glee at having saved the soap. She grabbed the top of his head to try to push him under. He was much too strong. Her advantage had always been the element of surprise, but Jack was ready for anything now. He grabbed her and swooped her into the air. "I think someone needs to learn some manners." He threw her into the water with ease. When she popped back up and pushed her hair out of her eyes, she saw he was taking his shirt off.

"What are you doing?" Kat exclaimed, acting horrified.

"I might as well take a bath since I'm all the way in. After all, I did save the soap," he mentioned again while showing it off as if it were a prize.

Jack was undressing under the water. He threw his clothes and boots up on shore. He teased her as he lathered up, "Ah, there's nothing like a bath after a hard morning of dung picking."

"Give me that soap," Kat commanded.

"Now, that's not a very nice way to ask after pushing me in the water."

"Please, may I use the soap?" Kat asked nicely.

"Since you used your manners, yes," Jack replied. Jack threw her the soap and continued to lather up.

Kat kept her eye on him as she stood in the shoulder-deep water. Jack could tell she was undressing now. He hadn't even planned this, but it sure was working out nicely. She held her left arm across her breasts as she jumped out of the water to launch her wet clothes onto the shore. She began soaping up her hair. Jack rinsed his own hair and silently stared at her. "Stop looking at me," she commanded.

"I have to keep my eye on you. I can't trust you. After all, you were the one who pushed me in," Jack replied seriously.

"At least turn your back for a minute so I can go to shallower water to soap up."

Jack turned his back to her. She headed toward shallower water, all the while keeping her eye on him. Hurriedly, she scrubbed her body.

"Need any help," Jack asked with his back turned.

"No, thanks," Kat replied. She finished lathering up and tossed the soap on the shore with the clothes.

Jack could hear her splashing out to deeper water to rinse off. "Can I turn around now?"

"Yes, you can turn around now."

Jack turned and looked at her. "You still have soap in your hair."

"I do?" Kat asked in surprise, feeling her hair. She dunked to get rid of any remaining soap.

To Jack's delight, it worked. Kat emerged and wiped the water from her eyes. Jack was nowhere to be found. Just then, Jack grabbed her leg. She jumped and squealed. Jack popped out of the water. "Ha!" he said. "You deserved that for pushing me in."

She lifted her hand to swat his shoulder. He grabbed it midair and pulled her to him. He knew it was a dangerous move. They were both naked, yet he couldn't resist. It was like someone else was in control of his actions. Their naked bodies were touching. Kat's feet no longer reached the bottom of the pond. She had to encircle his neck with her arms to stay afloat. Their naked bodies touched for the first time. It was both shocking and wonderful.

Jack was simply losing his ability to think. He kissed her tenderly, determined to keep their passions at bay. "Kat," he said, "you're in charge. You've got to make sure we stop, because I won't be able to. Can you do that?"

"Mmm hmm," Kat muttered against his lips.

He wasn't convinced she had any more willpower than he did. His only choice was to stop it now. Grabbing her under the armpits, he pushed her away from him. She looked disappointed as he said, "We better get back, Kat."

Kat watched him walk out of the water. She knew he was right. At least it was an opportunity to look at his beautiful body for a moment. She didn't even pretend to look the other way. He pulled on his pants and led Bullet away from the pond. Kat walked out of the pool and pulled her wet clothes on, too.

Their clothes had almost dried by the time they got back to camp. "What happened to you two?" Laura asked.

"Guess who pushed me in a pond?" Jack said with a sideways glance at Kat.

"Kat, you're wicked!" Laura exclaimed.

"No, I'm not. He's the wicked one. He grabbed my leg and yanked me in, too," Kat said, defending herself.

Trevor watched the exchange with curiosity. At least this Laura seemed to have calmed down. She genuinely seemed to like Kat and this Jack character.

"Well, Trevor, have you had some time to think about your behavior?" Kat asked.

"Kat, we are not untying him," Laura cut in. "I've been talking to him and watching him. I've decided I don't like him and don't trust him."

"You haven't been talking to me," Trevor pointed out. "Every time I open my mouth, you say, '*shut up, prisoner!*'"

"Is that true, Laura?" Jack asked.

"Yes," Laura admitted.

Trevor had a smug look of victory on his face until Jack followed up with, "Good girl, Laura." Jack left to go check on Ginger's leg.

They were all against him. He didn't blame Kat for not trusting him after all she'd been through. Thinking back to the days on the farm, Trevor felt guilty for not being around more. Avoidance had been his way of dealing with his family. He'd go to his uncle's farm to work and leave Kat at home to deal with it by herself. Then it all ended so badly, with Kat forced literally to run for her life. If he were Kat, he wouldn't trust himself either.

Laura was still keeping a vigilant eye on Trevor. She practiced her knife throwing as she gave him her most evil eye. She was getting really good with the knife, hitting the same spot over and over in the bark of a nearby tree.

Jack and Kat fashioned sticks to roast the rabbit meat over the fire. It smelled delicious.

"I have to go," Trevor announced. They all turned and looked at him in silence. "I have to *relieve* myself," he clarified, in case they didn't understand him.

"We know what you mean," Jack said. "I guess I'd better handle this one." He grabbed Trevor's arm and hoisted him to a standing position. Trevor's feet were still bound.

"Aren't you going to untie me?" he asked Jack.

"No. Now start hopping. We'll go behind those trees and you can do your thing. Do you have to do a big job?" Jack asked.

Both Laura and Kat began laughing. Trevor wondered how much longer he would have to endure the humiliation of being a prisoner. "No, I just have to…you know…"

"All right, but you'll have to manage on your own with the ropes on. I'm not going to hold it for you," Jack informed him.

Laura and Kat laughed even harder. Trevor rolled his eyes and began hopping.

Jack brought him back to camp a few minutes later and set him up against a tree a few feet away from where the other three were set to dine. They raved over how delicious the meat tasted and drank deeply from the canteens. "I swear, this Montana water tastes better than regular water," Laura said. Trevor recognized it as an attempt to make him suffer. He wondered if they would let him eat or drink but decided to keep quiet about it. Finally, Kat came over and set a plate of meat and a canteen in front of him. He was thankful for the delicious meal, and Laura was right about the water.

"Well, since we are stranded here, I think I'll take a little nap," Jack said as he stretched out his long body, tipped his hat over his eyes, and put his hands behind his head.

Laura headed down to the stream to wash clothes and dishes and Kat began preparing the rabbit hide the way Jack had told her. He wanted to keep every hide possible so they'd have plenty to keep them warm over the long winter. "We'll use them for blankets, coats, hats, mittens, rugs—everything," Jack had told Kat. She admired his inventiveness and how he thought ahead. It seemed he did a much better job of that than she did. Her big dilemma now was Trevor. She hadn't spoken to him much throughout the day.

When Kat had done all she could with the rabbit hide she set it aside. She decided she would show it to Jack when he woke and see what else should be done. For now, she would go help Laura with her chores. She stood to leave and turned to speak to Trevor. "Remember, if you hurt one hair on his head, I promise I will hunt you down and make you suffer. Understand?"

"Kat, I won't hurt him," Trevor responded.

Jack smiled under his hat.

Trevor knew Kat needed time to digest what he'd said to her. To pass the time, Trevor spent the day watching them. They all worked together so well and seemed so happy, even Laura, the mean one. He noticed that she didn't seem mean to the others at all. She just really hated him, Trevor deducted. He studied Jack. You wouldn't know he was a cold-blooded killer by watching him. There didn't seem to be an ounce of temper in the man, and he treated the women very well. Trevor noticed that Kat looked at Jack frequently as he slept. Trevor wondered.

That evening, Jack cornered Kat and told her they would be moving out again tomorrow. "You'll need to decide what to do with Trevor. I don't think he is much of a threat, but I want you to make the decision, he is your brother. Um, I think we should leave Laura out of this decision…if it were up to her he'd probably be hanging from a tree."

Kat sighed and wandered over to talk to Trevor. "So, Trevor, if you survive this, what are your plans for the rest of your life?"

He was glad she finally asked and had decided honesty would be the best policy. If they felt any deception at all he'd be done for. "Well, now that I'm convinced he is not out to harm you, I'd really like to join you. It's too late in the year to travel any further west on my own. I do not want to go back to Missouri, and I'm not interested in going south. I really like this land and I'd like to make my home here, maybe try farming."

"Jack, could you come here?" Jack came and stood by Kat's side. "He wants to join us, maybe try farming."

"Join us? Farming, huh? Interesting. Can we trust him, Kat? Because you know, if he pulls any funny stuff, I'll have to kill him. Are you going to be okay with that?"

"Yeah, I'm okay with that," Kat answered without hesitation.

Trevor wondered how long they would continue to talk about him as if he weren't there.

"Laura!" Kat hollered across the clearing. "Are you okay with Trevor joining up with us?"

"When hell freezes over!" Laura hollered back.

"I'll go talk to her," Kat whispered to Jack as she turned and headed in Laura's direction.

CHAPTER 17

"Kat, I just don't think we should do anything to compromise all we've worked so hard to accomplish!" Laura was quite adamant. "There's something about him that irritates me. He has been a pain in your side this entire journey. Doesn't it ever end? I just can't comprehend why you would want him to join us after all he's done to you."

Kat took a deep breath and explained everything Trevor had said to her. After almost an hour of talking, Laura reluctantly agreed to let Trevor join them.

Trevor watched the two talk from a distance. He just couldn't understand why that woman hated him so much. His challenge, he decided, would be to find a way to win her over.

One condition of Trevor's acceptance into the group was that he be tied up at night. Laura insisted on it. She thought it was best to exercise caution, and she also told Kat she wouldn't be able to sleep knowing he was free to attack them.

Kat spoke with Trevor and filled him in on their routine and goals, and their expectations of him. She also reiterated what would happen to him if he harmed Jack.

Trevor accepted their rules, relieved and happy to be traveling deeper into Montana Territory with them. He would continue to keep an eye on Jack, but he liked what he had seen so far.

The next morning, Kat untied Trevor for the first time. Rubbing his wrists and ankles, he enjoyed the feeling of freedom. He knew to move slowly and not cause any anxiety among the group, especially with Laura. The woman barely needed a reason to kill him, and he wasn't about to give her one.

Ginger's leg seemed fine, which was important given the challenging terrain they had to tackle. They traveled a bit over rocky hills before finding a smoother path to follow. Midway through the day, they were crossing flatlands again. They did the usual hunting, fishing, and scouting. Kat was becoming quite a hide collector. She had done what Jack suggested and cleaned every animal skin from their hunting excursions. She was getting better each time and was now a bit embarrassed about the first few she'd done. Still, she kept them all.

Trevor kept quiet and did as he was told. Laura glared at him often and he walked on eggshells around her. Kat and Jack did a fairly good job of accepting Trevor into their party, giving him assignments and talking more and more with him each day. For Jack, it was quite a relief to have another man around. He worried about what might happen to the women if anything happened to him. He didn't know the Indian tribes in the area. He knew some tribes respected their women and treated them very well and others didn't. There was power in numbers and Trevor added strength to their party. Jack found him to be very hard working and amicable. Even the way he handled Laura impressed Jack.

Kat was secretly thrilled that Trevor was traveling with them. He was the only decent part of her past and she felt he could do so much better for himself if he were not around Boris and the boys. Kat knew there was much more to Trevor than he had shown up to this point in his life. By the third day of traveling, Kat was finally convinced he was not out to hurt Jack. The two men began to talk and make plans together. Trevor's presence helped to lift the workload.

Laura was still sullen.

One evening, Kat waited until Trevor and Laura had fallen asleep. She went over to talk to Jack. "I'm worried about Laura. She seems so angry with Trevor. I don't understand why she hates him so much. Any idea what we can do to get her to loosen up around him?"

"I think she's just trying to show us how tough she is. In fact, I bet she doesn't even realize it. What would you think about sending them on a chore together? She'd be forced to warm up to him," Jack offered.

"Or she'd kill him," Kat countered. "But I think it's a good idea. Let's give it a try."

"Tomorrow will be the test. We'll find a way to get them together and see what happens," Jack said while looking deep into her eyes. He was quickly losing interest in talking about Trevor and Laura's problem. "Hey, Kat?" Jack whispered. "Do you want to go swimming with me again, soon?"

"Jack!" Kat said. "You're hopeless. Besides we're not near water right now."

"We don't really need the water. We could just pretend."

Kat looked over to see if the others were sleeping. Once she was convinced they were, she encircled his neck with her arms and kissed him sweetly on the lips. "Goodnight, Jack, and thanks for giving Trevor a chance," she added.

It was time to execute their plan. The sun was up and Kat walked over to Jack and handed him some gear. Jack told her he had an idea.

"I'll follow your lead and hope it works," Kat murmured.

The party rode hard all day. Jack felt the urge to get settled and he pushed the group to move faster. They skipped the noon meal and only took a short mid-afternoon break. It seemed the country grew more beautiful the deeper they traveled into Montana Territory. It would soon be September. Time was running out if they planned on being prepared for winter. Jack liked this part of the country but still didn't feel he was quite "there." He hated to put the effort into building a cabin just to leave it behind when warm weather hit again. He'd give it a few more days, and if they didn't find the right spot they'd head back to this valley.

With about three hours of daylight left, Jack announced, "Let's stop here for tonight."

The others pulled the horses to a stop by a grove of pine trees. Trevor and Laura dismounted. Kat read the look Jack threw her, which said, *stay on your horse.*

"We need meat—some berries would be nice—and plenty of firewood. Kat, you and I will get the meat. Trevor and Laura, find some berries and bring back plenty of firewood.

Jack and Kat galloped off. Trevor read the look on Laura's face as she witnessed Kat and Jack's sudden exit. She was not happy.

Trevor on the other hand was thrilled. This was just the opportunity he needed to win her over. "Come on, partner. Let's get to work." Trevor smiled.

"I'm not your partner!" she replied as she followed him along the grove of trees.

Trevor noticed some berry bushes but decided to ride on by. Laura saw them too and said, "Here are some berries."

"Good eye, Laura," Trevor praised as he turned his mount around and headed back to the bushes. They both dismounted and began picking berries in silence.

Trevor gave her a sideways glance and popped a berry in his mouth. "Laura, these are delicious. Here, try one, we won't tell Jack and Kat we snitched a few." Before she could protest, Trevor put a berry in her mouth. She had no choice but to eat it. It was deliciously sweet. "Aren't they good, Laura?" Trevor asked, trying to pry a little bit of conversation out of her.

"Yes, they're delicious," she admitted reluctantly.

"If only these bugs would leave us be." Trevor swatted around his head.

The bugs were thick. Laura was busy picking berries (and eating one every now and again) when she suddenly dropped the handful she was holding and grabbed her eye.

"Ouch!"

"What's wrong?" Trevor asked.

"One of those damn bugs flew in my eye," Laura growled, "and it really stings." She was trying to work it out, but to no avail.

"Laura, let me see," Trevor said.

"No, just give me a minute; it will come out. Oh-oh-oh." It wasn't working its way out. Trevor bent down by Laura, who was sitting on the ground now.

"Here, hold still. I know a little bug removal trick." Trevor leaned Laura back and tilted her head to one side. Laura obliged, only because it was stinging so badly. Trevor took his canteen and flushed the invaded eye from the inside corner out with cool water.

"Is that better?" Trevor asked in a gentle voice while looking into her red eye.

"Yes, I think it's out," Laura hesitated to admit.

"Let me have a look. You could still have some bug parts in there. You never know, he may have left a leg or wing behind," Trevor gently teased.

She pushed his hand away and growled, "I'm fine!"

"Well, here," Trevor continued, seeming unaffected by her harsh retort. "Hold this to your eye. It will bring the swelling down." Trevor handed her his handkerchief, which was doused with cool water. He didn't give her a chance to refuse, as he gently placed it on her eye and brought her own hand up to hold it in place. "You rest for a minute and I'll finish picking the berries. If you hadn't eaten so many we'd have plenty by now," Trevor teased.

Laura sat and watched Trevor pick the remaining berries. Since he was not looking at her, she took the opportunity to stare at him. He was a mystery to her. It was such a strange story, his absentee relationship with Kat. How he had followed her all this way. And now his sudden interest in her life and even wanting to be a part of it. Laura tried to comprehend the reason for it. She also couldn't help but notice the muscles in Trevor's back as he reached into the bushes for more berries. He had powerful arms and strong hands. He really had a pleasant voice, too. It was deep, strong, and sincere. Laura shook her head. What was she thinking?

Trevor could feel her eyes on him. He took his time picking the bushes clean to give her time to calm down and think about what a good guy he really was. *Yeah, fat chance,* he thought.

"How's your eye?" Trevor asked as he put the berries in his bag.

"Fine," Laura answered shortly.

"Good. Let's continue with our chores. I think firewood is next on our list," Trevor continued, ignoring her curtness. He mounted his horse and Laura followed. They came across a fallen tree. Trevor dismounted and cut off the dried branches with his axe. Laura gathered them into a bunch. "These branches will make great kindling," Trevor said in an effort to keep the non-threatening conversation going. Laura kept working silently.

"There. That should be enough. Let's tie this bundle to the back of the packhorse." Laura helped him lift it onto the horse and held it as he secured it to its back. "These pines will make cabin-building easy. They are so straight and plentiful. Jack is right about gathering furs. I'm betting Montana winters can be pretty cold. Does cold weather bother you, Laura?"

"I don't know. Winters weren't very harsh where I came from."

Trevor was thrilled to get more than a one-word answer out of her. "Where do you come from?"

"Tennessee."

"Were your parents farmers?" Trevor was working it hard.

"No."

"What did your father do?"

"He was a doctor."

"Ah. That explains your smarts." Trevor threw in a little flattery and moved off it again so she wouldn't become suspicious. "My father, Boris, is a farmer, but not a very good one. He is lazy, inconsiderate, and likes to use other people. I don't know how much Kat told you, but if it hadn't been for her, the farm would have been in shambles. My brothers aren't much good either. They like to drink, and when you have Boris as an example of how to behave, you're likely to turn out rotten. I must say, I wasn't much help to Kat either. I hated that farm and I was always ashamed of everyone in the family, except Kat. I escaped by going to my Uncle Jacob's farm and helping him. He was my mother's brother and a very good man. Uncle Jacob was ten times the father

Boris was. You know, at first I was so angry with myself for leaving Kat to fend for herself, but then she never would have escaped to a new life and this beautiful country if it hadn't happened. Still, it kills me to think what Harley did to her." Trevor was looking directly into Laura's eyes.

By now she had let her guard down completely and was listening intently to Trevor's words. She could tell he felt true regret.

"Men are supposed to protect women, and I left Kat all alone. Laura, it gives me a knot right here." He pushed his fist to his stomach and began to forget himself as he spoke. "If Kat hadn't killed him, I would have." Trevor was gritting his teeth by now and Laura could see the hurt and anger.

"Trevor." It was the first time she'd spoken his name, and Trevor jerked his head back to look her in the eye. "Harley didn't rape Kat, if that's what you're thinking. He intended to—there is no doubt about that—but Kat killed him before he had a chance."

Trevor's entire body seemed to release the months of tension he had been carrying. "He didn't? She did? Thank you, Laura!" Without thinking, he put his arms around her and hugged her. "You don't know how much better you've made me feel." He released her and held her shoulders at arms' length. "If only you knew the agony I've felt since it happened." Trevor realized he was touching her and had even hugged her. "Oh, I'm sorry!" He released her and began picking up wood. "I know you hate me, but I will always be grateful to you for telling me. That's just something I couldn't bring myself to ask Kat."

They picked up the rest of the wood and headed back to camp.

Jack and Kat had caught some fish, left them at the campsite, and rode off again.

"Well, it was nice of them to leave the fish for us to clean." Trevor smiled. "Guess I better get to work."

Jack and Kat watched them through the telescope from a beautiful little clearing, "Jack, I think it might be working. At least they aren't fighting, as far as I can tell." As Kat handed the telescope to Jack, a small rodent ran right in front of her foot. "Aaaah!" Kat jumped back.

Jack laughed at her. "Are you going to tell me a big brave girl like you is afraid of mice?"

"I'm not fond of rodents," Kat admitted.

"So, you don't want me to bring one home to our cabin as a pet?"

Kat turned and looked at him.

"What's that look for?" Jack asked softly. He was standing very close to her now. He grabbed her hands and held them in his. "Kat, you and I haven't talked about it, but I want to build a cabin for us. You and me. Yes, Laura and Trevor will have rooms—on the other side of the cabin. But you and I will be sharing a room. Forever. I love you and I want to be with you always." Jack began to worry when Kat just stood there saying nothing. It seemed like forever, and then finally she broke into a slow smile. She threw her arms around his neck and hugged him tightly.

"Do you mean you want to marry me?" Kat asked.

"I guess I didn't say that exactly, did I?" Jack said. He then knelt down on one knee, held her hand in his, and smiling broadly, he said, "Will you marry me, John Deer?"

"Yes!" Kat tackled him in joy.

He lay on the ground with Kat sprawled on top of him. They were both laughing. Jack rolled her off and cozied up beside her on the ground. The wind gently bent the tall grass back and forth around them. He lovingly stroked the side of her face with the back of his hand as he spoke. "Kat, don't think I want to marry you just because you are amazingly beautiful. Or because you can hunt and fish and probably provide better for us than I could. Or because you're the only woman around." He smiled at her. "I love being with you, talking to you and working with you. Let's face it—we make a great team."

"That we do. I didn't think men like you existed. I guess I got lucky."

Jack leaned down and tenderly kissed the tip of her nose, which made Kat smile. Her lips were irresistible. Just one kiss, Jack told himself. Kat must have been thinking the same thing. She encircled his neck with her arms and brought him to her. When their lips touched, it was with pure love and appreciation for one another. As they kissed, the sweetness turned to hunger and longing. Jack couldn't get enough of her. He pulled her on top of him so he could touch. He ran his fingers through her thick, silky hair and caressed her back. His hands stretched down and over her firm, round buttocks. A hand encircled her thigh and slowly brought it up around his waist. Kat was completely aroused by his touch and by the fact that he was aroused. She moaned as her thigh rubbed up the length of him.

They were now lying on their sides, and it was Kat's turn to touch Jack. His kisses were sending uncontrollable urges through her. She didn't know what women were *supposed* to do; she could only do what she wanted to, and there was plenty she wanted to do right now. Her hands ran down the length of his strong back. Somehow knowing it would drive him crazy, she edged her hands into the back of his pants at the waistband and brought them around ever so slowly to his stomach. Her fingertips brushed the edge of his arousal, doing as much for her as it did for him. That wasn't enough for her; she brought her hand out of his waistband to the outside of his pants and rubbed slowly down the length of it. It was his turn to moan but it was more of a low growl.

Jack, with his one remaining ounce of sanity, said, "Honey, there's no turning back now. Are you okay with this?"

Kat said nothing. She answered by reaching up and ripping his shirt open down to his waist. Jack closed his eyes and moaned as he brought her lips to his again. It was his turn. He intended to enjoy her, slowly and lovingly. He knew it was her first time and he wanted it to be special for her. As if he were handling something very fragile, he unbuttoned her shirt buttons one by one. Kat was almost shocked at the things her mind was asking him to do to her. Jack gently pushed the shirt off her shoulders and took in the sight of her beautiful breasts. His lips met hers again, but only for a moment. His kisses traveled down her neck as his hand gently caressed her breasts. Kat could hardly stand it as his lips approached her breasts. She gasped as his warm mouth encircled an aroused nipple. She never would have dreamed that could feel so good. Jack's hands roamed her body freely. They were at her belt buckle and undoing her pants. Without consciously thinking about it, Kat was undoing his trousers—she never realized how erotic it could be to have him undress her.

Jack was determined to make this last as long as possible. He was enjoying every moment. The task of making his body wait was enormous. He was on top of her now and each enjoying the feel of the other's naked body. Kat felt no shame as she caressed his buttocks and she didn't hesitate to feel him down there. Curiosity and wonder took control over her actions. She was no longer allowing herself to think. He was lying between her legs now and was amazed he could keep himself from plunging into her. He did so because of his intense love for her and the fact that he wanted them both to enjoy this moment equally. He wanted the moment of their first joining to have deep meaning. He continued passionately kissing her as he lifted her leg up and caressed it. The tip of his arousal was now resting against her velvety lips. He was pleased with her response. She reached for him with her hips as if to pull him into her. He knew she was ready, but he also knew the reward of taking it slow. Jack stopped his kisses to look her deeply in the eyes. They both knew what was coming next. Ever so slowly, he entered her. Her eyes were filled with passion. The tip of his arousal touched her virginal barrier. He was consumed with love and appreciation knowing he would be the first she would let past. With a deep thrust, he entered her fully. She let out a small cry of shock and pain. He waited without moving for her to come back to him. Jack kissed her lips tenderly to show his appreciation. Kat smiled lovingly. She let him know it was okay by arching her hips to take him deeper. Their lovemaking lasted, as Jack had hoped. Never had he felt so in touch with a woman. He instinctively knew what pleased her and he gladly gave it. It was as much a pleasure for him as it was for her as he brought her over the brink into total ecstasy. She didn't hide her enjoyment, which brought him full circle.

When it was over, they lay, bodies glistening with sweat, still connected to one another. He showered her face in kisses until finally he spoke. He couldn't bring himself to part from her, so he stayed and whispered in her ear. "Kat, thank you for being the love of my life."

Kat replied, "You're welcome, Jack. I love you." They lay there together in the grass, enjoying what had just happened, until Kat finally spoke. "When can we do this again?"

CHAPTER 18

Kat and Jack headed back to camp, both attempting not look like the cat that swallowed the canary. Trevor and Laura were too consumed with their own thoughts to notice anything.

Kat and Jack filled the space with nervous chatter. "I see you found the fish we left. Hope you didn't mind, Trevor. You were always the best fish cleaner. I just hate it when I miss the little bones." Kat chattered on, "And look at all the berries you found. Mmm, they are delicious. Here Jack, try one."

Laura didn't say much. She was busy putting the food out so they could sit down and eat. Kat tried to get a feel as to Laura's mood. Had the experiment helped or hurt? She wasn't sure. Laura was hard to read. Trevor, on the other hand, seemed happy as a lark. Laura must have been a little nicer to him.

That night Laura had first watch. Kat and Jack thought it was important to give her watch right away so she wouldn't feel they didn't trust her. Besides, it was always easier to stay awake during first watch.

"Laura," Jack announced. "I want Trevor to sit watch with you tonight. He'll still be tied up, but I want him to go through the motions. If we decide to keep him, eventually he'll have to take a turn at watch. I'll walk the horses to the stream for water before I lie down. Kat, want to help me?"

"Sure!" They were off.

Laura stood there with her mouth hanging open again. This was beginning to become a habit with them.

Trevor resisted smiling.

"So, what do you do on watch?" Trevor broke in. He didn't want to give her a chance to protest.

"You sit with a gun across your lap and look out into the darkness. If you see an Indian or a wild animal or any sort of man sneaking up to you, you shoot them dead. You, however, will not be given a gun. We still can't trust you," Laura said.

"Sounds simple enough." Trevor walked up to sit on the rock beside Laura. She gave him a sideways glance and went back to checking her gun.

"You sure are handy with guns and knives, just like Kat. I thought Kat was the only woman alive who was so good at it, until I met you. Who taught you? Your Daddy?" Trevor asked, trying to draw Laura into a conversation.

"Huh. No!" Laura snorted. "My father was a great doctor, but he never gave women much credit. He thought we were only good for teaching, sewing, nursing the sick, and having children. I never understood that about him. He had to have noticed I was smart. I studied his medical books every night to try to get him to see how much I knew about his profession. He refused to see it or at least acknowledge it. The only time he noticed me was when I messed up. You just didn't make a mistake in our house or you heard about it from him. Mistakes were not allowed." Laura had said much more than she had intended to. In fact, she had intended to say as little as possible to this man, who had been smack dab in the middle of one of the biggest and potentially dangerous mistakes she had ever made—falling asleep on duty.

"You know, I just don't understand some fathers and mothers. They seem to do their children more harm than good. The harm you do by telling them they're stupid or lazy or by just ignoring them is far more than people realize," Trevor said as he moved the dirt with his toe. "My brothers heard it every day from Boris. *You're so goddamn stupid. You're good for nothing.* The insults went on and on. I guess I can't blame my brothers for behaving like they do. Kat was so strong not to believe Boris when he said mean things to her. She knew she couldn't stop him from saying those things, so I think she just put up an invisible wall and shut him out. It worked for her. I, on the other hand, left. I guess I wasn't as strong as Kat. I couldn't shut him out." Trevor looked up to find Laura looking directly at him. Laura looked startled when Trevor's gaze met hers. He smiled and asked, "So, who was it?"

"What do you mean?" Laura asked.

"Who taught you to shoot and throw knives as well as you do?" Trevor asked again.

"Kat."

Trevor smiled widely. "Of course. That makes perfect sense. She taught me a thing or two. Let's face it, she's just better at some of those things than I am."

Laura stared at him. She couldn't believe a man would admit a woman could do something better than he could. Especially when that thing was a "man's" task.

"Now mind you, there are a few things I'm better at than Kat, like cleaning fish." Trevor flashed those pearly whites at her again. In the dark, they looked even whiter than normal. Laura found herself smiling back at him. If she'd realized it she would have stopped herself. Trevor did realize it and kept talking. He was getting somewhere with her and he wanted it to continue. Trevor knew he was a good conversationalist. That skill helped him gain people's trust. People liked being around him. He continued talking, telling her amusing stories about growing up with Kat or the dumb things his brothers did.

What Trevor didn't realize was that he wasn't winning Laura over with his conversation skills. It was *what* he said. Laura listened carefully to every word coming out of Trevor. How was he continuing to say the right things, she wondered. He appeared to be a man that felt women and men were on equal ground. It also seemed he understood the effects harsh words had on children. He had had a bad upbringing and somehow came out of it with very little damage. It may have even made him wiser. Laura listened intently, amazed he hadn't messed up yet and let his true self show. No person could be that perfect. She would watch and study him and then revel when he did finally slip and reveal the true person he was. In the meantime, she would wait, watch, and listen.

Kat and Jack led the horses to the stream. They sat on a rock while the horses drank. Jack held Kat's hand and gently stroked her fingers up and down. Kat thought it felt wonderful. Jack spoke. "Today was wonderful for me. I have to force myself not to walk around with a big dumb dreamy smile on my face. I feel like I'm walking on clouds."

"Me too," Kat whispered. It was hard to keep it a secret but they knew they must. Laura was having such a tough time with Trevor, and Trevor might misbehave again if he knew the true nature of Kat and Jack's relationship. It was better that they kept quiet until things settled down. "I wish we could do that every day."

Jack smiled broadly. He loved how honest and uninhibited she was. He leaned over and kissed her gently on the lips. "I love you, Kat."

"I love you, too," she easily replied.

"We better get back and see how the two "non-love birds" are doing. We haven't heard any gunshots yet, so that's a good sign."

Kat and Jack strolled back into camp and avoided talking with Trevor and Laura. They were sitting on a rock in the distance and talking with each other, which was a great sign. They opted to not make a big deal of it and hoped it continued. Both rolled out their blankets on opposite ends of the camps and fell fast asleep, each dreaming about the other.

When Laura was relieved by Jack hours later, she went to bed but could not fall asleep. She was baffled by the fact that she had listened and talked to Trevor for three hours straight and that he hadn't messed up once. He would, she decided. She just had to give him the chance.

The camp was ready to move out at sunrise. They could all feel Jack's anxiousness to find his dream site.

"I am amazed," Kat said in wonderment. "You think you've seen it all, and the next day you run across something even more beautiful. Look at those rocks!" They had all stopped in awe. The rocks had a reddish tone and looked lumpy. "How did they get that way?"

"It makes you wonder," Trevor replied. He couldn't take his eyes off it. "I wish this were the spot. I'd come and look at that every day and never get tired of it. But this isn't it, is it, Jack?" Trevor posed the question to which he already knew the answer.

"No, but I feel we are really close. The land is getting richer. Water is plentiful. But it's got to be the right combination of trees, hillside, and streams. I just have a gut feeling it's out there—we are very close. I'll know it when I see it."

They stood there transfixed until Laura broke in, "Good, because my bottom is becoming permanently damaged from this damn saddle," she complained, rubbing her tailbone. "It seems I never get use to it!"

The others laughed. Whenever Laura put her ladylike manners aside and spoke her mind, it was always funny. On that note they all turned the horses and pressed on. They were all interested in reaching their final destination and didn't mind long stretches of riding without breaks. Even the horses seemed to know they were close and went forward tirelessly. They made very good progress that day and stopped early that evening at the edge of a mountain. After a short break, Jack announced he would ride ahead to determine what tomorrow's best route would be. There was still plenty of daylight left.

"Can I ride with you?" Trevor asked.

"You girls okay being on your own for awhile?" Jack asked.

In unison they snorted and replied, "Yes!"

Kat and Laura prepared for the evening meal. Then the girls just sat. It felt good to not be on a horse and not be doing anything. They always had a great time together and enjoyed each other's company. Laura asked Kat questions about what it had been like to be John Deer.

Kat told her how she was pretty sure she had gotten drunk the first day in the saloon. She recounted the first time she saw Jack and fooled him, and even how she learned to smoke.

"I can't believe you smoked. A woman. Oh, my God! I think I'll faint!" Laura mocked.

"Do you want to try it?" Kat asked mischievously. "We don't have to tell the boys."

Laura smiled back. "Why not?"

Kat snuck over to Jack's bag and dug around in it until she found the tobacco. She showed Laura how to roll the cigarette. Laura tried and did a very bad job. "Looks like the first one I tried," Kat said, and she laughed.

She rerolled Laura's and lit them both. She showed her how to inhale. Laura made faces and coughed but all in all did pretty well. "Yuk, that was disgusting," Laura said, "but it was fun."

"I thought so too, but I also kind of enjoyed it after a while. I can see how men like it. They don't seem to mind disgusting things." That made Laura laugh.

Jack and Trevor rode back to camp not much later. Neither Kat nor Laura admitted to smoking. It would be their little secret. The men, however, did look as though they had a secret. "What have you two been up to?" Kat asked suspiciously.

"We've got a little surprise for you two," Trevor teased.

"What?" Laura asked, her curiosity piqued.

"Well, we can't tell you now, but we'll show you after we eat," Jack teased.

All through the meal, the girls tried to pry it out of them. What could the surprise be? Trevor and Jack did a great job of keeping the secret yet sufficiently teased them. They inhaled the meal and cleaned up in a hurry.

"Are you sure your behind can take a little extra riding today?" Jack asked Laura before they mounted.

"Yes, and thank you—I appreciate your concern for my behind," Laura said sarcastically.

Off they rode with the girls still asking questions. The sun was melting into the horizon as they reached the "surprise." They came around a rocky formation and looked at the flat ahead of them. Both Laura and Kat looked puzzled.

"Jack, what is that?" Kat asked.

Before her was a small pool of water—at least she thought it was water. Steam was coming out of it and it seemed to be hot.

Jack looked at her and smiled. "It's called a hot spring. I heard about them, but I didn't think they really existed until Trevor and I happened upon this one. It's like a natural hot bath, and it's supposed to soothe aching muscles." Jack turned to Laura. "Laura, your behind came to mind when we found this."

They all laughed.

"So can we go in it?" Laura asked.

Kat was surprised. Laura wasn't normally comfortable around water.

"You bet. Trevor tested it out earlier and it's only a few feet deep," Jack replied as he dismounted.

"It's a little hot, but you get use to it after a few minutes," Trevor added, anxious to get back in it. He actually had thought of Laura's behind when he first saw it.

"Close your eyes, ladies," Jack announced, "unless you want to see all that Trevor and I have to offer!"

Laura gasped and turned her back as Jack started to undo his pants.

Kat just giggled and turned around.

"You don't mean to tell me you two are getting in there naked!" Laura protested.

"That's the only way to sit in a hot spring," Trevor said to Laura's back.

Laura was appalled. "I'm not getting in there naked, not with two men!"

"Laura," Jack tried to reason with her, "you can't see a thing. The water's too steamy, and we promise not to look when you get in and out. We will behave like perfect gentlemen. We promise. Besides we are all tired, achy, and sore. Our bodies need this. We were meant to find it. It would be an insult to nature to pass it up."

Laura was still hesitant. Kat leaned over and whispered to her, "Come on, Laura. I'll do it if you do. We're not in civilization anymore. Who will know but us? And who cares anyway? This is the day to try new things." Kat made a motion as if she were smoking. Laura smiled a little and a hint of adventure returned to her eyes. "Besides, you don't want to keep your clothes on and ride back to camp all wet. You'll catch a cold." Kat was doing her best to convince her.

"That does make good medical sense," Laura began to concede. "It wouldn't do me any good to have a cold *and* a sore bottom."

"Good! It's settled then." Kat spun around. "Trevor. Jack. Turn around and close your eyes. No peeking or we'll shoot you." Kat glanced back at Laura, who still had her back to the men. "We mean it. We'll shoot you," Kat added for Laura's benefit.

Trevor turned around. Jack still had his eyes on Kat. They had stolen secret glances and communicated often throughout the day with mere looks. Kat took a moment to drag her tongue across her lips, sending clear a message to Jack. Jack was stunned motionless. The effect she had on him with just one little gesture! Kat giggled and turned back around.

"Okay, Laura, it's now or never." Kat spun Laura around to face the men so they could keep an eye on them as they undressed. They removed their clothes quickly, as if someone would see them if they moved too slowly. Laura, in her playful way, turned her bottom and wiggled it at the men's backs. Kat laughed out loud and Laura joined in.

"What are you two up to now?" Jack asked with his back turned.

"Wouldn't you like to know?" Laura replied as the girls hurried to the edge of the water. "Don't turn around, yet," she added.

The girls gasped as they slid into the hot water. They sunk in up to their necks. "This is amazing!" Kat let the words out slowly. "It's even better than the hot bath I had at the hotel."

"Mmm," was all Laura could manage.

The sun had set, but a few shadowy lights lingered on the western horizon. It was beautiful.

"So, do you like our surprise?" Jack asked.

"Very much," Kat replied. "Laura, try this." Kat slipped all the way under the water and let the warmth engulf her entire being. She came back up and pushed her hair out of her eyes.

Laura followed her example. Laura stayed under the water for a moment. She reemerged and tossed her long hair back, smoothing it with her hands. Her eyes were still closed, giving Trevor plenty of time to look. To him, she looked like an angel, even when she was angry with him. Her skin was smooth and tanned. The color perfectly complemented her brown hair and eyes. Trevor found it strange how attracted he was to the way she moved. How her arm looked as she brushed her hair back. The way she walked. No one else walked like her. He thought it was odd; he had never noticed how anyone walked or moved before.

"I can't even feel my bottom now," Laura commented. They all laughed.

"This is so relaxing, yet energizing," Kat marveled.

"It's relaxing all right. I wouldn't say I have an ounce of energy, though," Laura added.

"Jack, can we have one of these where we settle?" Kat asked.

"Now, wouldn't that be perfect. We can always come back to this spot when our behinds are hurting."

"Ha, ha," Laura said weakly. Laura's eyes remained closed. Trevor had his head tilted back to the heavens and his eyes on the stars. Kat and Jack had theirs on each other, knowing they had the same thought running through their heads.

"This is heaven," Trevor said simply.

"Almost," Kat chimed in, knowing what *would* make it heaven.

"Back on the farm, Kat liked to take mud baths with the hogs. Remember that Kat?" Trevor offered.

"I'd almost forgotten about that. Thanks for bringing it up."

"Once, she was sitting on the fence by the hog pen when she spotted a mouse running along the top rail towards her. She screamed and jumped into the pen with the pigs. I laughed so hard. She was covered with mud and pig manure from her head to her toes. You could only see her eyes and her teeth."

"It was disgusting," Kat chimed in, "and I stank so badly! I could smell it in my skin for a week. I think I even got a little in my mouth."

"Oh, Kat, that's horrible." Laura had been pulled out of her trance-like state by the horror of Trevor's story. "What did you do to get it off you?"

"I went down to the icy cold stream. Trevor brought me a bar of soap and a change of clothes. He was still laughing at me. The water was so cold, but I scrubbed until I got it all off. The worst part was my hair. The smell really sticks."

Laura and Jack were laughing as they imagined Kat covered from head to toe. "All over a little mouse?" Jack asked.

"I told you I don't like mice. Looking back now, I'd have to say I'd take a mouse over a dip in the pig pen."

They soaked in the steamy water a long time. Kat looked over just in time to see Laura begin to slip under the water. She grabbed her and yanked her back up. Laura woke with a start. "Oh, my goodness. I was so relaxed I fell asleep."

"I'm ready to head back," Trevor said. "I'm getting hot."

"Oh." Kat sounded disappointed. "I don't want to leave yet, but if you're tired, Laura, we should go."

"You don't have to leave," Trevor said. "I'm ready to go. I can ride back to camp with her. You stay here and turn into an wrinkly old lady if it suits you."

"Laura, is that okay with you?"

"Sure." Laura was so relaxed she would have agreed to just about anything.

The men kept their backs turned while Laura got out and dressed. She leaned lazily against her mount as Trevor dressed and led his horse over to Laura. "Do you need help getting on your horse?"

"Oh no, I can manage." Laura hoisted herself on her horse and she and Trevor made their way back toward camp.

The moon was bright, and Kat and Jack watched them go in silence until they completely disappeared into the night. Kat couldn't get to Jack fast enough. He took her into his arms and kissed her deeply. Their bodies touched lightly in the hot, steamy waters. It was a strange and wonderful feeling. The night was still and the moonlight was magical. They explored each other's bodies in the steaming water until they could stand it no longer. Jack was sitting on a flat rock with his back against the side of the pool. He pulled Kat onto his lap in the water and slowly entered her. She moaned with pleasure. Kat knew she would never forget this night and the special lovemaking she shared with Jack. They took their time, enjoying each other. Several times during their rhythmic movements they stopped kissing to look deeply into each other's eyes. Seeing her eyes darken with passion was incredibly arousing to him. He pressed deeply into her and took her to even greater heights of passion. She clenched him tightly at the moment of their release.

They both knew they had shared something very special.

CHAPTER 19

The air was much cooler the next morning. "Is it my imagination or did fall arrive while we slept?" Trevor spoke first. The group was relaxed from the night before and the cool morning air was invigorating. They were now a smooth operation, each falling into their tasks like clockwork. They ate, packed, and were on the trail shortly after sunrise. As they rode past the hot spring on the first leg of the journey, each enjoyed their memories of the night before.

Rolling hills, green grass, and tall pines made up the scenery for most of the day. Off in the distance they saw a cougar. He had no interest in confronting the group. Instead, he looked at them for a few moments before turning and bounding off. They'd gone weeks without seeing other human beings except for the occasional curious Indian. Off in the distance, Kat could see great mountains. "Jack, are those the Rocky Mountains?"

"Yes, they are. Do you realize we may be the first white people to travel over this land? Lewis and Clark were here, but I doubt they were in this particular spot. It's rumored there are a few mountain men around here. Men that live by themselves, trap fur, and live off the land. They say they look like bears, all dressed in furs and with great long beards."

"Really?" Laura asked in wonder. "Are they dangerous?"

Trevor answered, "Oh, I don't think so, but if you see one I wouldn't just run up and introduce yourself. Living alone like that can make a man's mind change. Look at how strange Kat's become since she's left civilization."

"I didn't know her before so I just assumed she had always been strange," Laura piped in.

They all laughed.

"I hope you are all enjoying laughing at my expense," Kat remarked, glad to see the walls coming down between Laura and Trevor. A few days ago Laura wouldn't have even talked around him.

In the late afternoon, the four riders came to the crest of a hill. They all stopped abruptly as if they ran into a wall. Jack froze. Trevor stood there agape. Laura gasped and Kat whispered, "Oh, my God."

Kat continued, "Jack, this has to be it. Is this it?"

Jack lips curled slowly into a smile. "Yes, this is definitely it." He couldn't even bring himself to take his eyes off the valley before him. He didn't blink for fear it would disappear.

"It's perfect," Laura said.

"Perfect," Trevor agreed.

The valley had it all. To the north were great hills covered with rocks, grass, and pines. On the far west side was a small river that flowed south and eventually curved back toward the east end of the valley. In the middle was a great stretch of rolling pasture. Jack could already see the perfect spot for the homestead, toward the base of the great hills. It would provide protection from the winters yet set them up high enough to survey their land and the cattle he one day dreamed of raising. The woods would provide all the lumber and the hunting they would ever need and the river would provide their water. A small creek ran past the area where Jack wanted to build the house; it would be quite useful, he felt. It was perfect.

"Come on," Jack said as he urged Bullet onward. He had to get a closer look at the spot where the cabin would go. Each person in the party felt as though they were riding into a fairyland. It was so beautiful and seemed to be made just for them. When they reached the spot, Jack pulled Bullet to a stop. He dismounted and turned to the others. "This is where the house goes." They all nodded their heads in silent agreement. The view over the valley was spectacular and the great hills seemed to provide a protective wall.

From that day forward their mission changed. They had finally arrived. Trevor and Jack busied themselves with plans for the cabin while Laura and Kat provided their day-to-day needs. After Jack and Trevor surveyed the wilderness in all directions, they deemed it a safe place for Laura and Kat to hunt. Kat thought it was sweet how Jack wanted to protect her. She didn't think it was necessary, but nonetheless it made her feel special. What a feeling it was to be home, to find a place they could call their own. Kat knew she and Jack would need to have a talk with Trevor and Laura. They needed to tell them how they were in love and would be sharing a room in their new cabin.

"What are you smiling about?" Laura asked Kat as they headed out to do some hunting and exploring.

"I was just thinking about how happy I am. Can you believe it, Laura? We've found home. I feel like I've left the bad part of my life behind."

"It is amazing," Laura said. "I find myself grinning for no particular reason."

Kat was so glad to hear that. She worried about Laura's happiness. For Laura, it could be a life of isolation. Kat had Jack and that would always be enough for her, and she also had her stepbrother, Trevor. Right now it was exciting and new, but would Laura grow tired of such a secluded life?

Hunting was easy in this land. The game was plentiful. Kat and Laura never had to travel very far to find a meal.

Jack and Trevor worked hard. They began by cutting the tall pines and stripping them of branches and bark. The long logs would be their walls. The wood they didn't use became their woodpile for the winter. Kat and Laura helped when they could. During their breaks, Jack sketched out plans for the cabin's layout. He was also designing the stables. For now, neither structure needed to be too complicated, but it wouldn't be long before he needed to expand. In fact, Jack envisioned several expansions, and he needed to think of those things even as he began with the first phase of the home. Between the tools Trevor and Kat had either brought or stolen they had what was necessary to put up a simple cabin. Both carried an ax and Kat brought a sturdy saw. Kat had knives and Trevor had a shovel. Jack and Laura had left so suddenly, neither one came overly prepared for cabin building. Jack's hope was that the tools would not break before the initial cabin was finished.

The time was approaching when Jack would need to include Trevor in his plans. He was already asking about it. Jack pulled Kat aside and told her they needed to tell the others, or at least Trevor for now. Kat thought it was best if Jack told him. She wanted to be nearby, though, in the event Trevor did something stupid.

That evening, Jack and Trevor walked a short distance from camp. Laura had her back to them, but Kat had a full view of the two men. She could see that Jack was doing the talking, but they were too far away for her to discern Trevor's reaction. Kat realized she was holding her breath. Finally, she saw Trevor extend his hand and pat Jack on the shoulder. Kat was relieved. She honestly didn't know how Trevor would react. It could have gone either way. One down and one to go, she figured. The two men continued to talk for some time before heading back to finish the evening chores.

Just after dark, Jack asked Kat to help him with the horses. Kat gladly followed him. She was anxious to find out what Trevor had said. Jack had told him he was completely in love with Kat and planned to legally marry her if a man of the cloth or a judge ever came by. Until then, he considered himself married to her and would remain that way until the day he died. He also admitted to Trevor that it had been going on for quite some time, but out of respect for Laura and him they had decided to keep it quiet. "Trevor shook his head and then shook my hand. He said he had known it for a while now. Can you believe it? I thought we were being so careful. Anyway, he is very happy for us and gave us his blessing."

"Oh, Jack. I can't even tell you how relieved I am. It feels so good to have it out in the open," Kat said as she hugged him tightly.

"Well, not so fast," Jack said putting a halt to Kat's newfound feeling of freedom. "Trevor didn't think it was a good idea to tell Laura just yet. She's still somewhat skittish around him, and to learn about us might just put her relationship with Trevor back to square one."

In a way Kat was relieved. She feared the same reaction from Laura. Still, it would have been nice to have a completely open relationship with Jack, but she found it strangely exciting to sneak around. She mentioned this to Jack. He smiled and kissed her sweetly. He knew what she meant. They continued kissing for a while but knew they needed to stop. They were only a short distance away from the campfire, where Laura and Trevor sat. If either one decided to look their way they would have to wonder why they were standing so close to each other behind Bullet. Bullet began to nip at Jack's arm, interrupting his moment with Kat. "Why does he do that? Every time we are kissing or touching, Bullet does something to stop us. Do you think he's trying to protect me from you?" Kat asked.

"No. I think he's being selfish. If he's not getting any loving then he doesn't want me to. He's tired of me keeping him away from the love of his life, Ginger."

"I can't blame him," Kat said. "I know how hard it is to have temptation in front of you every moment of the day and not be able to act on it."

So, it went on as the three had decided. Kat, Jack, and Trevor now waited for the right moment to tell Laura. They would either wait for the perfect moment or until Laura was completely at ease and accepting of Trevor. Laura maintained a good poker face in the presence of Trevor. It was hard for any of them to read her. Trevor made a great effort to get into Laura's good graces, but there was only so much time in the day. Trevor and Jack were very busy with their projects and Kat and Laura kept busy, too. It certainly didn't leave much time for socializing.

The weeks wore on, and Kat and Laura used their hunting trips to explore the woods more deeply. Jack rode out a few times on his own and had even made contact with a nearby Indian tribe. Kat and Laura were frightened at first but felt better as Jack spoke about his encounters. Jack said they appeared to be a peaceful tribe and not bothered by their presence. They had a hard time communicating because neither spoke the other's language. Eventually they communicated via drawings in the dirt and signing. Jack learned that one member of the tribe could speak some English, but he was gone on a hunting trip.

They told Jack there was a white man's fort about a two-week's ride south of where they had settled. It was a stop on the Oregon Trail for settlers to resupply. The army kept it stocked. Jack got the impression the Indians didn't think much of the army. Communication about the upcoming winter and animals was exchanged. The Indians told Jack snow could come tomorrow or not for a couple months. It was not predictable. That worried Jack. He needed to get the cabin up. Members of the tribe had obviously been watching, because they asked about the brown-haired and black-haired girl and about the other man. Because Jack felt it was safer to say so, he told the Indians Laura and Kat were their wives.

Laura rolled her eyes.

"What else did he say?" Kat was very interested now.

Jack got into the story now that he had their attention. "He said *beware* of the ghost of the crazy mountain man. After midnight, he comes out of the mountains and steals beautiful women."

"Oh, Jack." Kat slapped his arm. "Stop trying to scare us."

"Maybe he didn't say that, but he did talk about the wildlife around here. He mentioned big bears and cats and he drew a picture of a huge cow or deer or something like that. It had funny flat antlers, or horns, and he had a name for it that I can't remember."

"Are you going to talk with them again?" Laura asked.

"I'm sure we will. We just kind of ran out of things to say this time and he and his men turned around and left. It was strange, but it must be their way."

Kat wanted to see an Indian up close. From a distance she had seen them from time to time. She thought they looked magnificent from afar and thought she'd be even more impressed if she could get a good look. They stood so straight and tall and had a mystical presence. They seemed to appear out of nowhere and then disappear again.

It wasn't long before Kat got her wish. She and Laura had ventured out on foot. It was a beautiful fall day. The air was still and crisp. The dry late-fall veg-etation rustled beneath their feet. There was only one problem. They had let down their guard. Kat and Laura entered the clearing without even pausing to look and listen first. The mighty roar snapped them out of their daydreams. It was a sight like Kat had never seen. The creature was on its back haunches and stood over twelve feet tall. An Indian boy stood frozen in front of the great bear. Kat and Laura witnessed the horrible act of the giant bear's arm swoop-ing down, connecting with the Indian's shoulder, and sending him through the air. He landed hard some distance from the bear.

Kat froze and remembered Jack's words. *Don't run.* She had already dis-missed the advice Jack had given her *to* run if she saw an Indian. Besides, the Indian was in no condition to pose a threat to Kat and Laura. The bear was another matter. Kat and Laura were just yards away from the creature. For now, however, the bear's fury was still directed at the Indian boy. Kat and Laura had the same idea. They pulled their guns, took aim, and shot the bear. Kat's bullet hit his throat and Laura's glided between its ribs and through the bear's heart. He took several steps on his hind feet and then went down like a fallen tree. His head bounced off the ground just a few yards from Kat and Laura.

The girls paused for a moment and looked around. They weren't sure if bears traveled alone or with friends. This one seemed to be alone. As if they both remembered at the same time, Kat and Laura turned their attention to the fallen Indian. In seconds they were at the boy's side. He was moaning and possibly in a state of shock, but he was conscious and alive. Laura's instincts kicked in and she immediately went to work examining his wounds.

"I think his arm's broken, maybe some ribs, and he's pretty torn up—but first we have to stop the bleeding." As Kat listened to Laura's diagnosis, she felt sick. She had skinned animals before, but seeing another human's flesh opened up like this was too much for her to take. He had been mauled, and with only one swipe of the bear's massive paw. She found herself shaking. Laura looked up at her and ordered her to get the cloth from her saddlebag.

Kat obeyed and returned with the cloth. Laura spoke soothing words to the Indian boy as she applied pressure to his gushing wounds. He yelped in pain and then passed out. "It's better this way," Laura commented as she worked. "Now we don't have to worry about him resisting." Laura moved his arm around now that the boy was no longer conscious.

About that time, three Indians on horseback bolted into the clearing and headed for the boy. The one Indian seemed quite upset and jumped off his horse before it even came to a stop. Kat took a few steps backward and considered Jack's advice to run. Her gut told her to stay.

Laura completely ignored the other Indians and continued to work on the boy's arm. Even in all the confusion, the three Indians seemed to sense Laura was attempting to save the boy's life. So they just let her work. She wrapped the arm she had reset as best she could and applied direct pressure to try to stop the bleeding. She enlisted Kat's help to work on another gaping wound on his chest. Kat did as she was told.

The blood was beginning to clot just as the rain began to fall. "We've got to get him out of the rain and keep his body temperature up. Let's take him back to the camp," Laura instructed.

They laid a blanket on the ground and placed the boy in the center. Kat and Laura picked up either side; it was then that the others helped. The Indian men stepped in and took the handles of the blanket from the girls. Although the ground was uneven, the Indians moved with ease and quickly made their way in silence to camp. Because of the seriousness of the situation, the girls forgot to be afraid of the Indians.

Camp now consisted of a large two-roomed lean-to. It wasn't much, but it would shelter them until the cabin was done. It hadn't rained until today and luckily the roof didn't leak.

Kat and Laura placed the boy on a soft animal hide. Laura checked his dressings and felt the boy's head. He was pale and cold and still unconscious.

"Kat, start a fire and get more blankets. We have to keep him warm," Laura ordered.

Kat did as she was told and leaned over Laura. "What else can I do to help?"

"Put pressure here, and here." Laura said. "I don't know if he'll make it, but we are going to keep trying."

"Laura," Kat said in a low tone, "these Indians look really mad. If this boy dies, I think we may be in trouble."

"I'm not looking at them; we have to be concerned about this boy first. Where the hell are Jack and Trevor anyway?" Laura said without taking her eyes off the boy.

"That's a good question. We could really use their support now," Kat muttered back.

Kat and Laura worked on the boy for over an hour, applying pressure to stop the bleeding and positioning him so blood would flow away from the wounds and back toward his heart. They also wrapped him in blankets and kept the fire stoked to keep him warm. Laura had Kat elevate his feet. Kat didn't know why Laura was asking her to do these things. Kat made the decision to have Laura teach her about her medical techniques; they could come in handy out here, Kat figured.

The three Indians didn't talk to the girls, but they did talk to one another. Kat glanced up at the Indians. One had left. Kat and Laura did not even know when he had gone.

"Hmm," Kat said to Laura, "now there are only two of them. One left without so much as a goodbye."

"Maybe he went out to whoop it up with Trevor and Jack," Laura added.

"I don't think they're into fun," Kat retorted. "I've never seen anyone look so expressionless. I'm going to name him, *Haven't Had a Good Laugh in Years*.

"And I'm going to name the other one, *Twin of Haven't Had a Good Laugh in Years*." Laura joined in.

Just then Trevor, Jack, the missing Indian, and an old Indian woman rode into camp. They all dismounted and the old Indian woman immediately went to work. She opened a leather pouch containing different herbs, mixed them in water, and then held them over the fire.

Trevor and Jack went quickly to Laura and Kat's side. "What happened?" Jack asked.

Laura and Kat told them the story.

"Is he going to live?" Trevor asked Laura.

"I don't know," Laura answered. "I reset his arm and the bleeding has slowed considerably. He's lost a lot of blood and there is a very good chance of infection. I'm sure the bear didn't wash his hands and clean his nails before he sliced him open. I'm hoping she's brewing up some kind of disinfectant," Laura said as she tossed her head in the direction of the old Indian woman.

"How have these fellows been behaving?" Trevor asked, referring to the Indians.

"Pretty much like they are now," Kat answered. "They've been watching and not saying much. We're thinking they're going to kill us if this boy dies."

"They aren't going to kill us," Jack reassured Kat. He put a hand on Kat's shoulder and said, "I'm sorry we weren't here for you two. I hope this hasn't been too frightening."

"An encounter with the biggest animal I've ever seen, a poor boy maimed and clinging to life, and some angry-looking Indians who may want to kill us.

It's been a piece of cake." Laura was obviously more upset than Kat had realized.

Kat looked up at Trevor and Jack and lifted her brow. The boy was definitely not out of the woods yet, which was upsetting Laura. She was determined to keep him alive.

The old Indian woman edged in past Laura and put the herb-soaked cloth on the boy's wounds. It smelled horrible. Laura watched with great interest. The old woman could tell Laura was interested and showed her what she was doing.

Jack and Trevor had gone off to talk to the Indians. It seemed to Kat like a normal exchange. Maybe they weren't going to kill them after all.

The boy began to stir. He moaned, and the old woman talked soothingly to him. He was in some pain, but not as much as Kat and Laura would have suspected. It must have had something to do with the medicine the old Indian woman used. Still, he looked pale, and it would take some time for him to recover if he didn't die of infection.

Night was falling. Kat brought out food and made some broth in case the boy was able to eat. He wasn't but did manage to drink some water.

"I wonder what his name is," Laura said to Kat.

"His name is Tucam." Kat and Laura jerked their heads up in surprise at the Indian who spoke. "He is son of *Twin of Haven't Had a Good Laugh in Years*."

They were embarrassed but also intrigued. "You speak English?" Kat asked the Indian.

"Yes, I learned from a trapper. He lives in those mountains. It is helpful to know what the white man is saying."

"I bet it is," Laura said. "So, does anyone else speak English?"

"No."

That was a relief. They had only offended him, although he didn't seem very offended.

Jack walked back into the shelter to check on the boy. "Jack, he understands English," Kat warned him.

"Yes, I know. We have spoken before. It's been a big help."

Kat looked at him impatiently. "It would have been a big help if you'd told us."

Laura turned to the one who could speak English. "I've done all I can for him. His bleeding has stopped, which is very good. I'm hoping what she put on him will help prevent an infection. That's the biggest danger now, that and fever. I wouldn't recommend we move him until he's better."

"He shall stay here and she will stay with you." He was referring to the old woman. It didn't seem to bother her to stay with them, and Laura was glad for the help. Plus, the old woman seemed to know a few helpful tricks.

Kat walked away. She wanted to stretch her legs and take a break. It had been a harrowing day. She sat on a rock some distance from the campfire. The cool air helped to clear her head. Jack followed her out there and asked her to take a walk with him. After they were safely out of sight from the others, Jack grabbed Kat and held her tightly. "Oh, honey, I'm sorry you went through that alone. I was so frightened when I saw you with them."

"Really, you didn't seem frightened," Kat replied. She was a bit surprised by his reaction.

"If you could have felt my heart pounding in my chest you would have known. I wonder if this was a good idea, bringing you and Laura so deep into the wilderness. What if something happens to Trevor and me? You two would be left alone. I couldn't bear the thought of something happening to you."

Kat was deeply touched and wanted to reassure him. "Laura and I can take care of ourselves. Look at what we did today. We killed a bear, saved a wounded boy, and met our neighbors. I think we'd do just fine, not that we ever need to worry about something happening to you and Trevor." Kat imagined something happening to Jack and she didn't like the feeling it gave her. She thought about the boy and how he hadn't planned to get in a fight with that bear today. His family must be so worried about him.

"We need to have a backup plan. A plan you and Laura must carry out if something happens to Trevor or me. I don't want you two out here alone."

"Jack, I don't like the way you're talking. Nothing is going to happen." Kat smiled up at him.

Jack realized how much in love he must have been if he was that concerned. He didn't know what he'd do if he ever lost her, and the thought of her being out here alone scared the hell out of him.

He smiled down at her, appreciating her positive yet naïve outlook. He kissed her and held her close. "I need to get you alone again," he whispered. Because of their hard work schedule and their effort to keep their relationship a secret, they hadn't had much alone time.

Back at the shelter, the boy rested peacefully. There was nothing else to do for him now. Either he would heal or he would die. The boy's father stared for a moment at Laura and then turned to the Indian who spoke English and said something to him. "We will be back tomorrow," the English-speaking Indian said to Laura—and with that, they were gone.

Trevor watched from the shadows as the old Indian woman put a hand on Laura's arm and motioned for her to go to sleep. He saw Laura smile at her. Even from this distance, Trevor thought Laura looked incredibly tired. She rose with some difficulty and walked slowly away from the shelter. Trevor grabbed her arm out of the darkness. She gasped.

"I'm sorry. I didn't mean to frighten you. I just wanted to tell you what a great job you did today. You saved his life. The Indians were impressed, too," Trevor told her. He had been more than impressed as he watched Laura work with confidence throughout the day. She had been bent over the boy taking care of him for hours. Trevor put his hands on her shoulders and began massaging her tight muscles. He knew it was a risky move. Laura looked annoyed at first, but she didn't ask him to stop. In an effort to take the edge off and make his touch less personal, Trevor added, "Your muscles are in danger of seizing up. I'm no doctor—" he smiled, "—but if you let this go you're going to have back pains and headaches, and then you won't be good to any of us. Come over here and lie down by the fire," Trevor commanded. To his surprise, she obeyed. Trevor continued to rub and massage her aching muscles, and in no time she was fast asleep. He looked at her and realized how much he wanted her. He was trying so hard to be careful around her. He knew he had made some headway. Still, she was so resistant. What was it she had said? "*When hell freezes over.*" That was it. Trevor didn't hold out hope she would ever come to feel about him as he did about her. She simply tolerated him because she had no choice. For now, that was better than outright hatred.

The old woman boiled more herbs and administered them to the Indian boy. How fortunate he was that the two brave girls had entered the clearing when they did. They were an interesting tribe, the old woman thought. The two girls were so beautiful and the men cared for them deeply—she could see that without understanding their words. The brown-haired girl seemed to know much about taking care of injuries. She looked forward to learning more from her in the days to come.

The old woman shook her head as she thought back to the bear lying dead in the clearing. It was the biggest grizzly she had seen in her lifetime. Her people had called him Evil One. He had no fear of people and had often wandered close to campsites. Evil One was even thought to stalk men. He had killed an Indian Brave about this time last year and had almost killed another today. She thought these two white girls had been sent from the Great Spirit to rid their land of this evil. Their people had performed many ceremonies asking the Great Spirit to help, and he had. It was a great day.

In the middle of the night, the brown-haired girl brought her a cup of water and some food. They both looked at the boy. He was resting, and the bleeding had not started up again. The brown-haired girl was pleased as she felt his forehead; he was not running a fever. The herbs had done the trick so far. She nodded knowingly and looked forward to sharing what she knew with this young girl some day. The old woman was tired and gratefully took the blankets that were offered to her. It was her turn to rest.

The next day was a warm, dry fall day. The old woman was at the boy's side. She chanted her prayers and administered her medicine as the brown-haired girl watched with curiosity. It was late morning when the boy opened his eyes. He was weak but alive. She spoke to him in the language of their people and he was able to mutter a few words back. She smiled broadly. He was a special boy in their tribe and he deserved to live. She had lived for a long time and knew when one of her people would grow into greatness. Tucam was definitely one of those braves.

Tucam gave her a weak smile and she squeezed his good arm. He wasn't sure where he was or exactly what had happened to him. As he forced his mind back in time, he began to recall walking through the clearing and suddenly seeing the bear. He could still see it rising in front of him. That was all he remembered. The boy looked at the old woman. Had she said it was the white women who killed Evil One? The boy looked at the brown-haired woman with amazement. He had never seen a white woman before and thought she was a spirit sent to save him. His people had often talked about the Evil One. The Great Spirit worked in mysterious ways. He never would have guessed a white woman would be the one to rid them of this giant evil.

Tucam also knew he would live and that his purpose in life must be important if the Great Spirit chose him to be a part of this. He wasn't sure what it would be, but he figured it must have to do with these white people. The boy could no longer keep his eyes open. He was still so weak. As he slipped into unconsciousness he thanked the Great Spirit for saving him and promised to commit himself to his greater plan, whatever it might be.

CHAPTER 20

Over the next few days, Jack and Trevor worked long hours on the cabin. Kat loved seeing it go up while Laura practically didn't even notice. She was too busy tending to Tucam. He was an interesting boy. Laura guessed his age to be around fourteen. She talked to him continually although she knew he didn't understand. He mostly just stared at her.

By the third day he was able to get up and walk around. Each day the Indians came to visit. They always brought food and gifts. The girls found it very interesting. The Indian men spoke with Trevor and Jack but not to Kat and Laura. They often looked at them, however. Jack showed them the cabin and the Indians looked at it with great interest, nodding their heads as they touched the walls. The girls found it amusing when the Indians stuck their heads up the fireplace.

Finally, the day came when the old woman and Laura decided Tucam could go home. His wounds were healing nicely, he had no fever or signs of infection, and he had regained some strength. He even learned some English. Laura was amazed how quickly he learned. When the Indians arrived to take him home, Tucam's father and another Indian approached Kat and Laura. They dismounted and walked over to the packhorse they were leading. Kat and Laura were astonished as the two Indians brought the great bear skin rug with the head still attached and laid it at their feet.

Jack said to Kat and Laura, "It appears they are presenting you with a gift. It is customary to say thank you rather than stand there with your mouths open."

Kat and Laura thanked them in unison. The rug was enormous and they had worked hard to prepare it for the girls. A huge bag of dried bear meat was handed to Jack, "This should get us through the winter," Jack commented as he also thanked the Indians.

"I've never had bear meat," Kat said in astonishment, "or a bearskin rug, for that matter."

It was obvious to the four that Kat and Laura's actions had endeared them to the neighboring tribe. Jack no longer worried about Kat or Laura being left to fend for themselves if something happened to him or Trevor. They watched the Indians ride off, knowing they would see them again often.

"One more night under the stars, because tomorrow we move into our cabin," Jack announced.

"What?" Laura was shocked. "We get to move in tomorrow?"

"That's right," Trevor added. "You've been so occupied doctoring that you haven't seen your home going up right before your eyes."

Kat was concerned. She could no longer put off telling Laura about her relationship with Jack. She knew by the look Jack threw her that he was thinking the same thing.

"I'm going to the stream to wash up. Then I want a tour through my new home," Laura announced proudly.

Kat knew this was her opportunity. She got up and followed Laura to the stream.

"Are you as excited as I am?" Kat asked Laura.

"That's putting it mildly," Laura said with exasperation. "I'm used to being pampered, and look how I've had to rough it over the past months. No, really, I have enjoyed life in the great outdoors, but I am definitely ready to have a home. I was shocked to find out we were moving in tomorrow. I'm walking on air!"

Kat was even more nervous to tell her now. "Laura, I have some news you probably won't like." Laura spun toward her with a look that said, *Don't burst my bubble now.* It didn't help Kat open up.

"Promise you won't be mad at me," Kat began.

Laura replied, "Then don't say anything to make me mad."

Kat swallowed hard. "Laura, I began this whole trip without a plan. I was just running. Running from my past. Running from what I had done, and things just kind of fell into place for me. I got the posse off my tail. Trevor is with us now and our relationship is better than ever." Kat glanced up, but there was no change in Laura's expression. She continued, "I met you, which has meant so much to me. I've never had a female friend and didn't know what I was missing. Nothing made me happier than the day you told me you wanted to stay and build a place with us. But, Laura, I've been keeping something from you, out of selfishness, really. Because I want you to stay in this cabin and build a life here. Okay, here goes…" Kat looked up at Laura again. Her eyes had narrowed as she listened to what Kat had to say. This was going worse than Kat could have ever imagined, but she had to get it over with. She shut her eyes and spewed the words out. "Jack and I are in love. We are going to get married as soon as possible. Until then, he and I will share a room in the cabin and you will have a separate room on the opposite side. So will Trevor." Kat opened her eyes and looked at Laura. "Please don't leave us. I would just die out here without you, but I'll understand if you want to."

Laura just stood there looking at her in total silence. Her expression didn't change as Kat made her confession. Finally, she threw her head back in exasperation. "Kat!"

Kat's heart was beating hard. She was quickly formulating reasons for her to stay.

"What were you thinking? Oh, my God, I can't believe you've kept it in that long. For crying out loud, I've known for months! That was what you had to tell me? That was the big thing you were so worried about?" Laura laughed at her now. "You mean to tell me you thought it wasn't obvious to me? The way you two look at each other, the way you speak to each other. How you sneak off together. Of course I knew!"

Kat was shocked and relieved. Mostly shocked. She thought she had been so careful. Laura was very intuitive. Or maybe they hadn't been as tricky as she thought. Either way, it was a big relief to Kat. "Oh, Laura." She threw her arms around her. "So, you're not going to leave?"

"Hell, no," Laura replied with a giggle. "You're not getting rid of me that easily. And from now on, no more secrets between us."

"You're so right. I was just terrified you'd leave. I handled it all wrong. Thanks for not being mad," Kat said.

The girls headed back to the cabin arm in arm. Jack and Trevor saw the two approaching. Jack said out of the corner of his mouth to Trevor, "Looks like it went well."

As Kat and Laura walked past the two men, Kat said to Jack with a smile, "She knew all along."

Jack was speechless. How did women always know those things?

They were all in great spirits as they ate their evening meal. They joked and laughed and talked about their new home. Back East, people would think it strange for four unmarried, mostly unrelated people to live in the same home.

That's what was great about being out here. They were free to do what made sense without social standards interfering. One cabin to heat, cook in, clean, and sleep in—it was the only option that made sense right now.

Jack and Trevor sat whittling branches that would eventually become chair legs. The first priority was to get the cabin up. The second was the stable. Furniture was really the last priority, but since it was dark they couldn't do anything else.

Kat and Laura were busy sewing together coats from buffalo hides by the light of the campfire. The coats were very heavy but would be much needed once winter hit. Because they needed the biggest pieces of hide for Trevor and Jack, they made their coats first. The hides had been a gift from the Indians and they had suggested making coats as soon as possible. Kat and Laura didn't have coats yet, but they did have boots.

The Indian women had come by one day and measured their feet. Laura and Kat thought it was very strange, until they returned with beautiful, warm doe-skinned boots that went all the way up to their knees. They'd also presented both girls with a pair of rabbit-fur-lined slippers to wear inside the cabin. Kat had never felt anything so soft in all her life. The girls treasured the gifts and wished they had something to give back to the Indians.

This particular evening, Jack and Kat were not very productive with their projects. They kept stealing glances across the campfire.

Trevor and Laura didn't even notice. Laura was intent on her sewing and Trevor was too busy looking at Laura. Finally, Laura looked up and announced she was too tired to sew even one more stitch. "I'm going to sleep."

"That's a good idea. Tomorrow's a big day. We don't want anyone tired or grumpy when we move into our new home," Jack said as he rolled out his bed-roll.

In minutes they were all tucked in and ready for a good night's sleep. Kat and Jack lay there wide-eyed until they heard Laura's breathing fall into a slow, steady rhythm. Trevor hadn't moved in a long time either. Jack carefully got up and walked over to Kat. He smiled when he saw she was wide-awake and smiling back at him. She carefully got up and they quietly walked toward the cabin, hand in hand.

Jack opened the door and led her in. The moonlight came through the window at the end of the cabin. The ceilings were high; Jack said after living out in the open so much he couldn't stand to have the ceiling too close to his head. The kitchen was in the back of the cabin and a large dining and living area was in the front. To the left was Kat and Jack's bedroom. It was long and had a high slanting ceiling. To the right were two bedrooms, Trevor's and Laura's. "So what do you think of your new home, Kat?"

"It's far beyond my expectations. It looks so solid and warm." Kat turned to the fireplace and the enormous hearth. "This is my favorite part. I've never seen such a beautiful fireplace."

"There are so many things you won't have for a while, Kat. A nice bed, for one thing, real bedding, plates, pots, and pans. We'll be roughing it for a while," Jack said.

"Jack," Kat said to him softly. "We've always roughed it. This is no different for me. But it's a home. That's all we need right now. The rest will come eventually. Especially if we keep on the good side of the Indians."

Jack smiled and brought her close to him. "Are you glad Laura knows about us?"

"I'm so relieved. I never realized how much it was weighing on me." Kat said as she snuggled closer.

Jack's face was just inches from Kat's. He looked into her beautiful green eyes and still couldn't believe she was his. He couldn't imagine ever getting tired of looking at her. His fingers traced along her cheek and across her lips. Without consciously thinking about it, Jack found himself kissing her, softly and sweetly at first, then with more passion. They found themselves on the bearskin rug. Kat found it very erotic as Jack used his teeth to pull her shirt open. He looked into her eyes with an animal passion as he slowly removed her clothes. Kat thought he was wildly handsome and the act drove her crazy. He knew just how to touch her. Although it was mid-October and they were both naked now, neither was the least bit cold. He kissed her, everywhere, and she was now wild with passion. Kat flipped him over and Jack pulled her on top of him. Kat so enjoyed the feeling of their naked bodies touching as they passionately kissed. Kat teased him with her movements until he could stand it no longer. He grabbed her hips and plunged into her. She threw her head back with a moan of pure pleasure. Jack thought he had never seen anything so beautiful as the moonlight reflected off her face and breasts. Her soft silky mane of hair shone as she tossed it down her back. To him she looked like a magical creature. They made love for hours. That night in the cabin symbolized the start of their lives together. They fell asleep exhausted in each other's arms, yet woke twice during the night for more lovemaking.

The next morning Kat was embarrassed as she heard Trevor knocking on the door. They had both slept late. "Do you two plan on helping us or are you catching up on lost sleep?"

Kat was horrified.

Jack just smiled. "We'll be right out," Jack hollered to Trevor. "Don't worry, I pulled the lock latch through," he whispered to Kat as he saw her startled expression. When she relaxed, Jack began passionately kissing her again.

Kat and Laura spent the morning putting their few belongings into the house. They had some pans, a skillet, utensils, clothes, knives, plates, and a mirror. Kat proudly hung the animal skins on the wall. She had collected several by now, and they would help to insulate the walls when the winter winds came.

Jack and Trevor began work on the stable. The animals would need shelter, too. Whenever Laura and Kat could, they helped. Some of the lifting was too physically demanding for the girls, but the extra hands to hold things in place sure helped. It was truly a labor of love. The work was hard, but Kat thoroughly enjoyed it. It was their place, and she was around people she loved. She hadn't had such feelings in her life since before her mother died. Kat believed she was the luckiest of them all. She had a husband. The thought made her smile. She had a best friend in Laura and a real brother in Trevor as well.

Kat frowned as she thought of Laura. Poor Laura—at least she had Kat, but that was about it. For as much time as they all spent together, she was very good at avoiding Trevor. It became clear to Kat that she must get Trevor and Laura on better terms. Kat just didn't understand it. Trevor was always kind and polite and he was always so up beat. Negative, ornery people annoyed Kat. They always brought the mood down and made life miserable for other people. She thought of Mr. Dickerson from the wagon train. It must have been hell on earth to be married to him or have him as a father.

What was it that made Laura avoid Trevor? He always treated her with so much respect—he acknowledged how talented she was with her doctoring and was genuinely impressed with her newfound hunting and riding skills. Jack had probably had the right idea earlier when he forced them to spend time together by leaving them alone. After all, look what happened whenever she and Jack were alone. Kat giggled out loud without realizing it.

"What are you laughing at?" Laura asked.

"Oh, I was just thinking of Jack," Kat answered.

"I see," Laura said, and she smiled.

Laura was especially pretty when she smiled. It really made her eyes twinkle.

"I think we're going to be very happy together," Kat continued, unable to contain her happiness.

"You two are perfect for one another. You complement each other very well and I can tell he absolutely adores you. The way he looks at you when you're not looking. It's actually funny! I can't even imagine you two bickering," Laura said with a smile.

She could tell Laura had no ill feelings about their happiness. "What type of man do you want to marry someday?" Kat asked.

"Hmm." Laura put some real thought into it before answering Kat. "I want a man who is strong and hardworking, but much more than that. Let's see. He has to be happy and sweet. My man must respect me and support me, not try to keep me under his thumb. And he must be light-hearted. I don't tolerate grumpy people like Mr. Dickerson." Having finished her description, she went back to her work.

Kat just stood and looked at her. She couldn't believe her ears. That settled it. She had to get Trevor and Laura alone with each other.

The stable was progressing nicely. Jack and Trevor even built a snow fence connecting it to the house. Now if a winter storm hit, they could still get to the stable to care for the animals by following the fence. In the dark of night it would be easy to get lost in a blizzard on the way to the stable.

It took them seven days to finish the stable. Now that the walls were up they could take more time working on the inside. It was much larger than Kat had imagined it would be. Jack said they would need several horses, some mules, and some oxen to handle the ranch work he had in mind. He had wished they had the oxen as he built the house and stable.

Back in late September, they had spent several days gathering grass from the flat lands that would serve as food for the livestock during the winter. Kat thought it was overkill, but Jack wanted to be prepared. She had to appreciate that.

Her plans to get Trevor and Laura alone had to wait for now, as they were too busy finishing the stable. By nightfall they were all so exhausted no one had the time or the energy for the trickery Kat had in mind.

Finally, Kat saw her opportunity. The house and stable were finished. There was plenty of wood cut for the winter. The horses had all the hay they could dream of and Kat and Laura had plenty of skins for making rugs, wall covers, and warm winter clothes. Their home was like no other they had seen back home. The skins added a beautiful, warm touch.

"I've never worked so hard in all my life!" Jack exclaimed, finally able to catch his breath. "What do you say we take a little break and ride over to the hot spring this evening? My aching muscles deserve it."

"That's a great idea!" Laura replied. She had loved the hot spring and thought about it every day since.

Kat and Laura packed warm clothes and some food and they were off. The horses even seemed to know this was a special treat. They were high-spirited and playful the entire way there.

Kat and Jack let Laura and Trevor lead the way. They stayed back a bit in order to give them some alone time.

"So, would you ever have thought you would be here a year ago?" Trevor asked Laura. He looked straight ahead.

Laura looked at him. Had he read her mind? That was exactly what she was thinking. "Never in a million years." Laura forgot herself and continued speaking. "I thought I would finish school, continue to study medicine, and help my father until I got married. Then, of course, I would have to quit. I really liked helping my father with patients."

"Why would you quit?" Trevor asked.

"Because married women don't work like that," Laura answered. She couldn't believe he even had to ask, yet his question made sense.

"Well, I understand, sort of, but if you know how to help people and there are people who need help—" Trevor lifted his gaze and looked at her, "—why wouldn't you? Just because it's frowned upon? I say if you want to keep doctoring people, you should. You're the doctor in this group. None of us have that talent, so I say even if you get married ten times and have twenty kids you should keep doctoring!"

Laura raised her eyebrows. It made perfect sense to her. She was a bit ashamed of herself for spouting out something she didn't believe but only said because it's what others had always told her.

"So, you wouldn't be angry if you married a girl and she wanted to doctor or teach or work in the saloon?" Laura posed the challenge.

"Well, not work in the saloon, but any of those others, sure, if that made her happy. From what I've seen, if the woman of the house ain't happy, ain't nobody happy!"

That made Laura smile. It was so true. Conversation with Trevor was always interesting. Laura found she was letting her guard down and she chastised herself.

Trevor continued asking her questions and Laura quickly forgot her resolve to put up her guard. He asked her about resetting Tucam's arm. What happens if you don't? Why do injured people get fevers? Laura was happy to answer his questions, and the best part about it was that Trevor truly was interested. Laura was a bit surprised when they rounded the bend and came upon the hot spring. Time had gone so fast talking to Trevor the entire way. Suddenly she remembered Kat and Jack. Laura turned back and there they were. She didn't even realize she hadn't spoken to them the entire way. Laura saw they were engrossed with one another and probably weren't even aware of them.

The group dismounted and followed the same routine as last time. Jack and Trevor undressed, to their underwear this time, and slipped into the warm, therapeutic waters. They turned their backs while the girls did the same. Kat snuggled up to Jack. Laura smiled to see her friends so happy. However, at that moment she also felt a little lonely. What would it be like to have a man wrap his arms around her like Jack did with Kat?

"Doesn't it feel good to be ready for winter?" Kat said as she leaned back against Jack.

"I wish we had a few more supplies," Jack said. "It would be nice to have some tea, sugar, flour, blankets, coffee, and canned food."

"Well, if we happen to come across a general store I'd also like some medicines, soap—some books would be nice—and cloth to make a fancy dress. Just in case I get invited to a ball." They all giggled lazily at Laura's order.

"Whoever goes to the store, bring me back a couple of oxen and mules so I don't have to break my back building the next addition to the house and stable," was Trevor's request.

"Kat, what would you want?" Jack asked.

"Nothing. I've got everything I need right here." Jack smiled at her statement. "Oh, I guess you could pick me up some candy," she added.

"Kat used to eat all the candy at Christmas time. She used to lick the candy sticks to a sharp point and threaten to stab the rest of us if we didn't give her some of ours. Most of the time it worked. I'm grateful just to be here today." Trevor's comment made them all laugh, even Laura.

"I'm very hot!" Kat announced suddenly. "I have to get out. Turn your heads."

"Kat, you don't want to leave yet do you?" Laura asked worriedly.

"Not just yet. I feel too woozy."

Jack looked at her with concern. "Kat, are you all right?"

"Just give me a minute." Kat rested her head in her hands as she sat on a rock by the waters edge. Suddenly she got up and staggered into the darkness. They could hear her as she vomited off in the distance.

Jack got out of the pool to go after her. She called from the darkness. "Uh, I'd rather you didn't come out here right now." Jack stopped in his tracks and turned to look back at Trevor and Laura. Laura was averting her eyes since Jack was only in his underwear. Jack didn't know what to do. He felt relieved as Kat reappeared in the clearing. She looked white as a ghost. "Whoa, I don't know where that came from," Kat said weakly.

"Are you still too hot?" Jack asked, afraid to touch her for fear she'd break.

"No, actually, now I'm really cold."

The night air was cold and Kat was soaking wet from head to toe.

Jack ran to her with a blanket. He held it up to shield her from the others. "Here, get out of those wet things and wrap up in this blanket." She was visibly shaking now. Kat did as she was told.

Laura got out of the pool, not seeming to care that she was only wearing her underwear. She grabbed Kat's dry clothes and brought them to her. Laura helped her quickly dress and then wrapped the blanket around her. Jack didn't even notice Laura's near nakedness. He was so concerned about Kat's sudden sickness.

Trevor, on the other hand, did notice. He stayed in the water and didn't even attempt to avert his eyes. Every inch of her underwear clung to the curves of her body and she looked absolutely beautiful. The moonlight added to the effect and almost made her garment appear more sheer. He hadn't noticed how tiny her waist was and what a flat little tummy she had. Trevor longed to span her waist with his hands. She had her back to him now and Trevor didn't hesitate to gaze at her shapely bottom. He couldn't believe his luck as Laura stood and turned his direction as she searched for Kat's missing boot. Laura's clinging garment accentuated the round swells of her beautiful breasts and the sheerness revealed her dark round nibbles. It was a good thing no one needed his help at this point because he would have been useless.

Kat sat down on a rock and Laura rubbed her arms in an effort to warm her up. "I'm feeling much better now. I'm just very tired."

"We'd better go back, Kat. You might have the flu and could have another bout of vomiting. A warm bed and some rest is what you need," Laura diagnosed.

"I think I just got too hot, and I did eat a lot for supper."

"Eating a lot for supper isn't unusual," Jack commented, "but you may have gotten too hot."

"You all shouldn't have to leave because of me," Kat said.

Quickly, Jack offered an idea. "You two stay. I'll ride back with Kat. She's right. There's no reason we all need to leave."

"That's a great idea," Kat agreed immediately. Although she still felt a little sick, she hopped on Ginger. At the same time, Jack grabbed his things and jumped on Bullet and just like that, they were gone.

Laura couldn't believe how quickly they left. She stood there in the night looking after them until she suddenly remembered she was in her underwear. Her head whipped around to look at Trevor in the warm pool. He was looking up at the stars overhead. At least he had been a gentleman and hadn't snuck a peak, Laura thought. Feeling she had been left with no choice and because she was getting very cold, she slipped back into the hot water.

CHAPTER 21

Laura broke the silence. "I hope Kat's okay."

"Oh, I think she will be. She looked much better once she threw up and got her warm clothes on," Trevor offered. "Do you feel all right? You ate the same fish as Kat."

Laura was moved by his concern. "Yes, I feel great."

"Good. Look." Trevor pointed up at the sky. "There's the Big Dipper and The Little Dipper."

"What?" Laura asked, looking into the sky where Trevor pointed.

"The Big Dipper and the Little Dipper. They are constellations. See, those stars form the Big Dipper, and if you look off the point of the Big Dipper you can see the Little Dipper. Hasn't anyone shown you constellations before?"

No one ever had, and Laura found it very interesting. Trevor knew a few more and pointed them out to her. Laura loved to learn and she was fascinated by what Trevor had to tell her about the stars. He told her a few things he had learned about planets, the earth, and the sun.

"How do you know those things?" Laura asked.

I read a book about a man named Copernicus. He lived long ago in Europe and he had several theories about the universe and how it worked. The church persecuted him when he published his findings, so he withdrew his statements. People were very ignorant back then. They were very full of superstition and felt believing in science was going against God. I think it was a ploy to keep the parishioners believing anything the church told them so they wouldn't question their leaders. But the truth lives on, and so did his writings. He was ahead of his day and now, in these modern times, people are more accepting of his theories."

"What else did he say?" Laura asked hurriedly, as if she couldn't wait to find out.

"That's about as much as I remember. I didn't get very far into the book. My brother, Henry, decided it would be fun to pick on me for reading. He took my book and fed it to the hogs. I was really mad at him for that."

"I'm mad at him for that!" Laura said with a scowl. "I wanted you to tell me more about it."

"There's one more thing to add to the list. Next time we go to the store we'll get a book on Copernicus," Trevor joked.

That made Laura laugh, but she did think it would be wonderful. She would love to read all about this Copernicus fellow and his theories. She stared into the sky, looking at the stars, and for the first time in her life was truly curious about them.

"Oh, look!" Laura actually shouted as she pointed to the sky. "A shooting star!"

"I missed it," Trevor said.

Laura was still excited. "I saw one once when I was a little girl. I heard they bring good luck if you make a wish. Oh! Trevor, look! There's another one!" Laura could barely contain herself.

Trevor had seen that one.

"And another! Trevor, is the sky falling?" Laura thought it was incredible, but she was also a little scared.

"No," Trevor said softly with his eyes on the sky. "It's called a meteor shower. I read about them, but I never saw one before."

"What's causing this?" Laura asked.

"I don't remember why, but it's happened before. Laura, be sure to make some wishes. I think we are in for some good luck."

Laura just looked at the sky in disbelief. She was moved when Trevor used her name, but she didn't know why.

It lasted about half an hour. Just when they had forgotten the outside world existed, they heard it. It sounded like a woman's scream and it was just over their heads. The horses bolted as a cougar leaped off a rock ledge over their heads.

It seemed surreal to Laura as she saw the short chase. She lost sight of the animals in the darkness but heard the carnage.

Trevor leaped out of the pool, grabbed his rifle, and ran in the direction of the attack. He fired one shot into the air. The cougar ran off, but the damage was done. Trevor fired the gun once more.

Laura had scrambled out of the pool once Trevor disappeared into the darkness; she was confused as to what she should do. Where did the animal go? She wished she could see Trevor. Did he shoot the cougar? Laura headed toward the sounds of a screaming animal. She heard another shot, and the pained cries of the horse abruptly stopped. Suddenly, Trevor was in front of her. He grabbed her by the shoulder and turned her around, walking her back to the moonlit clearing.

"Laura, it was a cougar."

Laura nodded but was speechless. Trevor continued, "He got Lady and hurt her very badly. I had to shoot her. He ripped her up and broke her back."

Laura's eyes filled with tears.

"She didn't suffer long," Trevor said softly as he held her. He had longed to hold her in his arms, but certainly not under these circumstances. Laura had become attached to Lady and was devastated.

Trevor was thankful she didn't have to see what he saw.

"You really had to shoot her? There was no other choice?" Laura asked through her tears.

"There was no other choice," Trevor confirmed. "Let's get dressed and hope Rusty wanders back this way. Otherwise, it's going to be a long walk home."

As they finished dressing, Rusty returned. Trevor was relieved. He helped Laura up onto Rusty's back and leaped up behind her. Laura had stopped crying by now, but she was still sad. What a strange evening it had been. Trevor wanted to say something to console Laura, but he didn't know what. "I'm sorry, Laura. I know you were very fond of Lady."

Laura started sobbing and Trevor scolded himself for making her cry again. "I know it doesn't make you feel any better, but I'm thankful it was Lady and not you. That cougar was right over our heads and could have chosen us instead of Lady."

Trevor decided to talk about something else to get her mind off it. "So, are you worried about spending the winter out here in the wilderness?"

"No, I think we'll get by just fine," Laura said through a sniffle.

"I think we will, too. Jack's the worrier of the group. He always wishes we had this or that. I think he worries about you and Kat. If it were just him, I don't think he'd feel the need to prepare so much."

"I think you're right, but it's cute that he worries so much. Did you see his face when Kat ran into the woods tonight?" Laura chuckled. "He looked absolutely dumbstruck. He wanted to do something for her but, of course, when someone is spilling their guts like that there's not much you can do."

Trevor was having a hard time keeping his mind clear. Laura's back and bottom rubbing against him was more than he could bear. Only with great effort did he dismiss all the lustful thoughts running through his mind.

"I'd hold back your hair if you were puking," Trevor said, and then, feeling it was too mushy a statement, he added, "On second thought, that wouldn't work very well, because then I'd probably puke right on top of you. I was thankful you and Jack had your attention on Kat, because I was sitting there plugging my ears."

Laura turned to look at him and smiled, "I believe that."

Trevor looked down into her beautiful eyes. He longed to kiss her full pink lips, which were slightly parted and very inviting. Ever so slowly, Trevor lowered his mouth towards hers.

Suddenly, Laura whipped her head back around. It startled Trevor and disappointed him. What was even more disappointing was how Laura turned cold for the rest of the ride home. He couldn't engage her in any conversation and she sat stiff as a board in front of him, making certain her body touched his as little as possible.

Trevor was frustrated; in fact, he was downright mad. He had done everything he could to win her over. That was it. He was out of ideas. He also didn't feel he deserved this treatment. They'd had a perfectly wonderful night, if you didn't count the puking and the cougar attack. From now on, she got the same treatment she gave him. Cold and rude. He didn't care how beautiful or intriguing she was. This just wasn't worth it.

Laura was mad at herself. She had let her guard down once again and he had almost broken through. That wouldn't happen again. He was trying to manipulate her as all men did. She saw through it. So what if she felt funny whenever she was around him. So what if she loved to talk to him. Trevor wasn't to be trusted. Or was he? No, she was being weak. She had been weak once before and she hated the feeling.

Once they were back at the cabin, Laura hurried into her room. The place was quiet. Kat and Jack were sound asleep. Laura was glad Kat was not sick, but she felt a little sick herself. It had been a strange and exhausting night.

Laura slept late the next day and woke to the sound of arguing voices. It was Kat and Jack. It surprised Laura, because they never fought. As Laura listened, she realized that most of the arguing was coming from Kat. Jack appeared to be trying to reason with her. Laura rose to see what was the matter.

"Kat, Trevor and I have discussed this, and it's got to be done and done now."

"No, it doesn't!" Kat fought back. "It's not necessary—we'll be fine."

"It's necessary now more than ever. We're down a horse and we need more supplies to get us through the winter. Trevor and I will leave this afternoon."

Laura stepped in. "Where are you going?"

"Laura, there is a fort set up along the Oregon Trail. It's a couple weeks ride from here, but we really need provisions to get us through the winter, just in case. If we leave now, we'll be back before Thanksgiving and before any heavy snow falls. If we wait, we could be snowbound and stuck for the winter. We spoke with the Indians and they told us about the fort and how to get there."

Jack turned back to Kat. "I've asked them to check on you two every day and they've agreed."

"Jack, no! You can't leave us!"

Jack didn't know what to do. He thought Kat was being completely unreasonable and he didn't know how to get through to her. He grabbed her hand and led her out of the cabin to talk to her some more.

Laura glanced at Trevor, before turning and heading back into the solitude of her room.

Trevor shook his head and went out to do some chores.

Kat and Jack walked a short distance in silence before they sat down under a tree. "Honey, I had no idea you'd react like this. I don't want to make you unhappy, but I'm going. You're not in any danger. Our Indian friends will watch out for you."

"I'm not worried about me." Kat broke into sobs just then. "I'm worried about you! What if you never come back? What if you get shot or attacked by Indians, get sick or fall off a cliff?"

Jack was shocked. Kat never cried. He smiled and pulled her to him. "Well, you've thought of everything. But nothing like that is going to happen to me. For goodness sake, Kat, I made it safely on a long wagon train west, and with your help I outfoxed a posse and outran a tornado. A little trip to get supplies is nothing."

"Then let me come with you."

"No. Now that we have this place we need to have someone here. Besides, we can't leave Laura here alone, and we don't have enough horses for all of us to go."

Jack knew she knew he was right although he could tell she wasn't completely ready to give in. "I still don't want you to go. I won't see you for so long." She began to cry again.

Jack didn't understand it, but in a way it made him feel good to know she would miss him so much. He knew he would miss her every moment he was away. And he knew it would actually be harder on her, stuck in one place waiting for him to return. They walked through the woods that morning and talked about the trip. They made love under a pine tree and Kat cried again.

That afternoon, Kat and Laura helped them pack and watched them ride off. Kat was not hiding her feelings and Laura felt heavy-hearted too. She wanted to cheer Kat up. She seemed so sad. "Kat, they'll be back before we know it, especially if we keep busy."

It seemed like a reasonable plan but was easier said than done. There wasn't much to do. They went on walks every day. The Indians visited daily and brought them plenty of food. They had done as much to the cabin as they could. There were no books or paper. Kat and Laura got very creative and found ways to keep themselves occupied. They made up games and did math problems in the dirt with a stick. Laura's math was more advanced than Kat's, so she taught her some of what she knew.

In the days that followed, Laura spent most of the time worrying about Kat. Her appetite was waning. She looked gaunt. "Kat, how are you feeling? You look peaked."

"I'm not very hungry lately, and I do feel sick a lot. Probably spent too many years abusing my stomach, thinking I could eat what ever I wanted. It must have finally caught up with me."

Kat was vomiting morning, noon, and night. Laura didn't know what to do. She brewed tea for her, which seemed to make her feel better. She kept a close eye out for fever but Kat's temperature remained normal. Some days she seemed better and some days worse. Was it medical or mental? Was Kat that disturbed about Jack leaving? She couldn't be. Laura remembered it had started before Kat even knew he was leaving. Laura found herself wishing they were back.

It had been three long weeks since the men had left. Kat seemed to be in a depression. She ate very little and spent a lot of time in bed. The Indians came by with food and provisions. Laura had an idea and kicked herself for not thinking of it before. She spoke to their Indian friends and asked them to send the medicine woman over to have a look at Kat. After all, she was out of ideas. Kat wasn't running a fever. She had no sores. Laura asked her if she had any aches and pains and Kat had said no. At times she felt fine but other times she was just plain old sick. Laura forced her to eat, despite the vomiting. She new she had to keep her strength up.

Kat appreciated Laura's doctoring and tried to act happy and healthy so she wouldn't worry. But the truth was, Kat was beginning to worry. At times she felt fine but at other times she felt awful. It seemed the food she use to love was now her enemy. Kat knew she was losing weight and even began to wonder if she would die before she saw Jack again. Physically she was exhausted and the stress of Jack being gone so long was wearing on her. If only there were some devise that would allow her to talk to him from far away. She just needed to hear his voice and then, she convinced herself, she would be all right.

Kat lay down on her bed late one afternoon to take a nap. She felt woozy and was thinking of Jack and wishing she could talk to him. Soon she was in a deep sleep. She began to dream. A tornado was coming and she had to tell everyone so they could get to the cellar. The wind was blowing so hard she couldn't get to the people she needed to warn. The dust was so bad she couldn't see anything. She was fighting to open her eyes so she could see, but the dust and wind were too much.

Suddenly, Laura and Trevor appeared before her eyes. "Get to the storm cellar! A tornado is coming!" Trevor and Laura obeyed her and asked her to come with them. "I can't. I have to find Jack and Mamma and Flex!" Kat searched and searched for her mother, but she was nowhere to be found.

Suddenly, Jack was beside her. He had Flex tucked under his arm. "There you are. I've been looking all over for you," Jack told her in her dream. He didn't seem worried at all about the tornado. He calmly walked her to the storm cellar and they joined Laura and Trevor.

"I'm so glad you found Flex," Kat told him. Although the storm raged on they all felt safe in the cellar, and Kat was so glad to see Jack. The storm cellar stank though. It had a strange odor Kat didn't recognize. She shook her head, trying to get away from the smell. It was then that she awoke.

Kat found herself lying in bed at the cabin. The old Indian woman was standing over her. She had her hand on her stomach and was chanting something. She was burning incense. To Kat's surprise, she discovered she was naked underneath the blanket. The old woman smiled and brushed Kat's hair back as she continued chanting. The incense made Kat feel funny, and it also made her hungry. The woman had her sit up and drink something that didn't taste very good.

Laura entered the room with a bowl of soup. She looked at Kat and smiled broadly. Kat wondered for a minute if she was dreaming again.

"Hey, Kat, are you up for some soup?"

It sounded delicious. Kat sat up and hungrily ate the soup. To her surprise, it stayed down. She even asked for more.

Laura looked at the old woman. "You were right—it worked." Laura was pleased with herself that she had sent for her and felt ashamed for not thinking of it sooner.

"Laura, what's wrong with me—and what did she give me to cure it?"

"Well, you're not cured yet. Only time can do that. But what she did do was administer a treatment of smelly herbs and strange tea. See, what you have is a severe case of morning sickness that lasts all day and night. Kat, you're pregnant!"

Laura bent over and hugged her friend. "Can you believe I never considered that as a possibility? I've just never known anyone who was sick all the time from it like you've been. I was so scared you had something much worse." Laura bent over her and whispered, "Didn't you notice you missed your monthly flow?"

"No, Laura, I've felt so rotten I didn't notice. But it makes sense now." Kat giggled. Being pregnant had never entered her mind. Kat had heard about women who had tried and tried to get pregnant. For some it took a long time. She'd even heard of it taking years, and sometimes several miscarriages, before some women had success. Kat giggled again.

The old woman stayed a couple of days to make certain her mixture would keep Kat's all-day morning sickness at bay. Kat and Laura were glad to have her company and her smile. She showed Laura how to make the brew and gave them plenty of incense to last them through the next couple of months. She expected the problem would subside naturally as Kat grew further along.

The days went faster now. Both girls were thrilled about the baby and relieved that Kat wasn't dying. Laura and Kat looked forward to Trevor and Jack's return home. They had been gone just under four weeks now, and the girls were hopeful they'd return a few days early.

It didn't happen that way, but the girls managed to keep their spirits high. They knew it was a long shot, but you couldn't blame them for hoping.

The fourth week turned into the fifth week. Fine, it was taking longer than they had estimated. They were annoyed that Jack and Trevor had given them best-case scenario. They should have known the last few days would be especially hard on them. Week six came, and Kat and Laura tried not to let each other know how incredibly worried they were.

When the old Indian woman came to check on Kat, Laura spoke to her about their concerns for Jack and Trevor. The old woman talked to her men and they said they hadn't heard anything, but that wasn't unusual in these parts. Tucam's father, who could speak some English, told them there were several things that could delay their trip and that they shouldn't be worried. They would wait a little while longer and then send a party to meet them on the last leg of the journey home, in case they were having difficulty.

Week six turned into week seven and then began week eight. It was very early in the morning when Laura woke up to Kat shaking her. "Let's ride to the Indians' camp and ask them to go look for them. I can't take this anymore!" Laura could tell Kat had been crying; she felt the same way.

On the ride to the camp on that frigid December morning, Kat spoke with more determination than Laura had ever heard from her. "I swear, if they don't go find them I'm going myself." Laura knew Kat was serious. Even in her condition, she knew she'd do it. Laura would just have to help convince the Indians to go.

As it turned out, it took no convincing. The Indians had intended to leave the following morning. Several of the braves were on a long hunt and would be returning by nightfall. By then, four Indians, including Tucam and his father, were preparing to look for Trevor and Jack. This made Kat and Laura feel better and worse. Because it took no convincing it told them the Indians had feared the worst, too.

At least it was something. Kat and Laura were sick of waiting. They discussed this on the ride back to the cabin. The weather was cold, crisp, and refreshing. And it was so still out it made the girls' ears ring. To their delight, big, fat snowflakes began to fall. It was beautiful, the most beautiful snow either had ever seen.

To their dismay, it didn't stop. By mid-afternoon, the beautiful fat flakes had turned into blowing, stinging snow. The wind was howling by evening. Kat and Laura bundled up and followed the snow fence to the stable to care for Ginger. The buildings were solid. No snow came through any cracks, and although you could hear the wind, it couldn't be felt through the walls. They numbly walked back to the cabin. Their numbness wasn't from the cold but from their despair. If Jack and Trevor hadn't already been killed, there was no way they could make it through this storm. It raged on for three days and three nights. What was worse was the very real possibility they would never know what happened to them. A cloud of depression hung heavy in the cabin.

CHAPTER 22

Trevor and Jack headed south at a good clip. Jack felt terrible about Kat's reaction. He wished he could have made her feel better, but it was impossible. She just didn't understand the need to supply themselves before winter hit. He would make it better, though, by riding hard and fast and making it back in three weeks instead of four. That would make her very happy.

Trevor was in favor of a speedy trip as well. He knew of the impending winter but was mostly interested in getting back to Kat and Laura. What if Laura became ill or Kat got hurt? Trevor didn't like to think of it.

The trip to the fort was uneventful. Although the terrain was rocky, the horses made good time. It seemed they were becoming quite adept at traveling across just about any terrain.

When they arrived at the fort, it was teeming with activity. It felt strange to be around people again. Both Jack and Trevor were surprised at how many people were there and that so much business was going on at this remote station in the wilderness. In the short time there, they saw several supply wagons. People were busy buying and selling items and there was much trading going on, especially trading of livestock. It was the very end of the season and people were doing their final dealings. Demand was greater than supply, but it was obvious these weary travelers didn't have the money to purchase all they wanted.

Trevor and Jack didn't have that problem. Trevor had saved nearly every penny he'd earned working on Uncle Jacob's farm and the other odd jobs he'd had over the years.

Jack had some money from the sale of his farm back in Missouri, which would have been plenty.

Laura even had a good stash. Her parents had been quite wealthy and Mr. Shafer and Mr. Appleton had managed to retrieve a great deal of it for her when her parents' wagon was washed downstream. She offered it to Jack and Trevor when they announced the trip.

But it was Kat who had come through with the big money. Her hands shook slightly as she showed it to Jack and Trevor. She was worried about what they'd think of her when she said she'd stolen it from Harley Sneed. Her worry disappeared when they both laughed and congratulated her on thinking to look under his mattress. Trevor was especially happy because Boris would never get a dime of the money he thought would someday be all his. They all joked about being independently wealthy and having nowhere to spend their money.

Jack and Trevor bought everything they could possibly need and then some. Thankfully, they made good time on the trip there, because going home would take considerably longer. Jack and Trevor bought a team of oxen and a team of mules.

The plan was to pull out the next morning—until Trevor woke up in the middle of the night vomiting. He was pale, weak, and sicker than a dog. Their trip would have to be delayed a few days. The severe case of flu Trevor caught lasted three days. He became quite dehydrated and wasn't able to travel for another three days. Finally, he regained enough strength to ride.

Jack was itching to get going, but at least the delay allowed him the chance to talk with people and catch up on some news. He even found a special gift to bring home to Kat.

To Jack's surprise, he ran in to the Shafers. Mr. Shafer told Jack how the train had fallen apart after they left. Dickerson was kicked out at the first fort for what he had done to Jack. "I don't know why you all left, but I'm sure you had a good reason."

Jack simply told him he had met up with friends and they planned to start a ranching operation. He told him John and Laura were with him and were safe. Jack discovered Mr. Shafer had wisely decided to spend the winter at the fort. He was helping the army with various tasks, and Mrs. Shafer and the girls helped in the laundry. It was a good temporary solution, one that would get them through the winter. The rest of the folks had traveled on to Oregon.

Trevor and Jack were never so happy to get out of a place. It was dirty and loud. They saw people they couldn't believe had made it this far packing up to continue westward on the Oregon Trail. Didn't they know it was too late in the year?

Travel home was slow. The oxen walked at a snail's pace and the mules were barely faster than that. Jack and Trevor had oxen back on their farms but neither had traveled long distances with them. They knew they'd be slow, but this was ridiculous. Oh, well, so they'd be gone six weeks rather than four. Kat and Laura would be worried, but they'd be safe and cared for. What's a little delay as long as they got home safely?

Then, the weather changed.

🍁   🍁   🍁

Kat and Laura awoke on day four. The snow had stopped and the sun was out. It was bitterly cold, and the landscape looked vastly different than it had just four days earlier. Several feet of snow now covered the ground. With their warm boots, buffalo coats, and fur-lined hats and mittens, the girls ventured out into the snow. Instinctively, they looked to the south, willing Trevor and Jack to appear on the horizon.

Feeling very empty, Laura and Kat went through their daily chores. Each worried even more as they realized how cold they were and that they'd only been out for a short time. If they had a dollar for every time their gaze went southward, they'd have been rich.

Their Indian friends came to check on them just after noon. They told them what they already knew. No one had been able to leave to find their men, and until the snow melted a bit they couldn't risk going out. Kat and Laura were disappointed but knew it was how it had to be. It had been a long shot anyway.

Tucam and his father cautioned the girls to stay indoors. They predicted the light snow would pick up and blow into the open areas. It would be like experiencing the blizzard all over again.

The Indians returned to their camp and promised to come again the next day. As it turned out, that never happened. The wind began to blow, and just as they had said, it picked up the snow, creating a ground blizzard. This went on for another three days.

"Laura, I don't think we're ever going to see them again," Kat said out of the blue on day three of the ground blizzard.

"You can't think that way. They may be stuck somewhere—they may not even make it home until spring—but we will see them again," Laura almost snapped at her.

She softened her tone and then said, "Kat, they'll be back, and you have to take care of yourself for your baby's sake. You can't get yourself upset. This pregnancy has had a rough enough start without you adding to it with negative thoughts."

Kat knew she had a point, but it had been so long. Another week went by, a week of stormy days mixed with sunny days. Soon, it was the day before Christmas.

Kat sat in a chair by the fireplace and reflected on the past year and how much her life had changed. She had been just a child last spring and now she felt like a woman. She had left her home, traveled great distances, made new friends, helped build a home, and was expecting a baby. She had loved and lost—and that thought made her sad. As Kat sat in front of the fire, she considered for a moment if it would have been better had she never experienced it at all. Would things be better if life had not changed for her, if she had stayed on the farm?

Kat slowly smiled, realizing that she wouldn't have traded it for anything in the world. Spending a few wonderful months with Jack was better than never having known him. Getting to know Trevor after all these years was worth it. And carrying a child that would be with her always to remind her of Jack definitely made it all worthwhile. Kat missed Jack terribly, but for the first time in weeks she felt her mood lift.

Tomorrow would be the first Christmas in her new home and she owed it to Laura to make it special. "We should have something special for our Christmas dinner. Got any ideas?" Kat asked Laura. Kat could see Laura was a little surprised by her sudden cheery tone.

It only took a moment for Laura to catch her excitement and come up with an idea. "Pumpkin pie. We still have some leftover pumpkins our Indian friends brought us. I don't have flour, but I can make a crust from cornmeal." The girls kept busy by making their Christmas pie. Laura told stories of the delicious treats her mother would bake up for them at Christmas time. She talked of the beautiful dolls she got every year as gifts but how all she had really wanted for Christmas were books. Whenever she got a book she read it at least ten times. She had even brought a few with her, but they had been swept downstream with everything else.

Kat laughed. "I always got things like knives or whips. One year I got a baby pig."

"I don't know what could possibly top getting a baby pig for Christmas," Laura snickered.

The daylight faded. It had been a sunny day and it began to warm up for the first time in weeks. Kat and Laura built a man out of snow and named him

Charles. As they headed in, it began to snow—the big, soft flakes they both loved so much. Trying not to feel melancholy, Kat and Laura prepared to go to bed. Kat was tired from all the fresh air and was looking forward to a good night's sleep. Before heading off to bed, Laura lifted the window flap on her side of the cabin to see if it had stopped snowing. "The snow is letting up, but it's still coming down," she announced to Kat. "Good night, Charles!" Laura said, acting silly as she waved out the window to him.

Kat laughed as Laura brought her head back in and shut the window flap. Laura was still smiling at her own funny comment, until she turned and saw the look on Kat's face. Both girls knew there was a problem. They had built Charles on the other side of the cabin. What had Laura seen? Kat grabbed the pistol that was sitting on the fireplace mantel. The door blew open and a huge figure burst into the cabin. Laura was sure it was one of those mountain men Jack had spoken about.

Kat screamed and ran full force into Jack's arms. He was bundled in his coat, full of snow and cold, but she didn't care. It was the happiest moment of her life.

"Oh, Jack, am I dreaming, or are you really here?" She wouldn't let go of him for fear he'd disappear.

"You're not dreaming. I'm really home," he said as Kat squeezed him tightly. "Hello, Laura. It's good to finally see you two again." He looked different to Kat. He was thinner and had a beard, but it was Jack. She kissed him, hugged him tight, then felt his face and hugged him some more. It still felt like a dream.

Laura asked, "Where's Trevor?"

A moment of dread hung in the air before Jack spoke. "He's putting the livestock away. I should go help him."

Just then, the door opened and Trevor filled the space. Kat ran to him and hugged him. "Oh, Trevor, you're alive! I was sure you were dead!"

"Well, thanks a lot!" Trevor laughed.

Kat pulled away from him and looked into his face. He looked older, all bundled up, but it was definitely Trevor. "What do you mean, 'livestock'?" Kat asked as if she had just heard Jack's statement.

"Kat, put your coat on and come see what we bought," Jack urged.

In no time, Kat pulled on her boots, heavy coat, and fur-lined cap and mittens. Jack led her to the barn to see the oxen and mules and the two beautiful horses he had bought. They were thin from the hard journey, but they were alive.

Kat and Jack's quick exit left Laura and Trevor suddenly alone. Trevor had never felt so uncomfortable as he turned to greet Laura. He knew he would have a hard time disguising how much he had missed her, but with Laura he knew he must keep it low key. He mustered all the composure he could as he turned to look at her for the first time.

Trevor's trepidation turned to surprise as Laura flew across the room and threw herself into his arms.

"Oh, Trevor, I didn't think I would ever see you again, and the thought of that was killing me. "Don't you ever leave me again!" she scolded.

Trevor couldn't believe his ears. He thought he was dreaming, or perhaps delirious from the cold. "Laura?" He pushed her away from him and lifted her chin so their eyes could meet. "Do you mean to tell me you missed me? Is that really what I'm hearing?" Trevor needed it clarified—it was so important to him. He continued, "Because I need to be clear on this before you trample all over my heart again. You missed me and you don't want me to leave you ever again?"

"Trevor," Laura replied with exasperation, "you're going to have to start listening to me better. I said *when hell freezes over* and I meant it. And I think hell *did* freeze over these past few weeks, wouldn't you agree?"

Trevor melted. She had finally let him in and he was never going to be on the outside again. He bent down and kissed her and she willingly kissed him back.

"What's that?" Laura asked as she felt something in his coat pocket.

"Oh, I almost forgot. It's Jack's present to Kat. Let's put it in your bedroom before I lose it."

CHAPTER 23

In the barn, Kat admired the team of oxen and mules. "Jack, what in the world took you so long?"

"Kat, everything that could go wrong did, from flu to livestock wandering off to sprained ankles and snowstorm after snowstorm. And do you have any idea how slow oxen walk?"

She shook her head no.

"I didn't either, but Trevor and I were determined to make it back alive. We had too good a reason. I'm so happy to be home and to see you again, and I promise we'll tell you all about it tomorrow. Right now all I want to do is hold you, kiss you, and do everything else we do so well together."

They couldn't wait a minute longer. They made love right there in the barn. Laura and Trevor could have walked in, but they didn't care. They had to.

Kat and Jack walked back to the house to celebrate the happiest Christmas Eve of their lives. When they entered and saw Trevor and Laura sitting by the fire, holding hands and talking intimately, they knew their lives had changed forever, too. Kat and Jack couldn't have been happier for them.

Laura jumped up and ran to Kat. "Kat, Kat! Look what Trevor gave me for Christmas!"

Kat had never seen Laura so excited. Laura showed Kat two beautiful books. One was about Benjamin Franklin and the other about someone Kat had never heard of before. A man named Copernicus. Whoever he was, it made Laura very happy. Laura then picked up a very thick book and she was beaming as Kat read the title, *Modern Medicine*.

Just then, Jack, sounding alarmed, asked, "Trevor, what happened to Kat's gift?"

"Don't get excited, Jack. I put it in Laura's bedroom for safekeeping until you were ready to give it to her."

Kat looked at Jack with a smile. "You got me a gift? Well, go get it. I'm not going to wait until Christmas morning if Laura didn't have to," Kat teased.

Jack and Trevor went into Laura's room. "Close your eyes. I didn't have time to wrap it."

Kat did as she was told.

Laura was smiling broadly, as were the boys as they emerged from the bedroom. Jack positioned the gift carefully in front of Kat, and when he was ready he whispered, "You can open your eyes now."

Kat slowly opened her eyes and all the possible gifts she had imagined paled in comparison to what she saw before her. She held her breath, her hands shook, and tears filled her eyes as she reached down to pick up the most beautiful little black kitten she had ever seen.

The others had to hold back tears as they saw how moved Kat was. None of them would ever know how much meaning the gift held for her and how she treasured it. The kitten stayed on Kat's lap the entire night as they enjoyed the best Christmas of their lives.

Trevor and Jack brought in the supplies. They popped popcorn and drank tea. Jack threatened to throw the kitten in a snow bank because it was getting more attention than he was. Trevor threatened to do the same with Laura's books.

"I didn't get you anything," Laura said to Trevor.

"That's because you didn't get to go shopping like I did. That's all right. I have a few ideas on how you can repay me."

They all laughed.

"I have something for you, Jack," Kat said smartly as she licked her candy stick to a sharp point and poked Jack in the arm with it, "but it won't arrive for another five months or so," she said as she rubbed her stomach.

Laura and Trevor watched Jack's reaction. He grabbed Kat and hugged her tightly. His eyes filled with tears and he whispered how much he loved her in her ear. It had been a year of incredible gifts.

"Believe me, that is quite a story, too, but we'll save it for tomorrow. For now, I just want to enjoy my good luck at being able to spend Christmas Eve with the people I love…and my gift." Kat lifted the kitten and kissed it on the nose. It mewed in appreciation. "And my candy."

And so they did. They talked, they ate, and they laughed together, and at midnight they wished each other Merry Christmas and hugged and kissed.

After the exchange of glad tidings they sat in silence and appreciated each other's company. The magical moment of silence was broken by a question that suddenly popped into Jack's mind.

"So, who is this Charles fellow, anyway?"

0-595-30231-9

Made in the USA
Monee, IL
17 October 2020

45462149R00114